TWO'S COMPANY

Bronwyn Forest

2

www.BOROUGHSPUBLISHINGGROUP.com

TWO'S COMPANY
Copyright © 2020 Bronwyn Forest

ISBN 978-1-951055-7 5-2

To my husband, M, my Always Fantasy Man

ACKNOWLEDGMENTS

Many thanks to friends and family who never let me give up on my dreams. Enormous gratitude to Michelle for taking a chance on Leah and Ash's story. And to Susan, editor extraordinaire.

TWO'S COMPANY

Chapter 1

The brass plaque read *J. Cranford, Managing Director.*

Not for long, Leah thought with a zap of excitement. She rapped firmly on the door and straightened her pencil skirt. A grunt greeted her as the door swung open.

The man who gestured her into the office loomed gray and cadaverous, looking like he'd bitten a lemon. "Julius Cranford," he murmured. "I suppose you're Ms. Bellerose?" He made it sound like an accusation.

"I am." Leah nodded as she gave him a professional smile and handshake. She waited for some kind of welcome, but none was forthcoming. *Ah, I see how it is*, she sighed to herself. *Well, two can play that game, Julius.* She became brisk. "Shall we discuss the transition of duties?" Without waiting for a reply, she placed her briefcase on the desk and settled into a maroon office chair exuding the chemical aroma of fresh upholstery.

Cranford lowered himself gingerly into the high-backed chair behind the desk. "There was no need for new office furniture. My old chair was perfectly fine. Waste of money." His tone implied this was all her fault as he surveyed the office with distaste.

"The company wanted to give the entire hotel a face-lift, Mr. Cranford." Leah removed a folder from her briefcase. "Let's review a few of the most critical items, then you can show me around."

Cranford frowned and steepled his hands. "Ms. Bellerose, I want it understood that I opposed this takeover and I do not need any help with the management of Charmant Forest. I've been running it expertly for well over thirty years and am very proud of how efficiently and professionally we do things. We are a well-oiled machine." His hangdog eyes surveyed Leah's smooth face, freckles, and sleek, auburn ponytail. "Over thirty years," he repeated. "Longer than you've been alive, most likely." He pursed his lips and sat back.

"You flatter me, Mr. Cranford. My age is irrelevant, of course, but for the record, I'm thirty-eight. I have two bachelor's degrees, two master's degrees, and I've worked in some of the most prestigious hotels in the world," Leah said coolly. "Now let's clarify. The buyout—I emphasize it was *not* a takeover—is the only reason this hotel is still in business. You must know that the bank was ready to foreclose on loans made over the years and that the company who originally owned the hotel had been trying to sell for nearly a decade."

She crossed her legs and smiled. "So, while I understand your attachment to your position, you do know that you would be unemployed now if it weren't for the Gerard Hospitality Group?" She paused, noting that two small pink spots had appeared on Cranford's cheeks.

"It so happens I advocated for you to stay and assist with the transition. To be my right hand, as it were, rather than being offered early retirement." *Though it wouldn't have been that early*, she couldn't help musing. Cranford looked about ninety. "I've drafted a list of items for us to address in my first week, along with some short-term and long-term goals. Here's a copy for you. Now, let's start with—"

She was interrupted by a bang as the door to the office was flung open. "Mr. Cranford, we have an emergency." A young woman with frizzy red hair rushed into the office. "There's a toilet overflow in room thirty-two—the same room where we had that electrical fire last week—and I can't get hold of the new maintenance man. There's water everywhere."

Cranford scowled at the woman. "Can't you see I'm in a meeting, Dahlia? Call Arthur or Hector." He rubbed his temple.

"They ain't here." The young woman was hyperventilating. "They went to town to pick up supplies because the regular produce delivery didn't happen today. There was some kind of mix-up on who was ordering or the payment or something." She stopped long enough to notice Leah. "Can you use a plunger?" she asked her.

Leah turned to Cranford with a raised eyebrow.

***

Thirty-two. Thirty-two. Where the hell was room thirty-two, for God's sake? Asher ignored his pager's shriek and jogged down the hall, past rooms twenty-five through twenty-nine. There the numbers stopped. He swore and pulled a map of the hotel from the pocket of his coveralls.

"Blasted hotel only has eighty rooms. How can it be so hard to find consecutive numbers?" He kept jogging and finally reached a staircase that led to a section he hadn't seen before, a corridor that seemed to be stuck onto the main building at an angle.

"Thirty, thirty-one..." He skidded around the corner and into the open door of room thirty-two, where water was pooling on the carpet outside the bathroom. An elderly woman with hair an unlikely shade of copper was wringing her hands.

"What took you so long?" she demanded. "I've never been so upset. This is disgraceful—"

Asher brushed past her and ignored the cry of "Really." He surveyed the problem and hefted the plunger from his tool belt, though he hated to even touch the thing.

"Get back," he growled at the woman, as she hovered over his shoulder. He stuck the plunger in the toilet and pushed it up and down. Nothing. How did these things work? Water continued to pour out onto the floor. A box of denture cleanser floated by his foot. Ash momentarily closed his eyes. *What did I do to deserve this?* he wondered for the hundredth time that week.

Oh, yeah. I was an idiot.

He plunged the rubber bulb up and down another time or two to no avail. His shoes squelched as he swore under his breath.

"What's happening?" shrieked the woman.

"Hell if I...What did you try to flush, anyway?" Ash tried to buy time to think. He banged the plunger into the toilet again, splashing both of them.

"I beg your pardon. What are you implying?" The woman was spitting on his neck as she squawked. "I didn't do any—"

A different voice broke in, catching Ash's attention.

"Stand aside."

He felt himself being shoved unceremoniously sideways and looked up in surprise. "Hey—"

A woman—this one much younger and emanating energy—was scrutinizing him from top to bottom, taking in his damp coveralls and plunger. "*You're* the maintenance man?" she asked, voice dripping incredulity. Without waiting for a reply, she leaned over in her trendy business suit, reached behind the toilet, and turned a knob. The water immediately stopped flowing. The woman straightened up and brushed her palms together. Her face was inches from his. He could smell her perfume over the commode water.

"I suggest you take a remedial plumbing course, *maintenance man*," she said. "Turning off the water is the first thing you do in a plumbing emergency. Most people who aren't plumbers know at least that much."

What...? Who did she think she was? Ash opened his mouth, but she was already turning away from him to address the hotel manager, who was hovering in the doorway. "Mr. Cranford, if this employee is part of the well-oiled machine you referred to, I propose that the machine needs significant improvement." Ash watched in stunned fascination as the woman's emerald eyes flashed, though her face was dispassionate as she swiveled back to him. "Clean up this mess and find a carpet shampooer," she ordered, then gestured toward the elderly woman guest. "Arrange a fresh room with *working* plumbing and, of course, there won't be a bill for this stay." Pivoting on her impressively high heels, she exited the room.

Cranford turned to speak to the babbling old lady hanging onto his arm. Taking advantage of the momentary distraction, Ash followed the imperious young woman into the hall. He had to stride fast to catch up with her. Damn, how did she move so fast on those stilettos?

"Hey, you." He caught up to her and grabbed her arm. "What do you think you were doing talking to me like that?"

The woman went stock still, stared down at her arm, which he dropped immediately, and then back up at him. The green eyes no longer flashed but were cold as arctic ice. "Don't ever touch me again," she said, voice oddly calm. "And to answer your question, I was talking to you as anyone talks to someone who's a complete incompetent. You should be glad I arrived when I did."

Ash's chest burned. "I'd just gotten here and would have taken care of things if you hadn't barged in. I don't need to take lessons from some overblown female ego in a tight skirt." Through the haze of temper, he noticed a tiny muscle jump at the corner of her jaw and felt a spark of pleasure at getting to her, whoever she was. She was attractive—damn attractive, actually—but if there was one thing he hated, it was a woman with a flaming-feminist, I'm-in-charge agenda to cram down his throat.

His voice was a growl. "Furthermore, don't worry about me ever touching you again because I don't plan on it. I don't plan on ever seeing you again. After you check out, which I hope is today, we'll never have to cross paths again, which will be a relief to both of us." He smirked, almost a smile, as the woman fixed him with a withering glance.

"Don't count on it," she said, swiveling to continue down the hall. Ash stood in shocked silence for a long second, then jogged to catch up with her.

"What the hell does that mean? Don't count on what?"

She stopped moving so suddenly he had to take a step back. Her crimson lips twitched with something like satisfaction. "You will see me again. That is, until you are terminated from your employment, which may be sooner than you think. I'm your new boss."

***

The lobby of Charmant Forest was designed as an arbor, ornamental trees filling a central atrium. With the recent upgrades, fresh paint, and new, antique-style furnishings, it was attractive but understated. Leah surveyed the space as she made her way back to the office and decided the interior design was acceptable. Her preference would have been to dispense with the shadow boxes of butterflies and ancient nature prints that hung on the walls next to the elevators, but overall, it was a place she could feel proud to manage.

Mostly, if it weren't for the fact that staff problems had already arisen on this, her first day. First a surly managing director, then a hysterical red-headed assistant, then a maintenance man who didn't know a plunger from his arrogant ass. But she'd dealt with it. That's why she'd been sent to this place—to take control, to clean it up. And that's what she intended to do.

Her heels clicked a staccato on the parquet as she strode through the lobby. She knew that Cranford was behind her, moving at a snail's pace, but she didn't slow down. He would have to get used to her not waiting around for him.

"Pssst. Miss, uh, manager?" A voice interrupted Leah's concentration as she crossed in front of reception.

She blinked to focus on the middle-aged woman behind the desk, who was holding a phone receiver against her palm. "Yes?"

"Miss Manager," the woman said in a smooth, Spanish-accented voice low with urgency. "Phone call for you or, uh, Mr. Cranford." She waved the phone in the direction of the older man, who was plodding toward them. "It's the *mayor*," she whispered.

Leah glanced toward Cranford, then back to the woman. "Transfer it to the office...Hilda," she finished, reading the woman's name tag. "I'll take care of it."

The phone was ringing when she strode into the office. She hit Answer, then Speaker. "Leah Bellerose."

"This is Mayor Philpott's office," a creaky female voice drawled. "The mayor would like to speak to the manager regarding an urgent request."

Leah pulled up her planner on her laptop. "This is Leah Bellerose, the new managing director. How can I be of assistance?"

"This is the secretary?"

"*No*, this is Leah Bellerose. I *am* the manager."

"Hold, please." A pause was followed by the phlegmatic rumble of a Gothic voice. "Philpott here. Who's this?"

Leah repeated her introduction of herself with barely suppressed exasperation. Whatever had happened to southern manners? And the last fifty years of social progress?

"Well, my goodness, Charmant Forest has gone and got itself a girl manager. Heard about the renovation but didn't know it came with new management. All right, darlin', here's what I need," Mayor Philpott declared. "The conference of regional mayors is being held next month and the venue in Charleston fell through. I volunteered to host. Can you do it?"

Call me darlin' again and I'll hang up on you, Leah thought, her temples beginning to pound. She looked up to see nervous, red-haired Dahlia and Cranford entering the office, Hilda right behind them.

Leah gestured for the little group to come closer and pointed to her notepad as she responded. "I'd like to accommodate, Mr. Mayor. Tell me more about what's needed." She scribbled notes and questions while the mayor spoke, and Leah looked to her audience for thumbs-up or down answers.

"Yes, sir. We do have a large conference room that can handle a hundred and fifty, with room for tables. Will you need all three meals that day?"

"The whole enchilada, sweetheart."

Leah continued writing. "I'll put together a proposal for you after I speak to my catering manager and have it to you by end of business tomorrow." She ignored Cranford's incomprehensible mumbling and spun away to speak in the direction of the back wall. "Yes, sir. Thank you, Mr. Mayor. I'll speak to you tomorrow. You're welcome." She stabbed the End button. "Sweetie pie, honey, darlin'," she muttered derisively at the device. Her sternum vibrated with annoyance. "Anyone have a Tums?" she said to no one in particular.

Now she had to deal with Cranford. Reluctantly, she turned in her chair to see the older man, Dahlia, and Hilda staring at her in horrified bewilderment. "What?"

"But we—"

"There's not—"

Dahlia and Hilda began speaking at the same time while Cranford was still drawing breath. "Wait, slow down." Leah held up her hand and pointed to Hilda, who seemed the most composed.

"Miss, we don't *have* a catering manager. We never have had." Hilda's face flushed with calamity.

Leah's eyebrows rose. "All right then. The events manager."

Hilda shook her head. "No events manager, neither."

Cranford broke in. "I always handled events myself. We didn't have many."

Leah tapped a finger on the arm of her chair. "Huh. That's unusual. But we can figure this out. I'll convene a meeting of the food-service staff and see if we need to hire some temporary help. Not a problem." She straightened her notes and looked away. "That's all. You can return to reception, Hilda." After a pause, she added, "Thank you." It was not her nature to put the social niceties first.

As no one made a move, her gaze went back to the little group. "What now?"

Dahlia and Cranford began talking at the same time and Leah held her hand up again. *Patience. These people aren't trying to kill you by irritating you to death.* "Dahlia."

The young woman's red curls fell into her face as she eagerly spoke. "Our ballroom is old as dirt. We rarely have meetings here, so it was left out of the renovations to save money. I *said* it was a bad idea not to fix it up. My stars, I recall telling Mama and Hilda, didn't I, Hilda? I did, and—"

Cranford picked up the message. "I was against this renovation from the beginning and now this. The mayors have never had a meeting here. It could be a great thing for the hotel, but not now. We aren't prepared. We'll be a laughingstock. It will ruin us."

Leah pressed her lips together. "Why," she began, so low that Cranford had to lean forward to hear her, "didn't you say that when I was on the phone?"

Cranford shrugged, his bony frame exaggerated in the loose gray suit he wore. "You didn't give me a chance." He pointed to the notes she'd scribbled. "You asked if we had meeting space for a hundred and fifty people and I answered in the affirmative. You didn't ask if we were prepared to host such a meeting."

Staring at him, Leah had the sudden urge to throw the notepad in his face. "Dahlia and Hilda, go back to your duties. Please," she noted as an afterthought. Once the women left, Leah turned back to Julius. "Listen to me. We're going to make this work. I've committed to the mayor and you're right—it would be great branding for the hotel. So, we *will* host this meeting a month from now." She pulled the notepad toward her and began to make a list. "Let's get started."

***

Ash watched from the railing of the second floor above the atrium as Leah strode across the space as if she owned it. Various curses crossed his mind, but he didn't speak them aloud.

A hiss escaped his lips as his eyes followed the tantalizing form of the woman who had humiliated him. "You think you're in charge, lady?" he murmured. He tapped a finger on the polished mahogany rail. "Well, you are in for a big surprise. Maybe not right away, but eventually."

This line of thinking, along with the anger that burned too easily in his body, was all too familiar – and he didn't like it. He resented the woman for lighting the flame under it, which he'd sought to dampen and control over the last few years. He'd never been a violent man, but his temper and impatience had bitten him in the ass more times than he cared to recall. The message he'd given himself lately had been that he'd conquered these baser elements. It was a source of pride that he could manage himself. Handle the world and its demons and idiots with calm, cerebral confidence.

Now that message was being challenged. Because there was nothing he'd like more at this moment than to send that woman crawling out the door.

As he watched, her shapely derriere disappeared down the hallway toward the office. He turned from the rail, determined to put the obnoxious, overbearing wench out of his mind. He had more important things to worry about.

Like keeping his job and getting out of the purgatory to which he was currently condemned. That bitch, whoever she was, was *not* going to be the source of his downfall.

Chapter 2

Leah flopped onto the couch and rested her aching feet on the ottoman. A long sigh escaped her. She reached for her wine glass and stared into its depths, wondering how an old hotel like Charmant Forest had managed to stay afloat for as long as it had. It was quaint, certainly, and on the outskirts of a charming, if faded, small southern city. But even with all the renovations, you could still smell the dusty fatigue of the place.

She studied the water-stained ceiling, the cracked and curling daisy wallpaper in the kitchen. "I've teleported to nineteen-fifties bad television architecture," she lamented.

The whole town was like that, right down to this retro apartment building. Cool in mid-century fashion, but too original to be in any way fabulous. There was flaking paint, creaky plumbing, and aqua tile in the bathroom. The refrigerator looked to be original to the building although she had to pound on the door to get it open. Her friends in New York would not be impressed. However, that hardly concerned her at this point. She had more important things to worry about.

The image of Julius Cranford's wizened features and stolid, belligerent manner prickled her sense of how management should comport itself. He was going to suck up a lot of her initial effort, like an energy vampire.

And that maintenance man. Obviously unfit for his job, completely useless for basic tasks, and rude on top of that. Undesirable qualities from both a technical and customer service point of view. Though his hair was dark, wavy, and thick and...*Strike that*. She was not going to think about his hair. He'd also smelled nice, she thought with a frown, which was odd. What kind of maintenance man smelled nice? He'd been angry and defensive when they'd talked in the hall. All she could remember from his appearance were cheekbones that looked like they'd been cut from granite, a slightly crooked nose, and a generous mouth, which had been lush and firm at the same time.

What would it be like to feel that mouth on mine? She groaned. Sometimes her hormones got in the way of her common sense. It was maddening.

"Why are men so impossible, Prunella?" she asked. The honey-colored Sphynx cat staring at her from the side table didn't answer, only yawned and lay down, splaying her hairless body across the glass. Her long tail curled languorously as Leah regarded her best friend. "Easy for you to say. You don't have to deal with them." She took a sip of wine. "Maybe I should get spayed. That would simplify things. I'll call the vet tomorrow and see when he can fit me in."

Her morbid thoughts were interrupted by the chirp of her phone. She glanced at the screen, heart sinking as she hit Answer.

"Barry," she sighed. "I told you not to call me anymore. We have nothing to talk about."

The man spoke fast. "Leah, if you'd let me explain one more time—"

"Really? Are you going to be *that* person, Barry? I'm going to have to block your number. You are turning me into *that* person." She hit End while he was still drawing breath. She rubbed her forehead and stroked Prunella, who had come to curl up on her lap.

"There's another one, Prune." She sipped her wine. "The original Deceitful Bastard. Just can't understand that lying is the number one violation in a relationship. There *is* no explanation, no excuse. Not ever." She snuggled the cat's golden nose. "You never lie to me, do you, baby girl?" She inhaled the feline's sweet, dusky scent. If only cats could be her sole social connections, life would be a lot easier. Cats never lied. You always knew who they were and where they stood.

Out of nowhere, a dense cloud of sadness descended over her, its thick, gray fog sticking in her throat. This was new. Her eyes began to sting and her nose prickled.

"Damn." She sat up, sucked in air and shook her head. "No one is worth this. No one. And certainly not *Barry*." The name came out like spit.

Barry had been in her life for too many years, ever since she graduated with her first degree in business. He'd supported her idea to go back to school for her master's, told her he loved her a million times—which she'd badly needed to hear after the way she grew up. Now she realized he'd spoken the words as a ploy because he knew how desperately she needed them. He had manipulated her. He'd *used* her. Used her for sex, for money, for affection, all the while seeing other women behind her back. Ugh. How gullible could a person be? There were a thousand clues—a million—none of which she saw. *How?* How could that have happened?

Her mother, the formidable Cecelia Sebastian Bellerose, would never have accepted that kind of con, no matter the cost. Evidence— the impoverished state Cecilia had been left in after she'd caught her husband gambling away the rent money. Despite his many excuses and promises, Cecilia had ended their marriage and never looked back. Leah sighed. Her mother hadn't graduated from high school and never read anything but supermarket tabloids, but even she saw through a man's pitiful attempt to excuse his bad behavior. After all her education and worldly experience, Leah wondered what was *her* excuse?

The sting in her eyes was angrily shaken off. "No self-pity, Bellerose," she commanded. "No silly emotional displays." Now that *was* something valuable she had learned at her mother's knee. Feelings were inconvenient and messy and got in the way.

"Except where cats are concerned," she cooed to Prunella, who was purring like a miniature lawnmower. "Cats are perfect and worthy of my love." She settled onto the couch and picked up the remote. Mindless channel surfing was one of her favorite activities, a sort of meditation, but she hadn't gotten far when her phone chirped again. A small alarm bell clanged in her chest, but the screen displayed a different name this time and she sat up straight as she answered.

"Good evening, sir".

"Leah, how was the first day? Anything I should know?"

Prunella yowled as Leah lifted her to the ground. Cat free, she rose and paced up and down the tiny apartment, phone to her ear. "As expected, sir. Cranford was not happy to see me, as you predicted, but he won't be a problem." She avoided mentioning how surprised she was at the hotel manager's age since she had no idea how old her boss was. He didn't look nearly Cranford's vintage, but better not risk offending the man who signed her paychecks.

"He agreed to work with you?"

"Well, as I said, he wasn't happy about it, but he seems to know he has no choice." Leah stopped to sip her wine and stare out the window at the darkened street. There were no streetlights in this part of the little provincial city. She'd have to wear a light when she went out jogging in the morning. "We reviewed the transition plan, and he didn't have any arguments, other than that he ran the hotel like a well-oiled machine for thirty years." That made her smile. Like it or not, Cranford was going to receive a crash course in hotel management from yours truly.

Her boss grunted. "Right. He should be grateful you campaigned for him to stay—at least for now. He has no idea how close he came to being the first one to be let go."

"Continuity is important, sir. The staff seem pretty cohesive, at least the ones I've met. They've been together a long time, so taking Cranford out too early risks alienating the ones we'll want to keep— if there are any. I have a feeling he'll select himself out in due time." A glow of confidence in her human resource instincts spread throughout her body. Or was it the wine? She placed her half-drunk glass on the counter and shoved it away.

"You're likely right," her boss was saying. "I leave it to you to judge. Charmant Forest was a gamble for this company, and we're hoping it pays off. If not, we may abandon the boutique renovation idea and stick to high concept, high-end acquisitions. This hotel is your shot, Bellerose. If you do well here, we'll consider moving you up to a larger endeavor. Our Singapore resort requires some fresh blood."

Leah's heart jumped. "Singapore?"

The man chuckled. "It's a recent acquisition, like Charmant Forest, but much newer, quite sizable, and, of course, in the heart of a vibrant city. I'm keeping an eye on it. The current management is doing an adequate job, but as you well know, the Gerard Group strives for more than adequate. We beat Hyatt in the Fortune 500 last year and intend to keep it that way."

"Absolutely." Leah's voice remained calm, though her pulse thrummed. Singapore? "I appreciate your confidence in me, sir. I won't disappoint you."

"See that you don't." The man's tone became brisk. "Well, keep me informed. I trust you to report in at least weekly on net revenues and any staff issues. We're going to turn this place around. By month's end, we should be prepared to transition all the deadwood out of Charmant Forest." He sounded pleased with his play on words.

"Understood. Thank you, sir." Leah ended the call and looked out the window toward the light coming from down the hill, where the old hotel loomed. Why hadn't she mentioned the unrenovated ballroom or the mayors' conference? Her belly tightened as she thought about the potential repercussions and forced herself to relax. She needed more information before saying anything to Gerard. She needed a plan. That was her strong suit. Gather comprehensive information, formulate a plan, then inform those who needed to know.

She couldn't wait to get started.

**

Asher sat at the hotel bar and surveyed the patrons. He'd ditched the monkey suit and changed into plain khakis and casual dress shirt, cuffs rolled up. No more maintenance man, at least for the moment, but not exactly a high roller either. Why bother? This place was a backwater. Lots of gray hair, a few younger couples and families, but no singles. That was okay. He was exhausted and probably wouldn't know what to do with a willing woman at this moment, even if he could find one.

Well, maybe that wasn't true. He stared into the dregs of his club soda and lime. It wasn't likely that the lack of alcohol would dampen his memory or his instincts when it came to the fairer sex, past assumptions be damned. It was possible sobriety might even help, bizarre as that sounded.

"Another?"

He looked up as the bartender spoke, realizing he'd been lost in his thoughts. "No thanks, Joey, I'm pretty beat. Got to get home."

Joey nodded as he wiped the bar. "You meet the new managing director today? Heard she spent most of the day holed up with Cranford in his office. I hear she's a real ballbuster."

Ash grimaced. "Yeah, I heard that, too." He slapped a tip on the bar. "I encountered her was more like it. Don't want to meet her again," he said, voice hard. Waving, he turned and left the bar.

Five minutes later he was in his apartment, such that it was. A damn subbasement, adjacent to the hotel's boiler room. No windows. Cement walls. Might as well be a prison cell.

Hell, right now it *was* a prison cell.

Setting his jaw against the frustration and claustrophobia raking at his insides, he opened his laptop and hit video call. His father's face appeared seconds later.

"Right on time," the older man said, glancing at his Rolex. "Though I'm a bit surprised I didn't hear from you earlier. You must have been busy with your janitorial duties." The corner of his mouth twitched.

"You have to get me out of here," Ash said. "Seriously. I don't care where you send me. Omaha. Lubbock. Anywhere but here."

His father chuckled but it didn't have a nice ring to it. "You're where you need to be, Ash. Besides, we don't own hotels in Omaha or Lubbock—though if you do well in Charmant, we might send you to, oh, how about Iowa? You could scout new locations for us."

Ash rubbed his forehead. "Very funny." He blew out a breath. "Dad, honestly, this isn't going to work. I'm wasted here. You know what I'm capable of—you've seen it. My skills could be increasing our profits somewhere else. Somewhere with a lot more potential than…this place."

The older man leaned toward the camera so fast that Ash sat back. "You listen to me, boy. I sent you to Charmant for a purpose. Yes, I *do* know what you're capable of and you know it as well. You're capable of getting blind drunk and making moves on my business partner's wife, nearly sparking a lawsuit. You're capable of revealing confidential stock information to a competitor. Almost had federal regulators on us for that."

Ash's retort was swift. "I was drinking then, and I haven't—"

"You may be thirty-nine years old, Asher, but you have a penchant for trying to destroy yourself and those around you like no one I've ever seen. Now, you can wreak havoc and throw away the natural gifts given to you, or you can straighten up and start acting like you deserve your name."

"That's not fair and you know it. It's been over a year. I've done everything you've asked with no complaints. Now it's time for me to—"

"It's time for you to continue restoring the faith of the board and paying off your debt," his father cut in. "I allowed you to work under my remedial tutelage, which put me in a risky spot with my top executives. Nevertheless, I did it."

"It was humiliating and unnecessary. And I don't need remedial anything. Don't forget who was top of his class at Stanford."

It was clear his father wasn't listening. "I don't have time to manage you anymore." The edge in his voice cut to the bone. "So I'll say this one more time, boy. I'm not sending you anywhere else but remember you're there in Charmant by choice. You're not a prisoner." Ash felt the cement walls breathing down on him as his father continued. "You can walk away any time you want. Go right ahead. But if you do, you're on your own, once and for all. I'm not opening the door to you again."

Silence stretched between them as the words settled. The rumble from the hotel's laundry room vibrated through the ceiling. Ash's eyes strayed to the office bar behind his father's mahogany desk, stocked as always with crystal decanters and cut-glass tumblers. He knew that in his father's hand, out of sight, was his nightly drink. Lagavulin Scotch, with exactly five drops of spring water. Ash could almost taste it on his tongue.

Forcing his mind back to the issue at hand, he met his father's steely eyes. "The new managing director you hired is a damn—" He stopped and sucked in air. She's what? A gorgeous bitch? An evil sorceress? "She's not a good fit here, I can tell you that. Too slick, too Big City. Has no feel for what this place needs or how it operates. She'll alienate people. Just watch."

His father's mouth twitched again. "Are you sure she didn't only alienate *you*, boy?"

Ash's teeth clenched and he relaxed them with difficulty. "I have to go. I'll call you tomorrow." He hit End and stared at the blank screen. "And don't call me 'boy'," he growled, as he snapped the computer shut.

Chapter 3

Leah scanned the banquet table, which held stacks of boxed lunches. An open box was in her hand, the pong of soggy bread, wilted lettuce, and plastic wrap gag worthy. Some kind of mystery meat and gray mayonnaise leaked out from mushy white bread, causing her to turn her head away. *You've got to be kidding me*, she thought. *I feel like I'm back in the trailer park.*

"Are they all this bad?" she wondered aloud as she tossed the open box on the table.

"That's how they always are," Dahlia Markley said. She shrugged and pulled her messy red curls into a lopsided ponytail. "When we started ordering from Leroy's down the street for our meetings, it kind of lowered morale, but Mr. Cranford said it's cheaper than using our kitchen. And anyway, we have to save our resources for our guests at mealtimes."

Leah pressed her lips together and stared at the young woman.

"That's what he said." Dahlia bit her lip.

And because a man said it, you went right along with it. Brilliant. Leah launched into action. "Go get me the largest garbage bag you can find. And send your mother in here. Please," she added as an afterthought. She began herding boxes to the end of the table as Dahlia trotted out of the room. A moment later, Estelle Markley, head chef and restaurant manager, trundled through the doorway. She was barely five feet tall, heavyset, and wore a stained apron over her skirt. Wiry gray hair was pulled into a topknot. Bright blue clogs contrasted with what was otherwise a colorless facade. She looked like she brooked no nonsense from any man—or woman.

"You wanted to see me?" Her voice was clipped. "I'm in a dilly of a hurry. We have nearly a full house at the moment and lunch is only an hour away."

Leah nodded and extended her hand. "Mrs. Markley, I'm Leah Bellerose. We haven't had a chance to meet, but I've been speaking to Dahlia. She's lovely, by the way." It never hurt to compliment someone's child.

Mrs. Markley softened as she shook Leah's hand. Her grip was robust, like her appearance. "She takes after me, not her daddy. So, what can I do for you?"

"Well, as you can see," Leah said, "we are preparing for a staff meeting, and the food is entirely inadequate. It's inedible." Dahlia appeared at her side with a large garbage bag. Leah began sweeping the boxed lunches into it, then stopped, chagrined. "Wait, should we send these to the homeless shelter or something?"

Dahlia's gaze was goggle-eyed. "There ain't no homeless people in Charmant." Her head tilted. "O'course, there was Junior Slokum. After his head injury at the sewage plant? Used to sleep behind the Piggly Wiggly and run down Main Street in his altogether. Lordy, was that a sight. But then his Aunt Birdie took him in. She's a saint."

Leah stared at Dahlia, then turned to Mrs. Markley with effort. "I need food for the meeting. It doesn't have to be anything fancy. Do you have enough of whatever you're preparing for the house today?"

Mrs. Markley was clearly trying to decide between indignation and flattery at being asked to help. "I don't think we have enough to cover all the staff in a meeting, no. It's very last minute," she added pointedly, peering at Leah.

"I see," Leah said, shoving the last of the boxes into the garbage bag and stamping it down with her foot. The heel of her Valentino went straight through one box and caught. "Shit," she murmured. *Great show, Bellerose. Smooth move.* Dahlia handed her a napkin and she removed the condiment-covered shoe to wipe it off. "Work with me here, Estelle. What can we feed these people?"

Mrs. Markley stared at Leah wiping her shoe and seemed to come to a decision. "I do have some bread, fresh baked."

Dahlia nodded vigorously. "Mother makes amazing bread. And we never get any of it. She pitches a hissy if I touch a piece."

"Good. You have enough?" Leah stepped back into her shoe and tied the garbage bag.

"I think so. I sell some to the grocery down the road, but—"

"They aren't getting any today. What else?"

"Well...I have plenty of cheese. And Dahlia can go down to the farmer's market for some fruit. Peaches are in." Mrs. Markley seemed to be getting into the spirit of things. "I'll make some fresh lemonade. Easy and inexpensive."

"Perfect. That's all we need." Leah handed Dahlia the garbage bag. "Excellent problem-solving. I'll see you both back in this room in"—she glanced at her watch— "thirty minutes."

She watched the two women trot out of the room and wondered what kind of parallel universe she'd stumbled into. A dilly of a hurry? A hissy? She felt like she'd been dropped into an old episode of Mayberry RFD. That wasn't a tragedy, of course, but she'd left small-town life behind a long time ago and had no intention of going back.

Mrs. Markley was, however, someone Leah could relate to. She was obviously a woman in charge of her realm, even if her realm was only the kitchen and restaurant in a small hotel in a provincial town. It was reassuring to know that Estelle Markley was on top of things there, which would mean Leah herself would have less cleanup to do in that department.

The problem of the unrenovated ballroom and the need for all hands on deck for the mayors' meeting would have to wait until later in the afternoon. A general staff meeting was always the top item. First things first. Put out the biggest fire, then the next big fire. She sucked in air and sat down with her notes.

Half an hour later, Leah sat in the nearly filled Staff Conference Room, a glorified break room behind the hotel kitchen. She rapped on a water glass to get the slowly assembling group's attention and suppressed the urge to shout. *Does everyone here move in slow motion?*

"Make sure you all have your name tags on. Finish getting your food and have a seat. We need to start." She gestured to a couple of confused-looking housekeepers and tried to offer an encouraging smile. "Meetings start on time from now on. Thank you." She stood next to Cranford at the front of the room and ignored his hostile expression. If meetings hadn't started on time before, that was going to change immediately.

"Is everyone here?" she asked him. Unwittingly, she found herself scanning the room for the maintenance man.

Cranford took his time answering but made sure his voice carried. "This is mostly the managers and shift supervisors, Ms.

Bellerose. Not everyone can attend these meetings, as I'm sure you understand. Our staff have actual work to do."

Julius, Julius, Leah mused. *You have picked the wrong person to do battle with.* She didn't blink an eye as she addressed the group. "Some of our most important work is team building. For those of you I haven't already met, I'm Leah Bellerose, the new managing director of Charmant Forest." She waited a beat as the murmuring died down. "Mr. Cranford has been kind enough to fill me in on how things have been running, which I've seen for myself over the last twenty-four hours, and I can tell you there will be changes." She stopped as whispers simmered again, then held up her hand for silence. "For those of you wanting to work hard and further your careers, there's nothing to worry about. I'll be conducting performance reviews over the next few weeks since I understand those have not been done in some time."

Another poisonous vibration from Cranford was ignored. She continued, "I'd like—"

A hand waved in the air. "Excuse me, miss," a man said in a thick Spanish accent. He rose to his feet. "Do performance reviews mean raises? We haven't had raises in a long time."

Leah clasped her hands in front of her and reminded herself to be patient. "What is your name?"

"Hector." He smiled, seemingly proud of his name.

Leah waited, then asked, "Hector *what*? And what do you do?"

"Hector Duran. I am the manager of all housekeeping." He raised his fist in victory as several people whooped.

Leah nodded. "Thank you, Hector. I can tell you that the company will consider raises once we have gotten all administrative and human resource issues cleaned up. That may take a while, but I assure you it's one of my priorities."

An avalanche of questions about potential raises cost Leah nearly ten minutes and she dragged the meeting back to order with effort. Her forbearance was wearing thin. Obviously, these people had been ignored for too long. It was understandable they were clamoring for answers, but it was her job to maintain control. And that was her specialty. Still, not for the first time, she felt the weight of her responsibility. It was as if she were trying to lift a pallet of stone by herself. It felt physical, which meant she needed to off-load some things. "Let's park this issue and move on." She ignored the grumbles and consulted her staff list. "Who manages the grounds and land—"

A movement at the corner of the room caught her eye, and she looked up. The incorrigible maintenance man from the day before slipped into a chair in the back and slouched in his seat, trying to avoid being noticed, which irritated her even more than the sight of him.

Leah's chin rose. "And you are...?" she demanded, fixing him with a hawk like gaze.

The man glanced from side to side. "Me?"

Leah was silent, waiting.

The man unhurriedly straightened in his chair before he answered. "Asher. Asher Banks."

Asher Banks. Interesting name. The thought came involuntarily: *I wonder if he still smells good.* Leah snapped herself back to attention. "And what is it you do here, Asher Banks, other than *not* plumbing, that makes you twenty minutes late for a mandatory meeting?" The twitters in the audience told her she'd gotten everyone's attention. The days of slack management were over.

Banks rose from his chair unbidden and regarded her for a moment longer than was comfortable. He was taller than she remembered, with broad shoulders. His blue maintenance uniform couldn't conceal his athletic form—rolled up sleeves revealed muscled forearms covered with the right amount of dark hair. She suppressed a tiny shiver as he met her gaze in unspoken defiance. "I work with Arthur in maintenance...*as you already know*, Ms. Bellerose." He paused a beat. "I was assisting on an important matter having to do with lawn care."

He must think she was an idiot. "A lawn emergency?" She couldn't hide her sarcasm. Of course, she shouldn't be calling him out publicly, but it might do well to demonstrate in front of everyone that she wasn't going to accept lame excuses for tardiness or poor performance.

Banks's jaw visibly tensed. "You could say that."

"Hmm." Leah considered this. "Who is the landscaping and grounds representative here?"

A woman in dirty blue jeans, plain-faced, and strikingly barefoot rose to her feet. "That would be me," she said. "Karen Pembroke. At your service." Everyone laughed.

Leah remained sober. "Thank you, Ms. Pembroke. Is it true that Mr. Banks here was 'assisting' with lawn care today?" She smiled tightly as the landscape manager considered her answer. "It's not a trick question, Ms. Pembroke. Just need to get a sense of how things run."

The young woman stuck her hands in her pockets. "I guess it's true. I mean, yes, it's true. That is, he was assisting our assistant."

Leah's eyebrows rose. "Assisting your assistant?"

"Let me explain." Asher Banks strode forward, and Leah was struck by the way he moved. Easy. Loose limbs, but exuding coiled energy, like an animal on the prowl. Not easy to look like that in a jumpsuit. Leah's face tingled and she frowned.

Asher stopped and leaned a hip against a table at the front of the room. "We have a grounds assistant—Arthur's son, actually—who needs some help sometimes. He's good with machines but has a hard time reading instructions, so I was helping him out today. I lost track of time. It wasn't his fault."

Karen Pembroke spoke up. "Our riding mower was due for a tune-up. William's done it before but needed a little refresher. I was busy with some new plantings, so Ash volunteered."

Leah shook her head. "I'm confused. We have a grounds assistant who can't read? Who vetted this employee?"

Another man spoke up. "I'm Arthur Jones." Leah watched the man struggle to stand, his large frame slowing him down. He wore a faded blue jumpsuit with a name patch on the left breast. His light brown skin was mottled, making him appear elderly, but his eyes had a youthful twinkle. "I've been at Charmant Forest for near on forty years since the textile mill closed down. It's been my life. When William was born, we knew he wasn't gonna be no college material, so I started training him to work with me." He paused and mopped his face with a handkerchief.

That's a real handkerchief, Leah realized. Textile mills. Barefoot employees. Yep, Mayberry, all right. What next, Aunt Bea with an apple pie?

Arthur continued. "My William's a good boy, and real helpful. He's worked here, helping with maintenance and grounds and housekeeping, for about twenty years now." The man nodded at Leah and sat back down.

"All right." Leah drew a breath. She would deal with this charity case later. "I think I'm getting the picture. For now, please remember that everyone is expected to attend these meetings and arrive on time. We have a lot of things to cover during this management transition, and I expect your cooperation." She looked pointedly at the infuriatingly attractive form of Asher Banks, then emphatically away. "Back to the agenda."

***

Asher watched Leah try to recover the meeting and almost felt sorry for her.

Almost, but not quite. The fact was she was a Class A bitch—even if she did look like sin in that tight skirt—and wouldn't last in this job. The problem was that she might destroy the hotel before his father came to his senses and got rid of her. That would be a disaster because this project was his last chance to prove himself. It was true he'd had an early start at the executive level and had pissed it away. A second chance hadn't gone all that well either, so this was his penance. Starting at the bottom to earn his way back in. If everything went as planned, he'd be back in an executive position by the end of the year, preferably as far from this place as was humanly possible.

Until Leah showed up, he'd been confident everything was on track. He'd gotten into the good graces of most of the managers, except for Cranford, who was a lost cause. That was okay. Cranford was weak and obviously on his way out with Leah's arrival. It presented Asher with a dilemma.

I'm going to have to make nice with Leah Bellerose. The thought caused his fists to clench. She made him...what? Angry? Exasperated? It was hard to know exactly. She represented everything he disliked in a woman. Bossy, overbearing, blindly confident. Uncaring. Maybe even narcissistic. All while wrapped in that killer body, with that silky hair he could almost feel against his skin, smelling like an exotic bloom, and walking around in those damn spike heels.

She was the devil.

His father's voice echoed in his head. *Keep your friends close and your enemies closer.* It was a critical lesson in business and life in general, one he'd seen his father employ any number of times to powerful effect.

Well, one thing Asher knew how to do was turn on the charm. It was one of his best and worst traits. And now he'd have to use it on Leah Bellerose.

He considered his tactics as he ran up and down the hotel's back staircase a few times. This was the only way to burn off his frustration lately, and today he needed it more than ever. Once he'd worked up a good sweat, he felt better and had a plan. Landing at the bottom of the stairs, breath returning to normal, he reveled in the looseness of his muscles, the sense of calm that descended on him.

He checked his pager. No messages. He had time before he had to meet Arthur to begin an inspection of the fire extinguishers, so he took a chance and headed to The Cove for hydration. Joey was alone behind the mahogany bar, cutting lime wedges.

"Ash the Man," Joey proclaimed. "What brings you here in the middle of the day?"

The barstool creaked as Ash sat. "Just needed a drink and a friendly face." He gestured to the soda hose. "The usual." His hand tapped a rhythm on the old wood as he watched Joey fill a glass and adorn it with a slice of lime.

The bartender slapped a napkin down under the fizzing glass. "What's on your mind? You look kinda amped."

Ash frowned. "I'm okay. Just had a good run to burn off the crazy, you know?" He took a long swallow of club soda.

"I get it." Joey's eyes flicked to the doorway, its carved arch bordered by topiary. "Uh-oh," he murmured, "here comes—"

"Well, well. I see that maintenance duties aren't stretching your limits today, Banks," a voice behind him said.

Ash swiveled on the barstool to meet the cool, emerald gaze of Leah Bellerose, flanked by Dahlia Markley and Hector Duran, both looking out of sorts. Ash regarded her, suppressing a sardonic reply, then spun back to face Joey. "On a break," he declared.

He smelled her perfume as she came closer. An exotic bloom, all right. Like something beautiful but poisonous in the jungle. It hit him square in the gut.

"I wasn't aware that staff breaks take place in areas where we serve hotel guests." Her voice was low and icy calm, completely unruffled and infuriating. "That's something we'll have to change."

She moved into his line of vision. "Now." Her gaze flicked downward, practically drawing an arrow to his seat on the barstool.

Ash directed his attention to his glass. He drew his forefinger around the rim in a leisurely fashion, then raised the glass to his mouth and took his time drinking the carbonated water. At last, he turned back to Leah, trying to maintain his calm. "Did you need something?" The internal fire he felt at being this close to her, to the anger below the surface, was barely suppressed as he held her gaze defiantly.

A flicker of irritation in her eyes gave him a warm glow of satisfaction but was short-lived. "Meet us in the ballroom in two minutes," she ordered, then turned on a high heel and stalked away. Dahlia and Hector ran to follow her.

"So that's how it's going to be, eh?" he muttered, throwing a tip on the bar. Joey looked at him silently as he scooped up the change. The look seemed to say, *Good luck with that, man.*

***

Julius Cranford retrieved a key—an actual key—from his pocket and inserted it into the lock of the ballroom's double doors. His skeletal fingers twisted the creaky key back and forth. Leah tapped a rhythm with her toe as she waited, annoyance skittering down her spine. This place was straight out of a gothic novel. Dahlia's nervous energy was palpable next to her, and Hector's hang-dog expression created an aura of doom around the little group. Thankfully, Hilda had gone back to cover reception—one less edgy personality for Leah to deal with.

The tall doors groaned as they swung open slowly, and a dank waft of stale air rushed over them.

"Ugh." Leah's hand covered her mouth and nose involuntarily, then waved in impatience. "Lights, please, Julius." She strode into the dark cavern and was greeted with a flickering, yellow-tinged sputter of light from the dust-covered chandelier. The room came into focus.

"Lordy," she heard Dahlia mutter as she entered the room on Leah's heels.

"Indeed." Leah sighed and took in the sight of the ballroom, which surely hadn't been touched in half a century. Faded wallpaper in an antiquated flower pattern hung and puckered, wrinkled carpet emitted a rotting smell that clotted the air. On the far wall, tall windows were obscured by heavy drapes, thick with dust and cobwebs.

As if to highlight the decrepitude, a stained banquet table sat on its side at one end of the room, legs sticking out into the funky air.

Cranford turned to Leah. "There's no way this room will be ready for the mayors' meeting. And no funds to ready it." His tone was triumphant.

Leah ignored him and trod across the carpet, heels sinking into the moldering carpet. She turned to Hector. "Mr. Duran, please take notes." She began to tick off the items that needed attention as Hector frantically scribbled on a notepad. "We'll need estimates on both cost and timeline for stripping this wallpaper and painting, replacing the carpet, and cleaning the drapes and chandelier." She surveyed the windows and touched a cobwebbed curtain gingerly. "I think we can get away with keeping these, minus the dust. Twenty-foot drapes aren't cheap."

Hector looked up. "Miss, I have a cousin who paints. He works fast." His gaze went guiltily to Cranford, then back to Leah.

"Get him over here today." She pursed her lips. "You don't have any cousins who install carpet, do you?" She ignored Dahlia's giggle as Hector cocked his head.

"No, miss, but I have a friend. He put in a bid on the other renovations but lost out to a larger company." He rubbed his nose. "But he's fast, too."

Leah nodded. "Call him. I want estimates today. We need to know prices and timelines, the faster the better." She looked around in exasperation. "Where is that maintenance man?"

Everyone looked toward the empty doorway. Cranford shrugged. "Banks tends to work on his own time."

Leah felt her chest burn and heat crept into her cheeks. *Not for long, he doesn't.*

Chapter 4

"You wanted to talk to me?" Asher's tone was more compliant than she had expected, which put her immediately on alert.

Leah pointed at the chair in which she had sat when she first met with Cranford. Now, she thought triumphantly, she sat *behind* the desk. She opened a folder and glanced at the documents inside. When she raised her eyes, he was still standing inside the door.

"Sit down, Banks." She didn't have time to play games with this guy, even if he did smell good. Damn him.

"I'd rather stand. You can tell me whatever you need to tell me and I'll get out of here and back to work." He grinned at her.

Leah exhaled. "Mr. Banks—"

"You need to call me Asher. Or Ash. I prefer it."

Now she was irritated. She stood up and walked around the desk. "I will call you Mr. Banks, because our relationship is a professional one," she asserted. "And you will call me Ms. Bellerose. You will arrive for all meetings punctually; you will not argue with me, in private or in public. You will learn how to do your job or you will be term—"

She stopped as he stepped forward suddenly, coming so close she could see the pupils in his eyes dilate. "What the hell are you doing?" She was alarmed at the way her voice wobbled, the way her heart had started to thrum.

"*Ms.* Bellerose, let's be honest about something," Asher said, his voice a low, velvet rumble. "You and I got off on the wrong foot. But it doesn't have to stay that way. I admit I'm not an expert at my job, but it's important to me to do well here. Let's start over. Maybe we can even be friends."

"I don't make friends at work."

He crossed his arms and chuckled as his voice dropped half an octave. "This could be a first."

Leah's stomach fluttered. God help her, he was charismatic. And the temptation was there, she had to admit. His eyes were a deep, speckled, golden-brown topaz , his hair thick and wavy. There were smile lines at the corners of his eyes, which meant he laughed a lot. Then there were those cheekbones. Leah sighed inwardly. Why did it help a person's case to be so good looking? It didn't seem right. In spite of herself, she wavered. He *sounded* sincere.

Asher continued. "I can see the challenges you have here, to get the hotel into profitability, especially after the renovation investment. Staff's been here a long time, some probably too long. You're doing what you have to do. I get that." He grinned at her again. This time it dazzled. "So, is that all you needed to tell me? That I need to be on time and learn my job and respect you? Because I will and I do."

Leah tried to focus on a spot on the wall. Alarm bells were going off in her head, faintly at first, then deafeningly. This guy was trying to charm her. And he thought she was too dumb to recognize it. Thought she was another in a long line of brainless skirts he'd chased and seduced with his shallow, transparent allure. This wasn't the first time Leah had been underestimated by a man who pigeonholed her into his sexist image of a gullible female. The more she thought about it, the angrier she became.

Asher Banks thought he could come in here and be all Mr. Handsome-Sweet-Talk? He thought it wouldn't matter if he was the worst maintenance man in the world and flouted her authority in front of others and couldn't get to meetings on time or follow directions as simple as sitting in a chair? Well, he had another think coming.

He was still grinning at her. "Well, what do you say, Ms. Leah Bellerose?" His gaze seemed to go straight down to her toes.

Of course, she had more control of herself than that. She suppressed the frisson of heat that ran up her back and met his eyes squarely. "You're fired," she said.

***

For a long moment, neither of them spoke. Leah watched a shadow pass over the dappled topaz eyes, then something else moved in. Something primordial. Instinctively, she stepped back and glanced toward the door. If he lashed out in anger, could she make it? She'd violated a cardinal rule of management, which was never to terminate an employee without at least one witness. Under normal circumstances, she would not have made such an error, but she seemed to have forgotten—momentarily—the usual protocol.

Her lips parted to speak but before she could make a sound, Asher closed the distance between them. "In that case," he said, "I can do this." He placed his hands on either side of her face and bent to kiss her, his lips touching hers before she knew what was happening.

Leah's body tensed like a bowstring, her hands went to his chest to push him away, but then…she didn't. His mouth was warm, the kiss gentle but insistent. Her inhalation was full of him, his skin, his hair, his breath. For a split second, it was as if she'd been dying of thirst and he'd offered her water. She couldn't get enough. Thoughts evaporated as she went liquid. Her eyes closed as she pulled him in, kissing him back, feeling his hands move into her hair, hearing him groan as his tongue touched hers.

Then it snapped. Her eyes flew open. Tension slammed back into her body and she used both palms against his chest to shove him, hard. "Get away from me," she gasped, wiping her mouth. "Get out." Then, suddenly, she couldn't speak. Her hands were shaking. She swallowed, looked away from him and turned to move behind her desk. Without glancing up, she pointed to the door.

It wasn't until she heard the door close and she'd counted slowly to a hundred that she stopped shaking.

***

Ash slammed the door to his apartment and leaned against it, catching his breath. Running up and down the hotel stairs a few times had managed to drain away most of the resentment and bitterness he'd felt leaving Leah's office. Now he had to think. He couldn't let his father know he'd been fired. That would spell the end of his third and last chance to salvage his life. *This* was the time for immediate damage control, and it would have to be done the right way, especially after he'd kissed her.

Damn fool.

Asher had never been one to analyze his romantic or sexual entanglements with women, but this situation was hard to ignore. Why he'd done it was something he couldn't answer right now, and he wasn't going to lose sleep over it. It had happened.

And it had been amazing. Even if it had lasted less than ten seconds, it had been spectacular. This was surprising, and Ash was rarely surprised by something like a kiss. Maybe he never had been.

The way Leah had gone from ice to fire in the space of a heartbeat had been thrilling, a punch to the gut. He'd had a hard time controlling himself. She'd responded to him before she knew what she was doing. This told him something, though he wasn't quite sure what.

Ash cursed in confusion and strode to the minifridge. He extracted a ginger ale, sat on the sofa, and pulled out his phone. His job right now was not to figure out Leah Bellerose, Satan in heels or potential conquest—or both. His only task was to save his ass, otherwise, there wouldn't be a point in any relationships, intimate or otherwise. He might as well check himself back into rehab and be done with it.

Of course, he could always hop a plane to Kathmandu and start over with a clean slate, but he'd never liked yak butter.

He dialed a number and went into damage control mode.

Chapter 5

Leah handed the personnel file to Cranford and gestured for him to open it. "I don't get it. There's practically no paperwork on this guy," she accused. "Where did he come from?"

Julius Cranford's nose twitched as if trying to ascertain the answer to her question by smelling the folder. "If you'll give me time to review this information and make some inquiries, I will get back to you as soon as I can."

They were sitting in the corner of The Grotto, the hotel restaurant, the dregs of the lunch crowd slowly draining out toward the lobby atrium. On the table in front of them, Mrs. Markley's famous squash soup was congealing in bowls that had been pushed aside. Leah had no appetite after the morning she'd had.

"Unacceptable," she snapped. Cranford was hopeless. He had no management chops and was a drag on her process at this point. A total energy vampire. "I terminated an employee for cause, Mr. Cranford. There was no choice after he…After he was insubordinate in the staff meeting." She forced her breath to slow. "I need to complete the appropriate paperwork and call this in to corporate immediately." The image of Ash's face as he leaned in to kiss her blew unbidden into her mind, and she blinked it away.

Cranford cleared his throat with agonizing slowness. "I'll see what I can do, Ms. Bellerose," he allowed. "But the employee in question does inhabit an apartment here in the hotel and it will take—"

"Wait, what?" Leah's stomach lurched. "He *lives* here?"

"Several of the managers live here in the hotel." Cranford nodded. "They have to be available in case of urgent needs." He looked prim on this point, as if explaining something elementary to a novice. He reached for his tepid soup.

Shit. Leah sat back in her chair and tried to think. This was worse than she'd thought. Not only had she terminated an employee without any written warnings, but now she'd put him out of his home as well.

Jesus, Bellerose, you're turning into a marshmallow. The guy was insubordinate. She had more than sufficient grounds to terminate him and it was well within her authority to do so. If he had to find other living arrangements, that was his problem, not hers. Her job was to make the hotel profitable and efficient. Ash himself had admitted as much. She wasn't running a social welfare agency.

"I want him out. Today," she charged, trying not to watch Cranford spooning gelatinous soup into his mouth. She looked away as the yellow liquid dribbled onto his quivering chin. "Get me the answers I need."

Cranford studied her as he dabbed his face with a linen napkin. "I said I'll do my best." He folded the napkin back into his lap. "Of course, you'll have to be the one to tell him he needs to vacate the premises immediately. According to policy, he has three days to move out, unless otherwise stated. If you want him out today, you'll have to tell him."

Leah's eyebrows shot up and Cranford shrugged. "Did you make that explicit when you terminated him?"

"I didn't know I needed to."

His lips twitched. "No. You didn't. Nonetheless, it must be done."

Leah suppressed a scream. Could this day get any worse? The universe seemed to be testing her, sending her through the gauntlet to see if she could handle this job, this life. Well, she could. She squared her shoulders and stood up. "Where is this apartment?"

***

Ash found William in the potting shed with Karen. The doughy, balding young man was patting soil around some small Japanese maple trees sitting in enormous ceramic pots. He greeted Ash proudly. "Ash. We're taking these to the garden. Me and Karen. On wheels, see?" He pointed to the plant dollies and smiled, showing off a mouth with several teeth missing. His speech was difficult to understand, but over the last few weeks, Ash had become accustomed to it and seldom had to ask William to repeat himself anymore.

Ash raised his hand. "High five, my man. That's awesome." William beamed as Ash turned to Karen. "Ms. Pembroke, may I borrow William for a few minutes? I'll bring him right back to help you."

Karen brushed dirt from her hands and wiped them on her jeans. "Sure, but don't steal him for too long. I can't do without William." She smiled as William laughed and slapped the thigh of his blue coveralls.

"She can't do without me," William chuckled and shook his head in wonderment as he followed Ash into the hotel.

Ash clapped William on the shoulder. "A lot of us feel that way, dude." As he said it, he realized how true it was. There had been a few times over the last weeks when he thought he'd go crazy with boredom, anger, frustration. And each time, being around William had pulled him right out of himself. William's friendly nature, his willingness to help anyone and trust others, was a revelation to Ash. He'd never met anyone like him. Weirdly, none of his A-list friends from Stanford could hold a candle to the man loping alongside him.

He hadn't thought about it before this moment, but it was true. He was dying to get out of this place, but he realized that he'd miss William. Maybe he could come back to visit him.

Odd thought.

He looked over at the man as he led them toward the hotel offices. "William, I wonder if you could do me a favor?" he asked, a twang of guilt under his breastbone. Was he about to take advantage of this disabled man's guilelessness?

William's response was unquestioning. "Sure."

"I'm going to introduce you to a lady, a new lady who works here. She might be a little surprised to meet you." They turned into the office hallway. "You don't have to say anything, but if she asks you questions, answer them honestly." He paused, aware of the irony of what he was saying. William was incapable of telling a lie and wouldn't even understand the concept. *Great. Now I feel like even more of an opportunistic heel.* Ash grimaced in frustration. Of course, all he was doing was advocating for himself. Making sure Leah the Devil understood the reason he'd been late to the meeting. And if he hadn't made a real effort to get there on time, she didn't need to know that.

They rounded the corner to the manager's office, where the open door revealed Julius Cranford sitting alone at his desk, looking disoriented. He glanced up when Ash appeared. "Did she find you?" the older man asked.

Ash shook his head. "Who?"

"Ms. Bellerose. She was going to…She was looking for you." Cranford shuffled some papers on the desk. "I sent her to your apartment."

"You sent…?" Ash frowned and swore to himself. *Just deal with it.* "William, let's head downstairs." He turned, throwing Cranford a sour look.

William's face lit up. "Okay."

As they descended in the elevator, William turned to Ash. "Is the lady pretty?" he asked.

"Hm? Oh." Ash looked up and stared at his reflection in the elevator's mirrored ceiling. "Yeah, I guess she is. In an evil kind of way."

William's gaze followed Ash's and he laughed as he pointed to their reflections. "Is she *really* pretty?"

Ash closed his eyes and willed the elevator to reach its destination. "Unfortunately, yes."

William laughed harder. "Do you like her?"

The elevator doors opened at last. "She's my boss," Ash said. He gestured for William to follow him before the man could ask him anything else.

Their footsteps were soft on the scuffed linoleum as they approached the apartment. The door was open. Ash's biceps stiffened as he stopped in the doorway to take in the scene.

Leah crouched next to the shelves on the far wall, looking at his books and records. *The bitch has broken into my apartment. Is she spying on me?*

"What the hell are you doing?" Momentarily forgetting his mission, Ash strode into the room and faced Leah squarely as she rose in surprise. At least she had the decency to look uncomfortable at being caught. Her cheeks were pink, which was annoyingly attractive. Then she ruined it by opening her mouth.

"We need to discuss the terms of your separation from the company," she said, clearly regaining her bearing. "I came down here to find you, but you weren't here."

"Uh, yeah. I wasn't. But you broke in. To my apartment." It made him angrier to say it out loud. His fists clenched and he flexed his fingers to loosen up.

She crossed her arms. "I certainly did not break in. I have a master key."

"Ah, so that makes it okay to let yourself in and go through a person's things?"

She gritted her teeth. "I hardly 'went through' your things. It's not like there's much to go through." She scanned the tiny space, then her eyes rested on William. "And you are?"

William broke into a huge smile. "I'm William," he announced, patting his chest. He took a bow.

Ash suppressed a smile. He couldn't have planned it any better. "Ms. Bellerose, this is William, Arthur's son. He's the one I told you about this morning. When I was late to the meeting."

To her credit, Leah absorbed this information evenly as she shook William's hand and took in his appearance. "Well. I'm glad to meet you, William. I hear you're a great help to the staff."

"I am."

"Yes." Leah turned an accusing eye on Ash.

"I brought William to the office to meet you. To explain why I was late to the staff meeting." He tried not to look at her mouth, finding it distracting. "Cranford said you'd come down here."

"I see. You brought William to vouch for you." She sounded disgusted and turned to the handyman. "Thank you for your assistance, William. You can go back to work now."

William nodded at Leah solemnly and announced, "He thinks you're pretty."

Ash's heart sank. He opened his mouth to respond, but Leah jumped in.

"Oh, he does, does he? Did he say that?" She turned to Ash, stony-faced.

"Yep," William replied matter-of-factly. "He said you're pretty, but in an evil kind of way."

Ash shook his head. "Jesus Christ," he muttered. "William, you can go back to the greenhouse now. Thanks for...Thanks." He rubbed a palm over his face.

Leah watched William leave, listened for the sound of the elevator doors opening and shutting, then whirled on him.

"Are you demented?" she seethed. "Using that young man as your excuse for tardiness? You think that's going to make a difference?"

Ash blew out a breath. He'd gone this far. It was too late to turn back now. "I wanted you to understand the bigger picture. William is a valued member of the staff and contributes a lot, but he does need extra help sometimes. That's what I was doing this morning, which made me late." He reached into his pocket for his phone. "And there's this." He tapped it and held it out for her to see.

Leah squinted at the phone. "What am I looking at?"

"It's a receipt. For a plumbing and electrical course. I'm doing it at night starting next week. It's all the basics I'll need."

"Why?" The green eyes flashed.

"Why?"

"Yes, *why*? You've been terminated from your position. Why sign up for a course?" Her voice was calm, but her jaw muscle twitched, giving away her irritation. It gave him a small buzz of satisfaction.

"Actually, I signed up for it before you canned me. The truth is you were right. I need some training. More training," he corrected, hoping that sounded credible.

"Huh." Leah folded her arms and considered. Angling away from him, she walked around the small space, which Ash took as a good sign. She was taking time to consider his unspoken request to keep his job.

The silence was broken intermittently by the churning of the laundry one floor up. Leah's heels clicked on the old linoleum as she toured the tiny living area. Her attention was held briefly by a cheap poster print of a Monet garden scene. "It was here when I moved in," he muttered, not wanting her to think he stuck up cheap posters like a kid in a dorm room. She ignored him.

Ash examined his shoes and bit his tongue on additional comments.

She stopped next to his turntable. "You like vinyl." It was a statement, not a question.

"Yeah." He followed her, pulled an LP from the shelf. "These belonged to my mother. She loved jazz." Running his hand over the faded cover of Dave Brubeck's "Take Five" was comforting. It had been in his family home as long as he could remember, in a house long ago left empty.

"Great album." Leah tilted her head to survey the titles on the CDs sharing space with the LPs. "Still using CDs. That's retro. And eclectic taste. I don't think I've ever seen *A Love Supreme* next to *Love Over Gold.*"

"Well, they obviously go together. Miles Davis would have loved Dire Straits." He slid the Brubeck album back in place and waited.

Leah straightened, refolded her arms, and faced him. "Banks, why is there no documentation in your personnel file?"

That took him off guard. "What?"

"Your file. It's almost empty. Just a few forms that you signed when you were hired. No interview forms, no background check, no tax form. How are you being paid?"

Ash thought fast. "I was hired through a temp agency. They're the ones who pay me." He silently exhaled with relief. A temp agency was plausible.

A frown appeared on the freckled face and the emerald eyes narrowed. "There should still be forms. Where are they?"

She didn't believe him. Crap. "How should I know? Ask Cranford."

"I did. He said he'd look into it."

"Well, there you go. That guy's so old, he doesn't remember half of what he does. Who knows where he might have filed my onboarding docs." He inhaled and took a chance. "Listen, Ms. Bellerose. Give me another chance. I need this gig." She was watching him carefully now. "Just one more shot. Write me up if you want to. File a formal corrective action, put me on probation, but let me stay. For, let's say a month. Then reevaluate."

He waited, watching her breathe. Damn, the woman could keep her cool, he had to give her that. What would it be like to see her lose that control for longer than ten seconds? The thought caused a heatwave to roll through him. He refocused, remembering he had to play at being professional.

She was studying his face. "Is your mother still alive?"

Off guard again. This time it took a long moment to answer. He shook his head. "Fifteen years ago. I'd just graduated." He stopped, not wanting to say too much, not wanting to talk about it at all.

"I'm sorry for your loss." She unfolded her arms and chewed her lip slowly. "Alright. I'll give you two weeks. But I want your paperwork. If Cranford can't find it, you'll have to request copies from your temp agency." She turned on her heel and walked to the door. Ash watched her, uncomfortably aware of his attraction and equally baffled by it. How could someone so awful be so intriguing at the same time?

Leah turned in the doorway. "You're completely wrong, you know," she pronounced in that annoying, know-it-all way. Ash's eyebrows rose. She smirked. "Miles Davis would *not* have loved Dire Straits."

Chapter 6

The streets of Charmant were dark and silent at five thirty in the morning. The sound of her cross-trainers rhythmically hitting the pavement created a soothing backdrop for Leah's churning thoughts. Sweat trickled down her back and soaked her T-shirt as she crossed one empty street after another, her surroundings barely registering.

The confrontation with Ash still lingered, though why it bothered her so much made her gut roil with confusion. In her line of work, one couldn't be too emotional.

Strike that. One couldn't be emotional at all. And yet, that's exactly what she'd done. Not only had the employee in question kissed her after she'd fired him, she'd unquestionably kissed him back. Just for a few seconds, but it couldn't be denied. It was as if she'd entered another world, one where anything might happen. Or perhaps, a fantasy of which she'd had no awareness.

It was terrifying. Magical. *Disastrous.* If she thought about it for more than a few seconds, panic descended. Because after that kiss— whatever it meant or didn't mean—she'd reversed her decision and allowed Ash to stay employed, albeit temporarily.

How would that look if anyone found out? The career she'd always dreamed of, the chance to make her mark and climb the ladder of this powerful international company, was on the line. Creating the life she wanted, different from the life she'd been handed at birth, was so close—too close to jeopardize in any way. The weight of anxiety she'd been carrying squeezed down into a heavy knot in her stomach and she sucked in air to loosen up.

Mindfulness, Bellerose. Present moment. Leah closed her eyes briefly as she ran, feeling the breeze on her face. The scent of pine and oak and newly cut grass was a welcome change from the exhaust fumes of New York. Even the silence, so weird the first couple of days, began to sink into her skin.

I can handle this, she thought. *It won't be a problem at all. I'll write Ash Banks up, then have him answer directly to Cranford. He won't have to see me, and I won't have to see him. Problem solved.*

She turned onto Main Street and ran up the sidewalk, into the dusky morning. A few people were out, hosing off stoops or delivering supplies to stores that would open later in the morning. Not having been downtown since her arrival, Leah found herself relaxed enough by her run to look around.

A couple of old department stores had been converted to arts and crafts galleries, offices, and restaurants. There was a small library, a visitor's bureau—*who visits here?*—and an urgent care clinic curiously located within an old fire station. The architecture was interesting and mostly well-maintained. Overall, charming, in an Andy Griffith kind of way.

A coffee shop's lights were on a couple of blocks down, so she headed in that direction. She slowed to a lope, allowing her breath to even out. Hands on her waist, she continued at a brisk walk past an old office building adorned with concrete gargoyles, now coming out of shadow as sunlight seeped over the horizon. Several uniformed workers were leaving the building, carrying garbage bags. One of them looked familiar.

Leah continued slowly toward the small group. "Hector?" She was pretty sure it was him.

The man turned. *"Sí?"*

"It's Leah Bellerose. From the hotel."

Hector peered toward her in the gray light. "Miss Bellerose?" He smiled but sounded cautious. "Oh. Yes. I did not recognize you at first. You look different."

"Ah." She chuckled. "Right. I'm not usually covered with sweat at work." She fanned the T-shirt to dry off.

"That's not it." Hector handed one of his colleagues the bag he'd been carrying and nodded his thanks. "You look good. Relaxed like."

Leah stopped fanning. "Relaxed." She bit back on a snappy retort, wondering why the man's observation felt like an insult. "Huh."

Hector shrugged and grinned awkwardly. "Your job is high pressure, no?" He looked around, as uncomfortable as she was with the turn in the conversation. "Please excuse me, miss. I need to get back to work."

Leah waved toward the office building. "You work here? At night?"

The man nodded. "Six nights a week. For eight years now."

Her eyebrow rose. "That makes for a long workday." It was more than long. It was insane. When did the man sleep? How did he stay so cheerful? "Can I buy you a cup of coffee? Or a bagel or something? I was heading down to that café—"

He was shaking his head before she could finish asking. "Thank you, Ms. Bellerose. I need to finish up here and have a shower before I have to punch in at the hotel." He cocked his head. "Maybe another time?"

"Sure." She watched him go, wondering what else she didn't know about her staff. Including what they thought of her.

***

The ballroom smelled as bad the next morning, though the web-strewn windows had been opened overnight to air it out. Ash sucked in a breath and reminded himself he was engaged in a marathon, not a sprint, and patience would be needed to get himself out of this predicament. No matter how much mildew he had to endure. He unclenched his teeth and mentally prepared to go into project planning mode.

"Uh, Mr. Banks?"

Ash turned to greet Antonio Duran, Hector's cousin, as he entered the cavernous space. Ash's heart sank. Antonio was a kid, in his early twenties. However, the starched white dress shirt, carefully pressed jeans, and clipboard indicated that this young man took his task seriously. Maybe there was hope.

Ash shook Antonio's hand and gestured in the direction of the faded wallpaper. "Think you can get this paper down, the walls repaired, and fresh paint up in the next two weeks? We need it done before the new carpet goes in." No point beating around the bush. If Hector's cousin couldn't commit to the insanely compressed timeline, there was little reason to have the conversation.

Antonio Duran studied the dim space, the peeling walls, the soaring ceiling. His black eyes glinted. "Can you pay for two shifts of workers? I can have two teams in here, working around the clock. That's what it would take."

Ash didn't pause. "I'll have your contract drafted by noon. But I need your word. Payment will be contingent on the deadline being met."

Antonio smiled a Cheshire cat grin. "You know how to do business. But, with respect," he paused, considering Ash's maintenance jumpsuit, "do you have the authority to make this deal with me? Hector says you're solid. But you are, pardon me, the maintenance supervisor. Not the head manager, my friend."

His comment was not unexpected, but it burned. Ash drew a careful breath. "The manager, Mr. Cranford, has put me in charge of the ballroom renovation. I'm coordinating all the work being done. So yes, I have the authority."

Antonio nodded slowly. "Again, you will forgive me. I've heard that Mr. Cranford is no longer in charge. There is a new manager. A woman."

The muscles in Ash's arms stiffened. He took a step to widen his stance, positioning himself for battle. "Be assured, I have been given authority from senior management. That's all you need to know." He extended his hand again, effectively concluding the meeting. "Come back this afternoon with your team prepared to work. I'll have the contract ready when you get here."

***

Leah made notes on her daily task list as she zipped into her skirt and finished her make-up. She pulled her shoulder-length hair into a low ponytail and called it good enough.

Her tablet was propped against the vanity mirror, as usual. Multi-tasking was the only way she could get everything in her life taken care of. Some people said multi-tasking was impossible, but she was living proof that it was possible and necessary.

She reviewed her list, heart sinking on item one: Banks's performance improvement plan. Ugh. No way to avoid it. She'd have to see him to finalize it, but that would be it— she'd never have to see him again. And that would be a relief, right?

No doubt.

The hollow feeling in her solar plexus was a remnant, a ridiculous, useless leftover, probably from her time with Barry. Something to ignore. Like most emotions, whatever this thing was couldn't have any utility for her. She had to remain focused on her goals and not let anything get in the way. Her spine straightened at the thought. That felt better. Being determined was one of her strongest attributes. She shared that with her mother, who was known within family circles as the iron maiden. *That's me*, she thought. The "junior iron maiden," her uncle had always said. Cerebral. Unemotional. Just saying it to herself made her feel lighter.

She applied a final swipe of mascara and stood back. "How do I look, Prune? Ready to conquer the day?" The cat sat primly on the vanity, watching the morning ritual with silent reproof. Her long, golden tail flicked imperiously. When she realized Leah was looking at her, she raised her back leg languidly to lick a delicate foot.

"Thanks for the support," Leah murmured as she threw her make-up into a drawer. "Gotta get going, princess. Lots of work to do." She dropped a kiss on the cat's head and grabbed her tablet.

As she snapped her briefcase shut and slipped into her heels, a loud knock sounded in the foyer.

A sizzle of warning ran up her arms as she went to the door and glanced through the peephole. Exasperation tightened her throat as she flung the door open. "Barry, what the hell are you doing here?"

The man threw his hands open. "Leah, minxy, I had to see you." He brushed past her into the apartment. "I drove almost all night to get here. Do you have any coffee? Siri couldn't find a Starbucks around here."

Leah tossed her briefcase on the couch. "Barry, you have to leave. I'm on my way to work."

He ignored her comment. "Doll, you look amazing. Healthy. Small-town life must agree with you."

He didn't look any different, Leah thought. Dark blond hair cut too short for her taste, narrow nose, gray Nordic eyes. Preppy polo shirt and chinos. Totally vanilla.

And that comment about small-town life. He had to know that would trip every trigger for her. Was he *trying* to make things worse for himself?

Barry scanned the living room as he marched into the kitchen. "This place is a disappointment. Look at this hideous linoleum. I thought you said this job was a step up for you." He shook his head and began opening cabinets. "Is that rental furniture or something? I never pegged you as an Ikea person. Coffee?"

Leah bit back an urge to yell. "I'm leaving, Barry. Listen to me. I don't want you here. I have nothing to say to you. Leave." She gestured toward the door. *I'm always telling people to leave, to get away from me.* The thought appeared out of nowhere and she brushed it away. There was no time for self-analysis now. No time to figure out why she'd ever been attracted to this ludicrous, vain, lying son of a bitch.

On the other hand, maybe she'd never been attracted to him. In fact, that felt right. It hadn't been *him* at all. He'd said all the right things at the time when she needed to hear them, vulnerable as she had once been. A stupid kid. Talk about emotions getting in the way.

Well, never again.

Barry, beige-clad backside visible as he bent over, spoke from the muffled depths of the lower cabinets. "Seriously? No coffee?" He stood and beamed at her. "Come on. I drove all the way here. Let's talk. We can go for coffee and, you know, see where we land."

Leah pulled her phone out of her purse. "I'm going to call the police if you're not out of here in thirty seconds."

The man became serious as he approached her. "Leah, please. I'm sorry I hurt you. I've said I was sorry a hundred times. But you weren't perfect, either, you know. We hardly brought out the best in each other."

She could not believe her ears. "I swear to God, if you make this my fault, you're a bigger ass than I ever imagined possible."

"Okay, okay. But minxy—"

"I am *not* your minxy. No more. Ever." Disgust rose in her throat. *How* could she ever have been taken in by this guy? "And don't get any closer to me." She grabbed her briefcase and stood in the open doorway, waiting.

Barry's face was crestfallen, but she recognized that look and knew it was only the surface. He didn't care. He was hollow and emotionless.

Like me.

Suddenly she couldn't breathe. Her gut tightened into a knot so hard it felt like she was disappearing into it—an internal black hole that threatened to consume her.

His voice came from far away, and she realized her eyes were shut. He was still babbling. "Drove all night. I'm staying at the Hilton over in Southport. Coffee?"

Her temper boiled over, out of control, an emotion that had a use for once. *"Get out."* she snarled, throat raw with fury.

Chapter 7

"Is this clear? You understand the parameters here? You have two weeks from today to meet all expectations, otherwise your employment will be terminated." Leah slid the document across the desk to Ash, along with a pen.

He signed, reminding himself in time to stop after his middle name, Banks. It was tempting to tell her who he was, to blurt it out. But no, he couldn't. Part of the deal with his father was that no one could know or even suspect. He didn't want special favors from her, but his shoulders tightened at the thought of deceiving her.

Weird. He'd never had that stab of conscience with a woman before, or even thought about honesty in a relationship. It was a foreign concept. Then again, no other woman he'd ever met had looked or acted quite like Leah. Or smelled as good. Or caused him to burn inside at the memory of a stolen kiss.

"Banks? I asked you a question and I need an answer." The green eyes flashed accusation.

And no other woman has been nearly so maddening. It was as if itching powder had been thrown at him. She might be smokin' hot, but she was still a pain in the ass. She didn't deserve his honesty. His voice was clipped. "Sure, I get it, okay? It's a pretty straightforward concept." He stood, not waiting for a response.

She stood as well and wiggled her hips to straighten her pencil skirt. Dark gray today, topped by a snug, cleavage-enhancing jacket. He looked away, trying to ignore the physical response that ripped through him.

"You don't have to sound so sarcastic, Banks." She tapped the papers together on the desk. "I'm doing this against my better judgment."

Now he was mad, which was much more familiar than being turned on against his will. Here came his good old friend, anger. "Don't do me any favors, lady. I intend to be a model employee.

And let's be honest, it's not like I did anything all that terrible to start with." His voice was steely, the words volleying out. "Admit it. You were a hardass because *that's who you are*. End of story." Even as he spoke, he knew he was risking his shot, but he couldn't hold back.

He watched as her face went pale, then pink and she stared down at the desk for a long moment. A pang of regret, unexpected and sharp, spiked under his ribs.

"You bastard," she whispered. She tossed the signed document toward him. "Get out of my office. I don't want to see you again. Ever. You'll deal with Cranford exclusively from now on."

Damn his temper. He'd give anything to turn the clock back two minutes.

Ash was around the desk before he knew what was happening. His body moved with a will of its own. Her eyes widened as he approached, so fast she had no time to move away. His hands wanted to wind themselves into her hair as his gaze roved her face, those adorable freckles, that inviting mouth. "I'm sorry, Leah. I'm sorry I'm such an ass."

She stared, pupils dilating at his use of her first name. Her lips parted but she made no sound. She seemed frozen, exposed. It was disorienting. How did she go from raving harridan to vulnerable woman in the space of a heartbeat?

He continued, "You're giving me a chance to make things right, and I threw it back in your face. I wish I could say that's not like me, but the truth is, it is. It's exactly like me." His thumb itched to caress her cheek. "My emotions get the better of me sometimes, but I'm working on it. It's that you—" He closed his eyes briefly. "You seem to bring out..." He shook his head, more confused than ever.

"The worst in you? Is that it? I bring out the worst in you?" Her voice was unsteady.

"No, that's not it at all. You bring out something I don't understand. Maybe it's not even good or bad. But it's vital." He exhaled ruefully and glanced at the ceiling. "Jesus. Vital. When have I ever used that word?"

The emotions in her face were impossible to read as she swallowed and stepped carefully back, away from him. A tiny line appeared momentarily between her eyebrows, then smoothed as her features arranged themselves into their standard, businesslike appearance.

"All the more reason for us to focus on our respective jobs and not get in each other's way." She turned, breaking eye contact. "I'll file the corrective plan. That's all." She busied herself at her desk.

At first it was hard to move, but he rolled his shoulders to loosen up and drew breath. "Right." His hand was on the doorknob when she stopped him.

"Banks."

He turned back expectantly.

This time it was her voice that was steely. "I want those hiring documents by the end of the week. Submit them to Cranford. You needn't come to me about anything else."

***

Onward. No distractions. Focus. No need to think about the way her skin hummed from contact with Ash. No reason to linger on the way his eyes met hers, the way he looked at her like he truly saw her, not the professional woman she was trying to be.

Scratch that. The professional woman I am—*the bastard.*

Leah watched Dahlia scurry around the gleaming restaurant kitchen with the other staff prepping for the lunch crowd. The young woman's mop of red hair kept escaping from the scarf she wore wound around her head, her eyes wide with the effort of trying to get salads plated.

Estelle barked orders at everyone, most loudly at her daughter. "Get that hair of yours under a proper cap, girl, or you're going to housekeeping permanently." She turned to Leah. "I can't do a thing with her. She's always been scattered." Her tone softened. "But she has a good heart. Like her father. So, we do what we can." She brushed flour from her hands and turned from the bread-making station. "What can I do for you, Miss Bellerose?"

For a panicked split second, Leah couldn't recall her task. "Ah, yes." She cleared her throat. "I'd like to arrange sandwiches and coffee for the workers in the ballroom, so they can be as efficient as possible. Here's a schedule I've put together. Please see that it's carried out." *Ridiculous to even be standing here. I could have called the kitchen or emailed the instructions.*

But she'd had to get out of that office.

Estelle nodded and pinned the schedule to her corkboard. "I'll take care of it, Miss Bellerose. You can count on me."

Leah noticed several of the kitchen staff slide glances at their supervisor, silently signaling that it would be them, not her, carrying out Leah's instructions. "I know I can, Estelle. I'm counting on all of you."

Dahlia smiled shyly and tapped her foot as she placed cucumber slices on plates of greens. Management instincts on the alert, Leah took note of this. When she wasn't frazzled, Dahlia attended carefully to what was happening. Maybe the young woman wouldn't be so useless after all.

Leah felt her skills and experience coming together in this place. While her ambitions went way beyond this little backwater, no doubt being here was affirming her confidence in herself.

Simon Gerard had hired her to assess and reorganize the hotel across the board, to do whatever it might take to bring it to profitability— and no bizarre moments of hormonal weakness could change that. She had her eyes on the prize. Back to New York City, or even Singapore. Moving up the ladder to countrywide, maybe even continental leadership in the company.

Her breath eased. *I can do this.*

She exited the kitchen and nodded at Dahlia. "Keep up the good work," she said, hardly believing her own words. Compliments were not her modus operandi. But it seemed right for the moment, and Dahlia's blushing "Thank you" confirmed it.

***

Ash knew he was taking a chance. He also knew he was a cad. That he was inexplicably attracted to this gorgeous, obnoxious, impossible woman was something he couldn't hide from himself, but the truth was he also needed to stay in her good graces. His father would be checking up on him, no question. It was his job to impress Leah Bellerose with his commitment to the hotel. Staying on her radar, in the best possible way, was his ticket out of here and back into the corporate world.

Her office door had been standing open, so technically he wasn't trespassing. He positioned himself carefully in the chair and placed the file folder on the desk in front of him. His jaw set as he heard the click of high heels approaching, followed by the voice of Hilda Ruiz.

"The mayor said you should call him anytime, Miss Manager. *Dios mio.* He even left his home number. I told him that you wouldn't..." The voice trailed off as the two women came to a stop in the office doorway and stared at Ash.

Leah's face was expressionless, her voice flat. "Banks."

He stood up. "Correct." He offered a grin in Hilda's direction. "Good to see you, ladies. I wanted to—"

"I thought I indicated that you weren't to bother me." She moved briskly around him, to the other side of the desk.

Hilda glanced awkwardly from Ash to Leah and began edging backward.

"Stay, Hilda. We need to review the registration protocol for the meeting of mayors. Mr. Banks was leaving." Leah's voice was matter-of-fact, but her eyes flashed. Ash felt a spark at that, knowing he got under her skin.

Careful. Don't want to piss her off too much.

"Ms. Bellerose, I have some business updates related to the ballroom renovation." He gestured toward the file folder. "You can certainly take a look yourself, but I'd welcome the opportunity to present them to you and answer any questions or concerns."

He saw the internal debate happening, though it was almost instantaneous. It was a very slight softening, nearly imperceptible, but definitely a start.

"Alright." She exhaled and turned to Hilda. "I'll follow up with you later, Ms. Ruiz." Hilda nodded, relieved, and disappeared.

Leah studied Ash silently for a moment, then strode to the door, closed it firmly, and faced him, arms folded. "Business updates, Banks? Really?" She looked at her wristwatch. "You have two minutes." She moved back behind the desk but stayed standing, clearly not planning for a long conversation.

Ash's eyebrows rose. "Two minutes?" His head tilted quizzically. "In that case, I'll leave out the finer details, but the bottom line is that as of now we have contracts for both the wallpaper removal, painting, and drapery cleaning in the ballroom. They're both dependent on a firm deadline. Work starts this afternoon." He stood to face her and held out the folder in her direction.

Leah didn't blink or move. "What about the carpet?"

"The carpet?"

"The thing on the floor. You know. I'm sure you've heard of them."

Ash bit back on a sharp retort and cleared his throat. "We're still working on that."

"And the chandelier. It needs to be taken down and cleaned."

His fists clenched involuntarily. This wasn't going the way he'd planned. "The point is that we already have contracts for two big pieces of this project. I personally spoke to the contractors and emphasized the importance—"

Leah held up a hand to stop him. "Banks, I don't care who speaks to these people. Julius is in charge of making sure the contracts get done. I'm meeting with him later. That's all I need to know."

He stared at her, bewildered by duel feelings of ire and intrigue. Confusion over human motivation was unfamiliar to him. It was a central feature of business acumen to know your target's drivers, and he honestly couldn't figure out what hers were.

"Banks?" She interrupted his thoughts.

His eyes refocused on hers. "What makes you like this?"

A slender eyebrow rose. "I beg your pardon?"

He shifted his weight so he was leaning against the desk. "What makes you like this?" He gestured toward her.

She blinked. "Like what?"

"What makes you so able to dismiss people? So dispassionate? It's like you're covered in Teflon. And yet..." His voice trailed off.

Leah was frozen in front of him and for a moment, fear spiked. Had he gone too far and offended her past all salvation? His job, his entire future was on the line.

Before he could speak, she sat heavily in the new office chair, leather creaking. She spun the chair slowly toward the back corner of the room, effectively shutting him out.

For a moment, neither moved nor spoke. Then her voice floated to him, barely above a whisper, with a faint wobble. "Leave." Then again, this time more firmly. *"Leave."*

Ash's feet felt rooted to the floor, frustration, dread, and regret warring within him. At last, fists unclenching, he inhaled carefully and stepped around the desk to kneel in front of her. The surprise on her face was unmistakable.

Seeing her that way, the woman behind the curtain, broke something in him. Something old. Something ready to crumble.

"Leah, I'll leave you alone if you want me to. But…" He took her hands slowly, turned them over and kissed one palm and then the other. When she didn't resist, he continued, not sure what was happening even as it happened. He rose and pulled her to her feet, then took her face in his hands.

"I'll leave you alone if you want me to, but I want you to know I don't regret kissing you. I don't regret this"—he looked around the office, then back at her—"because in spite of whatever mask, or whatever it is, of professionalism that you wear like a suit of armor, you are like a magnet. You're a flame that keeps leading me back, even when I know it could burn."

She was watching him now, eyes tracking his, curiosity leading while hurt and anger lurked.

Ash rested his forehead gently against hers. "What is it about you?" He lowered his mouth and bit her lower lip gently, feeling her stiffen in his arms. "I can't stay away from you. How's that for doing something against better judgment?" Gingerly, he angled to cover her mouth with his, felt her breath, heard her moan as she softened against his chest. Then she was kissing him back and he was so shocked he almost lost it. Lightning raced through his veins as her arms wound around his neck, her hand to the back of his head, pulling him closer into her.

Her tongue was hot against his, her breathing fast and deep, matching his. They stumbled sideways and ended up half on the desk. A stapler skidded over the edge and hit the floor with a thud.

Leah nipped his lower lip, then gasped. "*Shit.* This can't be happening again. Shit, shit, shit." But she twined her fingers in his hair as she kissed him again. She tasted like mint and lip gloss and…her. It was an intoxicating combination. He felt drunk.

His mouth moved to her neck, kissing, grazing the sensitive skin with his teeth. Her head was thrown back, her throat exposed as he continued. The scent of her skin hit his solar plexus while blood roared in his ears. A tidal wave of electricity rose between them, hot and demanding. His whole body felt illuminated with it.

She was sitting on the desk now, her hands roving over him, driving him wild. Ash realized his eyes had closed, something he never did. "Leah," he breathed, forcing his eyes open. "I don't know what this is. But I want to find out." He paused as she pulled back to look at him. "Don't make me stay away from you. Please. I'll report to the old man but let me see you." He held up a hand as she started to speak. "Only away from work. Strict boundaries." He stroked her hair and fell into the depths of those green eyes, immersing himself in their possibilities. "Don't say no. If you can't say yes, don't say anything."

He traced her mouth with his fingers as he spoke. "I need something...something that's not a No in my life right now." He bent to kiss her again and realized she was looking at him in bewilderment, a tiny frown line between her eyebrows. "What?"

She shook her head. "I've lost my mind," she whispered. Her hand went to the back of his head as she pulled him closer again. "But I'm beginning to think sanity is overrated."

***

Leah watched Ash leave her office and felt a lightness she'd never experienced before. Her limbs felt like wings. Gravity had lessened. And yet terror vibrated under the surface.

What the hell had just happened?

An avalanche of emotions tumbled inside of her, threatening to suffocate her. Better to focus on the physical, which was much less threatening than anything to do with feelings. The chemistry between them was undeniable and incendiary.

Not that she had much to compare it to, but one thing was certain. That was the best kiss she'd ever experienced, something she'd never even come close to imagining. She was embarrassingly turned on, and despite fear and anger warring for attention under her breastbone, it was hard not to run after him.

For God's sake, the guy even looked good in a maintenance jumpsuit. What his physique was like under there was something she could hardly fathom.

A low buzz ran through her limbs, from her toes up to the top of her head. The guy knew how to kiss a woman, that much was sure.

And he hadn't even seemed to mind when her first reaction was "*Shit.*"

Another smooth move, Bellerose. Totally hot response.

She ran a hand over her eyes and made her way into the powder room attached to the office. Her reflection in the mirror caused her to grimace.

Awesome. Mussed hair. Lip gloss hopelessly smeared, cheeks embarrassingly pink. Eyes…Hmm. Her eyes were bright. Like they were lit up behind the irises. Strange. What did that mean?

"Probably high blood pressure," she mumbled. Hairbrush in hand, she did as much damage control as she could, applied fresh lip gloss, and patted cool water onto her cheeks. *Better.*

Then it hit her. She had kissed *the maintenance man.* She wondered if he'd finished school. He had said something about graduation. Trade school, perhaps? Leah had never thought of herself as a snob— she *wasn't* a snob— not by any means. Her beginnings could hardly have been humbler, but she'd fought and scratched and sweated every day for the last twenty years to get where she was today. Someone like Banks— well, he seemed content to be where he was. A man without aspirations from the looks of it. She couldn't possibly be comfortable with the thought of a romantic entanglement with someone without ambition.

Of course, he did have that Brubeck album, which was a bit peculiar—she hadn't pegged him for a jazz lover—but it had been his mother's, so perhaps that explained it.

Guilt tugged at her but she quickly dismissed it. This wasn't snobbishness. It was pure practicality. She was highly educated and had lived in the world's most sophisticated cities. She was connected to executives, business leaders, politicians, entrepreneurs. When she was done in Charmant, she was going to Singapore. It was impossible she could have anything in common with a small-town maintenance man.

That's a good thing, because this—whatever it is—with Banks can't go anywhere, she told herself, sucking in a breath as she examined her flushed face in the mirror.

She exited the restroom and was met by Julius Cranford coming into the office. "Ms. Bellerose, we have a conference call with Simon Gerard."

She stopped in her tracks. Leah wasn't prepared to deal with her boss right now. She could barely tell up from down.

"Now?" Her attention was snagged by the phone on the desk, its Hold light blinking furiously.

Cranford sat in the chair in front of the desk. "It was scheduled yesterday. Did you forget?" He pushed the blinking light. "We're both here now, sir."

Simon Gerard's voice rumbled from the speakerphone. "Good. Leah, I need a full report on all staff by tomorrow. The board is moving up its plan to evaluate staffing needs."

"Ah." Leah scrambled through the stack of papers on her desk as she struggled to order her thoughts. "That might be a challenge, sir. I still have some interviews to conduct." She booted up her computer. "I can give you a partial breakdown now—"

"No need for that," Gerard interjected. "I'll schedule a follow-up tomorrow and we'll go from there. Prioritize the management staff and anyone else essential to organizational operations."

"Roger that." Leah made notes as he talked.

"Remember we need to cut costs, but where those savings come from will be for you to determine. The board will rely on your recommendations for final decisions."

Leah nodded as she typed. "Thank you, sir. Until tomorrow." She blew out a breath as the connection was severed. She avoided looking at the older man, but she could feel his eyes on her.

Cranford's voice was flat. "They're going to let me go, aren't they? I'm the manager who's been here the longest, so I'm the greatest financial liability."

Leah hadn't planned on having this conversation today, especially not after the encounter with Ash. Her mouth still tingled from his kisses. She wanted to be at home with Prunella, a glass of wine in hand, with no one demanding answers from her. "No final decisions have been made, Mr. Cranford."

He nodded. "I've been lucky to be here this long. I know that. Charmant Forest has been like a home to me, the staff like a family. I know that might be hard for you to understand, but it's the truth."

Leah bristled. "It's not hard for me to understand. I'm not unfeeling." She shifted uncomfortably.

A sad smile tipped the elderly man's thin lips. "There was a time in my life, a very difficult time when I thought I'd go crazy, and I almost did, except for the friends I had here, and the routine of work." He raised his eyes to hers. "But that was a long time ago. And now it's time to move on."

Leah tried to offer him an encouraging smile. "No matter what decisions are made, the transition will take time. Nothing will happen overnight."

The man rose stiffly from the chair and Leah was struck again by how old he was. It was a miracle he'd stayed at the hotel this long.

"Thank you, Ms. Bellerose." He made his way slowly to the door. "I think I'll leave a little early today if you don't mind. Unless you need assistance with the staff interviews."

"Of course. I can handle the interviews." *That's my job now,* Leah thought. *Deciding who will stay. And who will go.* She watched Cranford hobble out and shut the door behind him, leaving her in silence. The sense of herself carrying a heavy weight came back. This time it was a boulder wedged between her shoulder blades. The image prompted her to straighten and shrug her arms up and down to loosen them. *You can handle this,* she told herself. *This is what you've trained for.*

Her thoughts were interrupted by a video call coming in. Simon Gerard again. His chiseled features and expertly cut gray hair were distinguished, as always, and she thought— not for the first time— that he must have been quite handsome as a younger man.

"Leah, are you alone in your office?"

"Yes. Cranford has left. I think he knew you and I would be talking again privately." If only it weren't now. She was still having a hard time concentrating.

"I need to ask you about a few people specifically. Cranford is out, obviously, and almost certainly"—he consulted his notes— "Estelle Markley and Arthur Jones. They've been employed the longest and are nearing retirement age."

Estelle and Arthur. Leah grasped for a way to buy time. "Sir, I haven't had a chance to formulate a plan on those employees. My instinct is that they might be necessary for the continuity of the other staff we want to keep. Would it be acceptable if I get back to you about them after additional interviews? I need to gather more data."

Gerard frowned his reluctance. "I suppose another few days won't hurt, but I do want to strategize with you before the final report goes to the board." He tapped a pen on his desk. "Now, what about this Hector Duran. He's head of housekeeping. It's unusual to have a man in that position. Any thoughts there?"

Other than the overt sexism of your comment? Leah felt an acid burn in her throat. "Duran is solid, sir. He's very connected to his housekeeping staff. I understand there's a significantly lower than average incidence of turnover as a result."

Gerard absorbed this information while he continued to scan his notes. "I see Duran has a noncompete agreement, indicating he has a second job somewhere. What do you know about that?"

Leah nodded. "He does have another job with a cleaning company that takes care of office buildings at night. I don't know of any issues around that. He has no record of tardiness or other performance problems. He seems well-liked and well-respected. Housekeeping is probably the most efficient department at Charmant Forest."

"All right." Gerard tapped a stack of papers into a neat square. "But let's keep an eye on it. We can't have a manager's attention diluted with another position or affected by fatigue. Housekeeping is critical."

"Agreed. Absolutely."

Continuing, the man ran his finger down a list. "That brings us to—Asher Banks. New maintenance manager. Hired about a month ago, after the renovation, I believe."

Leah felt herself grow warm and she shifted, hoping her face wasn't still pink. "Yes. I...he was...he is new, sir. I mean, newish. A month or so." She cleared her throat and pretended to rifle through papers on her desk. *Get a grip, Bellerose. Are you trying to advertise the insanity of the last few days?*

Her chin rose slightly, and she started over, voice steady. "Yes, sir, Banks is new on the job. He works primarily with Arthur Jones, I believe, and Arthur's son, William." A vision of William's broad, beaming face and good-natured innocence sent a calming wave through her body, and she felt herself relax into her chair.

Gerard was watching her. "How's he doing?" His face was expressionless, but something about the way the question was asked caused a distant warning bell to ring.

"Acceptable," she began. "I'll be honest, he's had some challenges in terms of his expertise on the job, but he's demonstrated a willingness to learn and increase his skills." Was she sweating? Did she get all the smears of lip gloss off her mouth?

And why did she feel she had to defend Ash to Gerard? She should be honest about his brashness and report that he was now working under a corrective plan— but the words wouldn't come out.

"I see." Gerard appeared thoughtful. "He's learning and trying to improve?" He sounded genuinely curious.

"Yes, I would say so, sir."

The man nodded and the corner of his mouth twitched upward. "It's always good to see employees motivated to grow their skill sets." He rubbed his chin. "How's his attitude?"

The question was unexpected. "Sir?"

"His overall demeanor on the job. How does he conduct himself? Is he respectful?"

Leah suddenly felt that Gerard knew something she didn't. Could he know something about what had happened between Ash and her? How would that be possible? She rubbed her arms, trying to shake off the sense of doubt and the fear that went along with it. "His attitude is fine, for the most part. I would say he, well, he has a strong personality. Not that I know that much about it. His personality, that is," she added quickly. *Crap. Turn this conversation around, Bellerose, before he digs in any more or you give any more away.* "Banks is invested in doing well here, sir. He's made that clear. And he is respectful," she finished, not quite meeting the man's eagle-eyed gaze.

Gerard studied her, then seemed to come to a decision. "Fine, glad to hear it. Let's move on. What can you tell me about Dahlia Markley?"

It wasn't until they hung up ten minutes later that Leah realized she'd forgotten to mention the lack of documentation in Ash's personnel file. Or that Gerard had not seemed interested in the attitude of any employee except Asher Banks.

Chapter 8

Leah kicked off her heels and picked up Prunella. The cat purred her welcome and nuzzled against Leah's cheek.

"Another day in the Twilight Zone, Prune," she said. "It gets weirder and weirder." She padded into the kitchen to get a glass of wine, then decided on seltzer. Opening a bottle of wine seemed like too much effort. Every cell in her body drooped with fatigue.

She popped a frozen dinner in the microwave and stared out the dusty window toward the lights of the hotel down the hill. It was a picturesque sight, surrounded by darkened trees, moonlight on a pond in the distance, not a trailer park in sight. In fact, if a person didn't care about decent restaurants or theater or culture, this town could be an appealing place to settle. There were benefits to smaller.

The microwave dinged and she plopped her supposedly Tuscan pasta and veggies onto a plate. It would have been easier to eat in the hotel restaurant, but she'd wanted to get out of there. And this wasn't so bad, even if it was kind of soggy. She pushed the broccoli around with her fork and went in search of cheese.

Her phone buzzed.

The number that appeared caused her to groan. "Not now," she mumbled as she hit Answer, telling herself to sound cheerful. "Hi, Mama. How are you?"

Her mother's voice was the same, tired and rough around the edges. Too many years of cigarettes and physical labor. "Hi, baby. I can't complain. How's my little girl? What's happening with that new job?" Leah heard the snick of a lighter and a deep inhalation.

"I'm fine, Mama. The new job is good. Just started the first of this week." Better to stay away from details. Keeping it superficial was always best. The truth was her mother didn't want to know the personal details any more than she herself wanted to reveal them. They didn't have that kind of relationship, which suited them both.

"That's my girl. You said the job was somewhere south of New York." There was a pause as she waited for an answer to the implied question.

Leah suppressed a sigh. She could try to leave out the particulars, but she wouldn't outright lie to her mother. "Pretty far south of New York. I'm in Charmant. You know, near the border."

Her mother puffed out a breath. "Charmant? Why, Maggie, that's less than two hundred miles from here."

Leah inspected a fingernail and wondered if she could get a manicure in this town. "My boss mentioned sending me to Singapore for my next assignment. But right now, here I am." She continued, an itch of irritation compelling her. "And Mama, don't call me Maggie. You know I don't go by that anymore."

Her mother huffed in indignation. "Now that I don't understand. But," she said, taking on the matter-of-fact tone her daughter had learned so well, "if that's the way you want it, so be it. Far be it from me to interfere."

Leah sighed and closed her eyes. "You've always been good at..." *distancing yourself* "...giving me space." *So, I come by it honestly.* Her head started to throb. "I'm aiming for senior management in this company. I'm here but probably not for long."

"Well, honey, I think that's great." Her mother blew out smoke and continued. "I hope you can get over here to visit before you head off to somewhere else. It's been a while. At least two years."

Leah ran a hand over tired eyes. "I'll try. Maybe on a weekend. But it's hard. The hotel has a lot of issues and I'm working long hours."

Cecelia Bellerose wasn't one to wallow in sentiment or play the emotions card. "You take care of yourself, you hear me? Don't let yourself get run down. Take your vitamins."

That was worth a smile. "I will, Mama."

"Oh, and listen, Mag—I mean, *Leah.* if you can get away for a visit, make sure you stop in on Cousin Doogie. He's been asking after you. And Aunt Sugar. Her heart's been acting up, and it would mean a lot to her to see you."

Leah stood at the kitchen counter and stirred shredded cheese into her pasta and broccoli. "I'll try. I will. Though it won't be easy to get away from work." Made all the more difficult by her visceral dread of returning to her hometown.

"All right then, baby. You stay in touch, now, you hear?"

Leah ended the call and stared at her food. It smelled revolting. The conversation with her mother triggered too many memories of frozen dinners and donated canned goods, meals served at a Formica table in a run-down mobile home. "Should have eaten in the restaurant," she mumbled as she dumped the plate into the sink and stuffed the food into the garbage disposal. "What a waste."

It wasn't late but her appetite was nil, and her limbs ached with fatigue. She changed into sweatpants and T-shirt, brushed her teeth, and fed Prunella. Then she made the rounds, checking and rechecking the windows and door locks. Too many childhood moves in sketchy neighborhoods had left a legacy of paranoia, especially at night.

She flopped onto the couch to channel surf and the doorbell rang. "Damn," she cursed, closing her eyes. Someone at the door at this time on a Friday evening could not be good. Checking the peephole had her cursing again. "Barry," she growled. She opened the door only wide enough to speak but kept her foot braced against it. "What do you want?"

The man held out a bouquet of garishly colored grocery store daisies and offered her a contrite smile. "I brought these as a peace offering," he began. "Just to let you know how much I regret hurting—"

"I don't like flowers. Strange you don't recall that from our *decade* together. Don't come back." She tried to shut the door, but he pushed against it.

"Leah, hear me out. I only want to put things right between us. To make amends." He continued pushing, not quite forcing the door open but creating space for a full confrontation. "You don't have to take me back or anything. Not right now. Just accept my apology." He held out the flowers.

Leah ground her teeth together. "Fine." She took the flowers and pointed out the door with them. "You can go now."

"Can't we talk for a few minutes?" He sounded pitiful. "I came all this way. Put more miles on the Beemer than I ever have, and you know how I love my Beemer. Please, minxy. I mean, Leah."

Pitiful. He was utterly pitiful. She considered. "If we talk, do you promise to leave and not come back?"

"Of course."

"Don't make me regret this," she said, already feeling regretful.

He raised his hand. "On my word."

Leah tried not to role her eyes. Like his word meant anything. Lying bastard. *One, two, three.* Deep breath. "Two minutes. That's all." She held the door open reluctantly. Better to give him two minutes than have him come back later.

"Great." He sauntered in. "Have you had dinner? We could go out or something. Are there any decent restaurants in this town?"

"One minute, fifty seconds."

He grimaced. "Jesus. Okay." He surveyed the apartment. "Do you still have that funny-looking cat? What was her name?"

Leah set her jaw. "Prunella. My baby for the last five years. Yes, I still have her." Unbelievable. What a jerk.

"Right, right. Prunella. I remember. She's, uh, cute." He looked around nervously. "Where is she?"

"Probably hiding. Or looking for a crucifix."

The reference was lost on Barry. He nodded and tapped his foot. "So...How are you?"

That did it. "We're done." Leah opened the door and gestured. "Out."

"But I still have time. Like, a minute or something."

"Well, silly me. I thought you wanted to apologize, even though you've already apologized a thousand times and I've said fine, I've heard your apology and I never want to see you again." She shooed him backwards toward the door.

He pouted as he went. "Leah, it hurts me so much to see you alone. I miss you, angel."

What a shitty actor. It was insulting that he'd spent ten years with her and didn't know she could see straight through his charade. "Barry," she said very quietly. "I accept your apology, so you can now move on with your life. Without me." She pushed the flowers against his chest, causing him to take a step back. As he did, a movement behind him caught Leah's eye, someone approaching from across the breezeway.

It was Ash. He looked so different than he did at work that she almost didn't recognize him. His wavy dark hair was brushed, his face freshly shaved. He wore jeans and a dress shirt with the sleeves rolled up. A silver watch glinted on his wrist. Without the maintenance uniform, he looked like an ad for something. What exactly, she didn't know, but whatever it was, she was pretty sure she'd buy it.

And right now, she was glad to see him.

As Ash approached, she shoved the flowers into Barry's chest again and looked him in the eye. Her voice was forceful. "Good-bye, Barry." Her gaze shifted to Ash as he reached the doorway. "Hello," she said, trying to sound nonchalant. "This person was leaving. You can come right in." She let go of the flowers, which dropped to the ground, and opened the door wider.

Barry's blandly handsome face went blank with confusion. "Who's this?" His words hung in the air, unanswered, as Ash sailed past him and into the apartment.

Leah couldn't ignore the frisson of light that suffused her as Ash smiled at her. He turned to address Barry, still standing in the doorway, flowers at his feet. "Good-bye, Barry," he said mildly and shut the door with a firm click.

He threw the deadbolt, turned back to Leah, and handed her a gift bag he'd been carrying. She hadn't noticed it until this very second. She was genuinely surprised. "What's this?"

"Snacks. For you. Seemed like you might need a treat after the week you've had."

This took her a moment to absorb. "You brought me snacks?"

He laughed. "Yeah, I'm crazy like that."

"But we…we hardly know each other." *Lame.* What a lame thing to say. She mentally grimaced and clutched the bag.

"Well, I wouldn't exactly say that," Ash said, his tone heavy with innuendo. Damn. Even his voice was sexy. "The last time I saw you— what was it? Five hours ago?— you stuck your tongue down my throat."

She bit her bottom lip. "Um. Yeah. About that—"

"Listen, Bellerose, let's not do a postmortem on that kiss right now, okay? Let it be what it was." He looked around the apartment. "Cool place. Lots of character."

"That's one way to look at it." She stopped, unsure where to go next.

"I like the vibe. Very mid-century without the pretension." He gestured to the bag.

Good. That gave her something to focus on other than his mesmerizing eyes and mouth. Leah pulled items out of the bag, her face lighting up as she went. "Crackers and tapenade. Very fancy. Tangerines. Smoked almonds— yum." She popped the can open. "I love these. Dried mango. Organic ginger tea. And this is...what is this?" The writing on the box was in French.

Ash grinned. "Truffles. Parisian chocolate."

Leah sat on the couch, gift bag on her lap. "Banks, where did you get all this? There's no specialty food store in Charmant."

He sat next to her and shrugged. "I have ways."

She ate some almonds. They were insanely good. "I see. You have 'ways.'"

He gestured. "What can I say? It's—" His attention was snagged by Prunella, who leapt onto his lap without preamble. "Oh. Who is this stunning, golden creature, may I ask?"

Leah licked smoked almond salt from her fingers. "That's Prune. Prunella. She's my baby."

Ash stroked the hairless cat's head. "She's a beauty. Totally exotic." He ran a hand down the velvety back and chuckled as she arched and bumped against his hand. "Honored to meet you, Prunella. I guess next time the goody bag will have to include kitty treats." The cat replied by cranking up her motor. Her purr reverberated in the room.

Watching him, Leah felt a lump in her throat. He wasn't putting on a show. He thought Prunella was beautiful.

Watch it, Bellerose. Don't go all soft because the guy's being nice to your cat. He's still a maintenance man.

Yeah, but a maintenance man with a stunning physique and peculiar charisma. A maintenance man who kissed like a bona fide gigolo. A maintenance man who had brought her food after shutting the door on Barry, which got him double points.

"Okay, listen, Banks," she said, turning to him. "I appreciate you coming over and I appreciate the treats. But we can't date. Even if you report to Cranford, I'm still the managing director, and that's not acceptable." She paused. Ash was watching her silently, his eyes focused on hers. He was listening—really listening—to her. Not in the way people listened when she was being the boss and issuing directives. This was something else entirely. Suddenly she felt exposed. Vulnerable. She cleared her throat and shifted into take-charge mode.

"Not only is it not good business practice, but given the situation with your corrective plan, a relationship could easily be misconstrued if anyone knew about it. There's a risk to both of us, not me. My career is important to me and I'm not going to risk it, and I hope you have similar concerns about your own situation. And then there's the personal side of things. There's no room in my life for personal entanglements right now. And no interest, either. Honestly. I recently got out of a bad situation with—well, with Barry." It was mortifying to say it out loud. *Why* had she spent so long with Barry? Why had she spent any time *at all* with him?

"So, obviously, I'm not in a position to...I'm not..." She stopped. Ash was still focused on her, a tiny curve at one edge of his mouth. "What?"

He took her hand. "Are you finished?"

She hugged the gift bag against her with her free hand. "No. I mean, yes. I am. Finished."

Gently, he took the gift bag and set it aside. "When we're at the hotel, we are Ms. Bellerose the managing director and Asher Banks the maintenance man. Away from the hotel, we're Leah and Ash. And we're going to be lovers."

A sound rushed out of her, and her breath evaporated on a whisper. "Lovers?"

"That's right. Lovers. As in, sleeping together. Making each other crazy with passion. Exploring each other's every desire."

She shivered at his words, speechless for the moment.

He continued. "Now, I don't know about the relationship part. My record in that department ain't so hot, either. But I'm not looking for great romance. So you don't have to worry about that."

"Ah." Leah nodded, a peculiar hollowness in her chest as she found her voice. "I see. So, we can sleep together"—her stomach tumbled as she said the words—"but we won't necessarily have any kind of actual...human connection." What the hell was she implying? She didn't *want* any human connection. No emotional entanglement was what she was aiming for. And this guy was offering it to her. She should be overjoyed.

"On the contrary." Ash raised her hand to his mouth and began kissing her fingertips. "Lovers have a very human connection. Of a kind." He turned her hand over and began kissing the palm. "Life will be easier this way. No more tension, no more tiptoeing around the attraction. Because, honey, if this isn't attraction, I don't know what is."

Leah shut her eyes against the war in her solar plexus. When she opened them again, he was tracing her lifeline with the tip of his finger. Suddenly she felt indescribably tired. The past week had caught up with her. Figuring out what was happening with Asher Banks seemed impossible at the moment.

"Ash." He raised his eyes to hers at the sound of his name. She could barely speak, feeling like she was going to topple over. "I can't do this right now. I'm exhausted."

He nodded slowly and pulled her toward him. She rested her head against his broad, warm chest and closed her eyes again. The last thing she thought before she dropped off to sleep was, *Damn, he smells good.*

Chapter 9

Early morning sunlight pinkened the bedroom through the veil of curtains. Leah's eyes flew open.

"Oh, God. What time—?" She rolled over to look at the clock and her world toppled upside down. Ash was lying next to her, on top of the duvet, shirt off, jeans on.

*Holy mother of...*Leah sat up in bed and clutched the sheet to her chest. Her T-shirt was flung over the chair across the room, as were her sweatpants. A spike of fear was replaced with momentary relief as she realized she was wearing the sports bra she'd donned under her T-shirt the night before, and, thank god, she was still wearing underwear.

"Thank you, Jesus," she mumbled as she threw the covers back. Her feet hit the floor as Ash's voice rumbled to life.

"Are you thanking Jesus for the fact that we slept together, or because we *didn't* sleep together?"

She grabbed her robe and avoided looking at the bare-chested reality of him, there on the bed. *Her bed.*

"I'm going to make coffee." As she fled the room, she heard him chuckle. When she returned to the room five minutes later, he was coming out of the bathroom, still shirtless, wiping his face with a towel. "I hope you don't mind I used a bit of your toothpaste," he said.

She forced herself to focus on the speckled brown eyes, not the sculpted pectoral muscles or his impressive biceps. She ignored the curling russet hair that lightly covered his chest and trailed down his firm abdomen before it disappeared tantalizingly into the waistband of his jeans. "Of course. Feel free to use everything. Make yourself right at home. In fact, go ahead and use my toothbrush, why don't you?" Irritation prickled her skin as she made her way into the bathroom. Why she was annoyed, she wasn't sure. Maybe it was that he was so damn self-assured. Perhaps it was because she didn't mind that he was here, which pissed her off royally.

He answered as she was shutting the bathroom door. "Oh, I brought my own toothbrush."

That had her flinging the door open again. *"What?"*

He shrugged. "Is it a crime to carry a travel toothbrush?"

She shook her hairbrush at him. "See? Now that's what's so vexing about you."

Ash laughed. "Vexing? That's a first. I've been called a lot of things, but never vexing."

Leah crossed her arms across her chest. "Well, you are. Vexing. Because you're so damn logical and confident and..." Her voice trailed off.

He grinned at her. "And?"

Her chin rose. "That's it, I guess." She shut the bathroom door with a snap. *Great. Good one, Bellerose.* That was telling him.

She took her time with a shower, then realized she didn't have any clothes in the bathroom. Fantastic. She'd have to head out in her robe to get clean clothes.

Ash was propped up on the bed reading Cosmopolitan magazine. He looked up as she walked by. "Did you know that twenty-eight percent of women say they aren't sure they've ever had an orgasm?"

Leah yanked open a bureau drawer. "Is that so?" *Don't look at him. Ignore him and he'll go away.*

"Apparently." He flipped pages. "Kind of hard to believe. Maybe because I've never witnessed that myself. Every woman I've been with has absolutely known—"

"Banks, I have to get to work." She extracted a clean pair of panties from the drawer, balling them up in her fist, and headed into the walk-in closet. "I'm not interested in the history of your love life."

A movement behind her suddenly had her on alert, and his arms closed around her before she could react. "Why not?" he breathed in her ear. "Jealous?"

She froze, white-hot light shooting through her body. "Don't be ridiculous," she half-stuttered. "I—"

He whipped her around to face him and took her face in his hands. "You *are* jealous," he said, his gaze piercing her. "Because you want me to possess you, and no one else."

Leah tried to laugh, but it came out like a hiccup. "That's absurd," she whispered.

His lips hovered over hers. "It's true. You want to be possessed. By me."

He brought his mouth to hers and heat rushed into her, her stomach, her limbs, her lungs. She could barely stand or think. For a long moment, the only sound was that of their breath, the deafening drumming of their hearts. It was almost too much. Leah's legs went soft, her arms were suddenly around him, and she grasped his body for balance.

That was the moment her thoughts disappeared, and pure sensation took over.

The kiss deepened, their bodies rocked together. The lace panties she'd been holding dropped to the floor, a blue dress on a padded hanger swung silently. She bit his lower lip, pulled it between her teeth, and sucked, hearing him groan. He reciprocated by pulling her breath into him, moving his mouth to her jawline, then her earlobe. The pressure of his lips against her skin was electric. Adrenaline exploded outward from her diaphragm to her limbs and she lost her balance.

He caught her and swept her up, then laid her on the floor, half in, half outside of the closet. His bare chest was against her breasts as her robe fell open. Warm, hard pecs against the softness of her breasts felt like all she'd ever wanted.

Strength. Strength to match hers. Strength to meet her softness.

The hair on his abdomen tickled her stomach, temptation incarnate, and she gasped aloud. His hands were all over her at one time, roving, caressing, setting a raging wildfire inside of her.

This is happening, this is happening, this is happening. Leah went weightless and nearly levitated from the sensations consuming her.

Ash moved to cover one breast with his mouth and drew hard on the nipple, causing her to cry out. It didn't stop but became more intense. Her hands dug into the carpet, trying to ground herself as he sucked first one, then the other nipple. It was as if he were trying to gain sustenance from her body. His breath was cool on her skin as he blew against the wetness left by his attentions. His teeth scraped gently against her ribs and then went back to her nipples again, biting softly, pulling each one into his mouth.

It was too much. Even this. Too much.

A deep yearning throbbed between her legs, where she felt a spurt of moisture. An urge to meld with him invaded every cell. When had she ever felt this? Was this desire? She moaned and reached for him, pulling him into her, hard. Tongues intertwined, they were one being, connected and alight with energy. Her mind was blank. She barely noticed when he drew away from her.

Raised on his arms, he looked down at her, eyes dark, countenance fierce. "Leah, you and I have been sparring long enough. Tell me now. Do you want this? I need to know because I can't spar anymore."

Her breath was short and it took effort to speak. "Yes." The word reverberated in the air and she was suddenly surer of this than she'd ever been of anything. "Yes." She reached for him.

Permission given, he tugged the belt of her robe and opened the garment to expose her fully beneath him. He made no apology as he beheld her, gaze roving from her face to her neck, her shoulders, breasts, her torso to her belly and down. "God, you're beautiful," he breathed, his voice full of wonder. "I want to get to know every inch of you." His lips moved against hers, to her ear and down to her neck. She arched beneath him.

The tip of his tongue was wet and hot as he traced a line down her neck to each breast. Sensation sizzled through her as he continued, moving down her stomach, nipping on each side of her belly button. He kissed the tender skin above her bikini line, moving across her body, from one pelvic bone to the other. Leah's eyes closed, her hands in his hair, all reason gone.

Ash moved back up her belly, kissing, licking, teasing as he made his way back to her mouth. "More of that later," he whispered. "I want to taste all of you. But not all at once." His lips covered hers again, his tongue entwining with hers.

Her hand found the hard ridge in his jeans, and she stroked it longingly. She wanted to see it, feel it, know it. This, too, was entirely new, entirely unexpected.

He groaned into her mouth and moved above her. His smell filled her lungs. Just this, Leah thought, was better than anything she'd ever had.

Ash's breath grew harder as his hand trailed down her belly to her thighs. "Now." His mouth covered hers. "You're mine." Leah moaned into his mouth as his fingers tangled in her nether hair and rubbed into her cleft.

Her pelvis lifted of its own accord, meeting his hand eagerly. As he stroked into her more forcefully, she felt a rising heat, followed by a wave of self-conscious fear.

"I'm not...I can't..." The words died on her lips as he moved against her, his mouth on hers. *I can't do this. I can't come with a virtual stranger. I can barely come by myself.* But the words were hollow. They had nothing to do with what was happening now.

What was this? *This* was something different than the world she knew. The world where she was in charge, where she called the shots, where men were concerned with their pleasure and nothing else. The world where that didn't matter because no one took care of her but her. She'd always taken care of herself, by herself. Until now.

Her mind couldn't make sense of what was going on and she went blank, overcome with the blazing heat in her body.

"Leah," Ash murmured against her, his hand between her legs, "breathe. Just breathe." There was a tiny smile in his words, the tone far from condescending. It was caring.

He continued. "That's it. Relax." His fingers stroked into her, circling her clitoris. "Take your time. There's nothing that has to happen." His mouth covered hers as she sighed, he drew her breath into him and gave it back, becoming her lungs, her air.

Her sex swelled with feeling, hot, slick, wanting more of his hand, his fingers, his being. Without thinking, her lower back went into an arc, pushing against his whole body. He rubbed rhythmically against her opening without going in while his thumb spiraled her clitoris, making her gasp.

She was an animal, every cell magnifying, sizzling, expanding. Her breath stuttered. There was an urgency building that shocked and frightened her. Her body seemed to have a mind of its own, running wild down a path she'd never traveled. Unconsciously, one leg rose and encircled his jeans-clad thigh, attempting to get closer to him.

Then her brain woke up. It wouldn't be fair to him to let him think she could do this. She knew what orgasm was, but it was an infrequent, hard-won prize. He didn't have to work so hard to do this for her, especially when it might well end in frustration. She had to tell him.

She pulled away from his kiss. "Ash, I can't...It's not you..." Her hands were in his hair, framing his face, getting his attention.

Ash went motionless, dark eyes clouded with concern. "You want to stop?" His hand stilled against her thigh.

Her damp hair clung to her cheeks as she shook her head. "No, no. But I don't want you to think you have to...I mean, it's difficult for me..."

Ash's face relaxed and his mouth twitched. "Are you one of the twenty-eight percent?"

"What? *No.*" Leah squirmed underneath him. "It's...not easy for me."

He scanned her face. "Leah, this isn't a test and you don't have to perform. You're not being evaluated." Pausing, he kissed her lightly. "This isn't something you're in charge of, remember? I'm in charge here." He became serious, pupils dilated in the dim light of the closet. "Listen to me. *I'm in charge.* Right now, in this moment, you are mine."

Adrenaline surged again. "It's...I don't want you to have to put out so much effort..." She swallowed but couldn't find the words to go on.

The hand moved gently back between her legs. "Let's start over. And sweetheart, believe me, this is not an effort." He half-groaned, half-chuckled, but was serious when he spoke. "Any man who ever implied that this was work was a lying, selfish bastard."

Leah felt her spine relax into the floor. *You have no idea*, she thought.

He began his ministrations in earnest and colors exploded behind her eyelids. It was clear he was a man on a mission—and she was his mission.

She bowed against his hand, instinct and primal desire taking over.

Want. I want...

Suddenly his fingers were there. Her mouth opened in a soundless cry as first one, then two fingers thrust slowly inside while his thumb continued the mad pressure around her clit. He pushed his hand against her, fingers going in to the hilt as her hips rose from the floor to meet him.

As he slowly withdrew, hand slick, Leah's hands gripped his arms, desperate. His voice rumbled in her ear. "Slow down, baby. Just feel." His teeth nipped at the skin on her neck, then his mouth moved over hers, his breath hard now as his fingers moved back in, pushing toward her cervix. Deeper, then deeper still. His fingers pressed upward, finding a place she'd never known was there, a place that sent a red-hot lightning bolt searing through her. She bucked against him and he continued, relentlessly pushing her past all reason.

No. Not yet. She tried to speak but couldn't, every muscle straining toward his hand.

"Ash—" She choked his name into his mouth, and he shushed her.

"Feel," he breathed, fingers twisting and thrusting into her soul.

Then it came. An energy so intense she couldn't breathe, her body straining and exploding outward, open eyes blind to her surroundings. From a distance, she heard something, her voice, but no words. A sound so primal it was alien to all she knew. Her body, the universe, convulsed and then convulsed again, spiraling out of control.

Her legs were around his body, her arms encircling him as he kissed her, whispering to her, though she couldn't hear him. She rocked against him, a wave of sensation and emotion welling up and spilling over. Tears rolled down her cheeks before she knew what was happening. Her throat was raw.

Waves of sizzling pleasure continued to pulse through her as her senses came slowly back to life. Her eyes opened on the ceiling, vision blurred with tears. Her back against the floor tingled, the skin on her legs registered for the first time the rough softness of Ash's jeans. She heard his breathing and realized he was still raised above her, eyes on her.

Slowly her gaze went to his. It was impossible to speak, but she could move now. Her hands went to his face and she traced his lips with a finger. His eyebrows rose as her hands moved lower and unsnapped the jeans. The evidence of his arousal was undeniable, sizable, and rock hard against her thigh.

That was what she wanted now.

She pushed the waistband of his pants down and he shimmied out of them as she shifted to remove her arms from the robe, leaving it to lie beneath them. In one swift movement, he extracted a condom from a pocket and rolled it on. Leah allowed herself to take in the full picture, Ash's tall, muscled form, dark hair curling across his chest, trailing down to the thatch between his legs. His cock was admirable, standing hard and high, as tempting as anything she'd ever seen. She felt her internal muscles clench in anticipation.

He held himself above her, took himself in hand, and began rubbing into her. She was so wet, the head of his cock slid easily up and down, harder and harder against her vulva.

He lowered himself to kiss her. "Now. Now. You are mine." She had no time to react. The head of his cock came into her and was held there while his fingers stroked her clit and the sensitive skin of her sex. He pulled the lips open wider as he pulled himself out, then pushed back in slowly. Barely in, then out again.

Leah bucked beneath him and found her voice again, at last. "Ash," she gasped. *"Please."* The first orgasm had been shocking, but it had left her bewilderingly primed and ravenous for more. She was a wild animal, voracious, feral.

Ash was silent as he continued to tease her, moving inside, then out again with infuriating slowness, all the while torturing her with his fingers.

Leah pushed herself up to meet him. "Please, Ash," she gasped. "I don't want to come again without you." It was true. She wanted to do this with him.

His eyes softened slightly at that, but he remained serious as he lowered himself over her. "Now," he whispered, and thrust slow but hard, stretching her, filling her. He held himself there, then pulled back and thrust again, this time with more force.

He reached under her knees to lift her legs so that they draped over his arms, exposing her utterly. Withdrawn almost completely, he reached between them to spread her labia, allowing his body to stimulate her directly. His tongue matched the thrusts of his cock as he began a slow pistoning against her. Leah's breath left her with the force of his penetration. Her fingers raked into his back, the sensations searing through every cell.

"I can't...Don't..." Her words choked into silence as white-hot light overcame her and she was subsumed. From a distance, she heard him groan, then exclaim, and she felt a force like she was being pushed from one dimension to another, through the veil of the physical into the ethereal.

Silent and fused, they arched together. The air shivered around them. She was drawing him in and merging with him, simultaneously defining and losing herself. Then slowly, so slowly, they returned to earth, breath becoming more audible in the morning quiet.

At last, after an eternity elapsed, Leah felt Ash's lips against her ear.

"I was wrong," he whispered. The heat of his voice and breath burned her skin.

With effort, she opened her eyes. His face was buried in her neck, his hair against her cheek.

"Wha...?" Her voice sounded weird and unsteady.

"Mmm...." He rolled on top of her and stroked her hair away from her face with a gentle hand. His gaze returned to meet hers, sober and almost alarming.

Her brain fog lifted, seeing his expression. "What's wrong, Ash?" She was suddenly struck with fear. What had she done? What had she not done? It was hard to think. Her body was still reverberating.

He shook his head, not speaking. A finger traced her mouth, then made way for his kiss, which became more erotic than she could have imagined, given what they'd done. They were both spent. How could a kiss be so magical? His mouth worshiped hers, echoing the entirety of what had transpired.

Finally, he pulled gently away and considered her again. This time, she was less panicked. After that kiss, it was clear he was not upset with her.

He drew breath. "I was wrong, Leah. You aren't mine."

A spark of confusion had no time to grow to a flame as he continued. "That is, it's not only that you are mine. Because you are. You *are*." He dipped his mouth to hers for another brief kiss. "But there's something else," he whispered, caressing her face. "Ms. Bellerose, it is also the case...that I am yours."

Chapter 10

"We can't have breakfast together."

Ash ignored Leah's proclamation and slid into the booth next to her. He waved at the waitress and turned back to Leah. "I'm here by coincidence. On my way to work. Happened to see you through the window and didn't want to be rude." The last couple of hours had been phenomenal and nothing could tarnish them. He wouldn't allow her words, her reactive Leah-ness to ruin his mood.

"Ash, we have to set some limits—" She was interrupted by the appearance of the waitress, a gum-chewing woman with a bleached blonde ponytail and long blue fingernails.

"Coffee. And fruit. And maybe some oatmeal. Are your eggs free-range? Okay, then two eggs sunny-side. And a double order of hash browns. I seem to have a huge appetite this morning." Ash tapped on the menu and winked at Leah. "Want anything?"

She stared at him, wordless.

He grinned at the waitress and glanced at her name tag. "I guess that's it, uh…Crystal. Thanks." He gazed out the plate glass window and read the name of the place, written in script on the window. "*Bluebell*. Never been here. Been eating at the hotel for the past month." Sighing, he studied the diner menu. "Not exactly Le Cordon Bleu, is it? Though I hear they make a mean peach pie."

"Ash, please be serious." Leah's voice was strained. "When you left my place, we said we'd see each other at work. We have to abide by rules. This morning was," she paused and scanned the nearby tables, lowering her voice as she continued. "It was…Hell, I don't even know what. Indescribable. A fantasy, even." She sounded wistful and bewildered. "But I can't do this with you. I won't." He looked up sharply and she bit her lip. "What I mean is, you made a proposal to me about keeping strict lines between our personal and professional lives, and I agreed to that. Sort of. God help me." Her eyes went to the ceiling.

Ash accepted coffee from the waitress and slowly stirred in cream. "Okay. You said to be serious." He placed his spoon carefully on the saucer and met her gaze. "Well, I am." He gestured at the little diner. "We're not at the hotel. We're two people having breakfast."

Her eyes widened. "Oh, for God's sake, Ash. Wake up. We're on the clock right now." She tapped her wristwatch. "Well, you are, technically. I'm salaried, so I'm not on the clock—though, to be strictly accurate, I'm always on the clock." He opened his mouth to speak, but she held up her hand. "No. This isn't negotiable. Besides, it doesn't matter. This is a public place, which means that you and I are not...ourselves." She stopped, hearing the oddity of her own words. "You know what I mean. Our...*arrangement*...must be private. Between the two of us." She exhaled. "No one can know. *Ever*." She picked up her purse and rose from the table. When she spoke, it was with pragmatic regret. "That's the way it has to be."

Ash felt his face heat up. She was right. But he hated it. For every reason she knew, and for reasons she didn't know, she was right.

Their *arrangement*. He couldn't blame her for the phrase. He'd said as much himself. But it sounded like something dirty, and not in a good way. Something shameful. And that's not what the last few hours had felt like for him.

It was his turn to exhale. "Don't apologize. I was..." The words came out before he could analyze them. "I guess I was trying to buy a little more time. Until I can see you again."

Leah's face softened and she looked about to say something but didn't. She nodded, turned, and left the diner without a backward glance.

***

"Good God." Leah cupped a hand over her nose and mouth as she surveyed the ballroom, which looked like a bomb had been dropped in the middle of it. Dust and filth hung heavy in the air, and the sound of workers coughing was audible. Moldering wallpaper sat in shredded piles around the room while men on scaffolds scraped and tore at the ancient wall covering, pieces and chunks falling like rain around them. The dapper young man standing next to Leah yelped as she grabbed his arm and dragged him out into the hallway, shutting the door firmly behind them.

"Mr. Duran, you have to set up some air filters immediately. Get your workers out of there until the air is safe. And get them some masks. I don't want a damn lawsuit on my hands." She was furious. Possibly fueled by frustration over her life in general but focused right now on the ludicrous scene in the ballroom.

"I...Yes, ma'am, I mean, I will get to work on that right now, but the manager didn't tell me—"

"I don't care what the manager did or didn't tell you. You're supposed to be the expert. Jesus, this is a fiasco," she muttered to herself as she brushed dust off her skirt. "Get everyone out of there immediately. I'm coming back with the key to lock up until things are set right."

Cranford was on the phone in the office when she arrived, ready for battle. He gave her a baleful look as he turned back to the phone. "If you'll pardon me, sir, Ms. Bellerose has arrived. I'll call you back shortly." He gingerly placed the receiver back in the cradle and steepled his hands with precision.

Why did that gesture annoy her so much? Leah wondered. Maybe because it seemed so schoolmarm-ish. Though she'd begun to wonder about Cranford and his history, he never failed to set her teeth on edge.

"Julius, please explain to me why you hired that kid and his team to paint the ballroom. And while you're at it, I'd like to see the contract. I'm assuming there's a reasonable break clause in it." She didn't bother to conceal her skepticism that there was any such clause.

The older man looked pained but nodded and picked up the phone. "I'll have the contract brought for you to review."

"Just email it to me." She set her jaw, anticipating what was next.

"Ah." Cranford tapped his foot. "Yes. Well, we've not made a copy as yet. But we'll do that immediately," he added quickly.

Leah sucked in a breath. *Patience, Bellerose. Losing your temper will not solve this any faster.* "I'm confused. Wasn't the document drafted electronically?" *Or was it handwritten, perhaps on a scroll?*

Cranford considered. "I'm sure it was. But the signatures haven't been photocopied as yet. Hilda can get that done right now." He tapped a button on the phone. "Hilda, please obtain the painting contract from Mr. Banks and make, uh, four photocopies of it. Bring it to me straight away." He hung up and faced Leah. "We'll have that in a jiffy."

Leah felt her mouth drop open and for a moment, she had trouble finding her voice. "You're letting the *maintenance man* carry the contract around?"

"I very much doubt he's carrying it around. My guess would be—"

"You don't know where it is? Tell me how that's possible." Her hand hit the desk for emphasis.

"Well, you see, Mr. Banks was the one who spoke to the contractors. He—"

"No, no. Now I'm truly confused, Julius." She sat opposite him and leaned on the desk, face suffused with disbelief. "What earthly reason would there be for that? Explain it to me."

Cranford stared at his steepled fingers, then back up at her. "I'm trying to explain it to you, Ms. Bellerose. If you'll allow me." He pressed his lips together primly.

Leah forced herself to exhale. She gestured for him to continue, barely containing herself.

"Banks was put in charge of arranging the ballroom renovation contracts, so—"

A gasp escaped her before she realized it. "What?" She leaned across the desk, causing Cranford to sit back in alarm. "What are you talking about, Julius? You put the maintenance man—Asher Banks—in charge of our contracts?" Even as she said his name, her chest thrummed with something nameless she didn't have time for right now. A swell of heat and confusion and desire and exasperation.

She couldn't deal with this, couldn't stay in this room. She rose abruptly.

Cranford was still speaking as she turned to go. "In all fairness, his official title is Maintenance Manager. He does have oversight responsibilities."

She put her hand on the doorknob, anxious to get away. "Where is he?"

"Who?"

"Banks." She wanted to scream.

"Well, I'm not sure. You could page him." Cranford blinked a staccato rhythm. "Ms. Bellerose, this isn't something to expend your energy on. There are larger concerns. Financial reports. Staff reviews."

Leah sucked in a breath, furious and afraid she might explode into a geyser of frustration in the presence of this prehistoric lunatic. She returned to stand square in front of the desk for emphasis. "For Christ's sake, Julius, can't you see how important this is? Putting someone like Banks in charge of contracts is incomprehensible. Maybe even cause for disciplinary action."

Cranford's rheumy eyes clouded. "That sounds like a threat."

"It's a potential *consequence*. For you, and for me. If I don't get a handle on this immediately, the project could tank and *my* head will roll." She smacked the back of a hand into her palm. "This renovation and the overhaul of staff are the criteria on which I'm being judged, Julius. We're talking about my career. Everything I've ever worked for."

She ignored the tug of dissonance in her belly, the tiny voice that wanted things to be different. Different with her life. Different with Ash.

Well, things *couldn't* be different. The situation was what it was. No point in getting twisted up about it.

Cranford stood and nodded to her. "I'll leave you to it, then," he said as he walked out the door.

***

Leah sat on a bench in the clipped garden, hidden by a Pyracantha bush. The thorny leaves of the hedge matched her mood. In contrast, sounds from the swimming pool behind the hotel drifted through the air. A family with young children played noisily in the water, splashing and shrieking happily. For some reason, this caused a sad, gray weight to settle over her.

She raised her face to the midday sun, closed her eyes, and willed herself to relax. *Be present and feel the moment*, she intoned. Calm your mind and solutions will come.

Or some such bullshit.

A shadow passed over her and she opened her eyes.

"Hello, lady," said William. He beamed at her, slightly slanted eyelids nearly shut with the hugeness of his grin. "Are you sitting on the bench?"

She smiled wanly. "Yes, I am, William."

He sat down heavily next to her. "I'm going to sit with you."

Suppressing a sigh, she scooted over. "Aren't you working?"

The man raised a lunch box, replete with action figure images. "It's my lunch. Tuna today." He opened the box and the tang of tuna fish wafted out. "Oh, look." William pulled a baggie out of the lunch box and held it up for Leah to see. "Fig Newtons." He laughed.

She smiled. "You like them."

"My favorite. You want one?" He held out the baggy.

"No, thank you."

"You don't like Fig Newtons?" He sounded incredulous.

It was hard not to chuckle at that. "I like them. But I'm not very hungry right now."

William nodded as he munched his sandwich, crumbs falling into his lap like confetti. "Eat when you're hungry. Sandwich first. *Then* cookies."

"That sounds right."

"My mom says."

"Ah. Well, your mom is right." Leah leaned back on the bench. "What work are you doing today, William?"

He swallowed and lifted a hand to count, pointing to the stubby fingers of his left hand. "One, I'm cleaning tools. Karen lets me clean the power tools, too, but you have to *unplug* them first. Two, I'm feeding the flowers. Fertilizer. And then three," he emphasized by repeatedly tapping his index finger, "I am helping Ash pull up the carpet in the ballroom. I'm his best helper, he says." He chuckled and shook his head happily. "I'm busy today."

"I can see that." Leah studied the man as he joyfully chewed his sandwich and slurped from his thermos.

William finished his sandwich and wiped his hands on a napkin. "What work are *you* doing today?" he asked her.

She was taken aback. "I'm...working on some things in the ballroom, too."

"You *are*?" He clapped. "We'll work together. We'll be Ash's helpers *together*."

"Oh." Leah's stomach clenched. Compartmentalizing anything to do with Ash was the goal of coming out to the garden. For all the good it was doing.

William's face crinkled in confusion at her tone. "You don't want to help Ash?"

"It's not that, William. It's that I…Well, Ash and I need to talk about some things." She stopped, unsure where she was going with this.

William peered at her thoughtfully. "Are you mad at him?"

Leah drew a careful breath. "Not mad, but we need to figure some things out. Like which of us does what job." Strangely, that sounded right.

William became serious. "It's important to know what you're supposed to do. And *not* do." He raised a finger to demonstrate the gravity of his point.

"Indeed, it is," she murmured, suddenly suspecting that this man knew more than most.

"Lady, did Ash do something he's not supposed to do?" He sounded genuinely worried.

She patted his knee, which was out of character for her but felt appropriate in the moment. "Not really, William. Ash is trying to do a good job. He's doing what he was told to do."

"He's not in trouble?"

She hesitated, then shook her head. "No, he's not in trouble." She exhaled.

Relieved, William nodded. "Ash is good man. He's a good boss for me and my dad."

"You like him." She couldn't help smiling a little.

William smiled back at her. "Yes." He picked up the bag of cookies, opened it, and handed her one. "Ash likes you," he said softly.

Leah suppressed an internal trill of alarm, accepted the Fig Newton, and took a small bite. "Is that what he told you?"

William tapped his chin thoughtfully. "Nah. I can tell." She raised an eyebrow, which William caught. "I can tell how he looks at you."

Leah licked crumbs from her lips. "And how is that?"

"Friendly. But also like he wants to hug you." William sounded very knowing. "You can *sometimes* hug friends, but if you *like* somebody, you want to hug them a *lot*. More than friends. My mom said."

She nodded. "Your mom is a smart cookie." She raised the remaining piece of Fig Newton and popped it into her mouth. William slapped his thigh and doubled over with laughter. As they walked to the ballroom together, Leah realized the weight in her stomach had disappeared.

Chapter 11

Antonio Duran's face went from engaged to terrified in a split second. His eyes slid from Ash's to something behind the maintenance man. "It's her," he whispered.

Ash went still. "Bellerose?"

Duran nodded. "And don't tell me she's not as scary as she seems." He glanced at the windows of the ballroom, obviously wondering if he could escape.

"Oh, she's as scary as she seems. There's plenty of bite in that bark." Ash turned slowly to face Leah and William, who were striding across the stained carpet toward them. He tore his gaze from her cleavage and steeled himself for what was to come.

She stopped in front of Ash but turned in the direction of Duran. "Is that you, Mr. Duran? Why are you hiding behind Mr. Banks?"

Antonio stepped forward quickly. "Good afternoon, ma'am. I was talk—"

"I can see." She surveyed the room. "It appears you've solved the dust problem."

"*Sí*. I mean, yes, ma'am." Duran nodded. He looked guiltily at Ash.

"That was certainly fast. Do you have a magic wand?" She smiled pleasantly but her eyes were all business. Ash almost laughed out loud as Duran fumbled to respond. By now, he understood the intimidating fierceness of Leah Bellerose better than most, but he also knew that at least half of it was smoke and mirrors.

"Yes, miss. I mean, no. No magic wand." Duran gulped. "It turned out that when you and I were...uh, talking...earlier, Mr. Ash was already out getting the air filters and masks. He got back right after you left."

Leah turned to Ash, a war of emotions and thoughts visible behind the screen. "How efficient, Mr. Banks."

He bowed slightly. "I aim to please, Ms. Bellerose." His mouth twitched a tiny smile as his gaze met hers. She looked away with barely concealed irritation, which somehow amused him. Other than being frozen out by her at work and mystified about what the hell was happening between them and the fact that his career was in the toilet, he felt good today.

"Well, Mr. Duran, you seem to have things well in hand." She spoke to Antonio briskly. "I'll leave it up to you to report to Mr. Cranford at the end of each day, to keep him updated on progress." She turned to William. "You have work to do here, William?"

The man clapped. "Helping Ash."

"Yes. I'll see you later. Thank you for..." She paused and Ash noticed something like true wonder cross her face. "For the cookie," she concluded unexpectedly. She made a beeline out of the room.

Ash motioned for William to wait for him and followed her into the hallway, having to jog to catch up. Not for the first time, he considered the miracle of high heels and how a person could move so fast in them. She gave no indication she knew he was behind her and he didn't want to yell and call attention to himself. A couple of housekeeping staff passed them, looking curiously over their shoulders at the chase, but Ash ignored them.

She reached the end of the hall and turned into the service entrance into the kitchens, where a number of workers hustled about, carrying trays and pushing carts. Just as he'd followed her through the swinging doors, she whirled around, causing him to nearly run into her. "Why are you following me?" she hissed.

He regrouped and glanced around. "Can we talk?"

"No."

"It's important."

She closed her eyes briefly in annoyance. "Is it related to the ballroom?"

"I'd rather discuss it in private."

He could see her internal debate, quick as lightning. Considering how to appease him enough to get through the moment. "Oh, all right." She noticed the door to the walk-in refrigerator to her left and gestured for him to follow her inside.

She stood in front of shelves filled with bins of prepared salads and vegetables and folded her arms. "What is it? Make it fast."

Ash leaned casually against the refrigerator door and smiled at her. "Have you had lunch?"

She blinked. "I beg your pardon?"

"Of course you haven't. You've been slammed all day." He scanned her from head to toe. "I like you in navy blue, by the way. Much better than the gray you usually wear. Though that's sexy, too."

"That's it." She lunged toward the door. "Meeting over."

He raised a hand to block her. "Oh, come on, Leah. We can't have lunch somewhere? Away from the hotel? Or even a five-minute conversation?"

The green eyes threw sparks as she struggled to hold her voice down. "We had an agreement. And so help me, Asher Banks, if you push me on this, I *will* fire you, once and for all."

He held his ground for a long moment, meeting her gaze with every ounce of energy she shot at him. It crossed his mind that maybe getting fired wouldn't be the end of the world. He could go work for someone else— someone not his father. And he'd be free to see Leah without the entanglements of business associations.

Interesting thought.

He sighed. If he got fired, there would be a record, which wouldn't be great for his resumé and future prospects. So, maybe that wasn't the best idea. Still, something to think about—once he got out of this refrigerator.

"Okay." He lowered his arm. "You win." He stepped aside to allow Leah access to the door. She looked surprised and—was it possible—disappointed at his acquiescence.

She reached for the door handle, then turned back. Her face tilted and her eyes narrowed. "How did it happen that you were put in charge of the ballroom renovation contracts?"

Now it was his turn to be surprised. He scrambled. "How did I...? It happened."

"Nothing 'happens,' Banks. Don't insult my intelligence." She shivered in the frigid air of the walk-in refrigerator and rubbed her arms.

He reached for her and ran his hands up and down her arms to warm them. She stiffened in resistance, but he persisted. At least she didn't push away. "Honestly, it's not a big deal. Cranford asked me to talk to the contractors and get their signatures." He hoped this sounded plausible. "It's no more than that. They report to Cranford."

Her eyebrows rose. "Do they?"

"Of course. You said so yourself, to Duran, a few minutes ago."

She snorted. "Well, that's no guarantee of anything anymore. The world seems to have turned upside down lately." Her tone was annoyed, but underneath, there was more. He didn't know what it was, but a vibration in his solar plexus told him it had to do with him.

"Listen," he said, tipping her chin up. "You are in charge here. Everyone knows it. I'm lending a helping hand to an old man."

She stayed with his gaze a second too long, and he found himself leaning in, brushing his lips against hers. "Everything's going to be okay."

He was astonished to see tears well up in her eyes then and he pulled back. "Leah?"

She hugged herself harder, shook her head, and blinked. "It's fine." She looked away from him and addressed the back corner of the refrigerator. "It that…" She stopped and cleared her throat. "No one has ever said that to me. At least, not like they mean it."

Ash felt he was missing something. "Said what?"

She looked back at him. "That things are going to be okay." Her inhale was sharp. "I've always had to tell myself that. Always taken care of myself. There was never a choice."

He pulled her in to his body and rubbed his hands down her arms, then her back, continuing to warm her. "So, when I say it?" He let the question dangle.

Her arms were around him then. She rested her head against his chest. He could feel her breathing against him. His hand rose to stroke her hair. His desire to comfort her was like a wave, an alien yet welcome sensation. It struck him that this went way beyond sexual chemistry, into a realm he had never known existed. One that could scare him if he thought about it too much. But thinking about it wasn't necessary right now.

"Banks." Her voice was muffled against him.

He loosened his hold on her and kissed the top of her head. The exotic bloom scent filled his lungs.

"We have to get out of here." She pushed away with resignation and straightened her skirt. A small smile flashed. "Maybe not the refrigerator next time."

He laughed. And as he waited for Leah to make her exit, giving her plenty of time to leave before he himself emerged from the walk-in, he felt the import of what she'd said.

Next time.

***

"Miss Bellerose."

Leah turned wearily in the direction of Dahlia Markley's salutation. The young woman's smile was disarming, though she didn't have the energy to respond. "What can I do for you, Dahlia? I was on my way back to the office to work on the catering plans for the mayors' meeting."

Dahlia's face softened. "You look peaky, miss. Have you had lunch? Or a break?"

She tried not to sound dismissive. "I'm fine."

"Nonsense." Before she knew it, Dahlia was linking her arm around Leah's and pulling her toward the back door of the kitchen. "I'm taking you out for a break."

Taken off guard, Leah was slow to react. "I'm fine, Dahlia. Just busy. What are we—"

Dahlia tut-tutted. "No one can run at full steam all the time without stopping to recharge." She pointed around the corner of the hotel garden. "Let's go to the Bluebell. Have you been there yet? Fifteen minutes and you'll be back." Her stride was determined, and somehow Leah kept on walking with her.

"Wait. Don't you have to help with the late lunch crowd?" Leah struggled to orient herself to what was happening.

"Oh, it's not much of a crowd today. Weekends, most folks go over to the Hilton in Southport. It's only a few minutes down the road and they have an all-day brunch. It's to die for."

Leah's ears pricked up. "Interesting. I'll have to investigate that." Perhaps Dahlia knew things that could help springboard some lucrative projects. From there, her mind flashed to other staff. She should be surveying them for ideas. Why hadn't she thought of that before?

"Besides, Mama told me to get you out."

Her attention snapped back to the red-haired woman tugging her along. "What? She did?"

"Mercy, yes. Said you looked about ready to drop. And I agreed." Dahlia opened the door of the diner and pushed Leah through it. "You need some peach pie."

Leah sighed. "Peach pie." She closed her eyes briefly. It seemed like small towns would follow her around forever, no matter how hard she worked to extricate herself.

Sitting across from Dahlia, not ten feet from where she'd sat with Ash earlier, caused a feeling of such bizarre derealization, she wondered if she was dreaming. She sipped the coffee the waitress brought without being asked and was assured by the scalding temperature that she was indeed awake, and all of this was happening.

She rubbed her forehead and blinked. "Dahlia, I'm confused. You and your mother are very thoughtful, but you're…" How to say this without being rude, or at least indelicate? "You are, well, hotel staff. And I'm the new managing director." She drew breath to continue, but Dahlia leaned forward and laughed.

"I know, miss. Ain't it funny, me bringing you here?" She shook her head in bemusement. "But Mama and me, well, we can tell when someone needs a little recharge. Oh, pie." She picked up her fork and gestured to Leah. "Try it. It's the only thing worth having here, but that don't matter to any of us." A huge bite of pie disappeared, and the young woman was blessedly silent while she blissfully chewed.

Leah considered the glistening slab of pie in front of her. There goes my sugar ration for today, she thought, even if I only have a couple of bites. She tried to offer Dahlia a brave smile and picked up her fork.

The fact that her appetite was nearly nonexistent was quickly forgotten as the pungent flavors of the pie exploded in her mouth. "Oh, my," she moaned. A second bite was followed by a third and a fourth.

Dahlia giggled. "See?" She spoke around a large mouthful. "They don't even offer ice cream or Cool Whip or nothin' because it's so good all by itself."

Leah nodded, mouth full. The rich, salty crust, exquisitely ripened peaches, and honey seemed to go straight to her bloodstream, sending a glow down to her toes. She had to admit she'd needed this, or something like this.

No, this. *This.*

She ate more, finally sliding the plate back, cleaned of every crumb. The coffee had cooled sufficiently, and she sipped as she sat back. "I can't believe I ate all that."

Dahlia patted her stomach. "I know. I say that every time." She blew out a breath. "But it helps. Lots of people go all day on a piece of this pie."

"Hm. I get it." Leah cleared her throat. She should try to wrestle back control of the situation. "As much as I appreciate this, Dahlia, it's important for me to remind you—"

"That you're the boss. I know." Dahlia's face was solemn. "But see, that's why this was important."

Would today ever stop being confusing? "I'm not sure what you mean."

"Well, you are the boss and you were getting, uh, well, frazzled. No offense. But you have to take breaks to keep going." Dahlia nodded to emphasize her point. "And we want you to stay, so it was kind of important to remind you about that. And to tell you about the peach pie."

Leah was dumbstruck. "You want me to stay? *Here?*"

"Of course, silly. I mean, yes, ma'am." Dahlia's eyes were round. "It's no secret that Julius won't be around much longer. He's getting *too old*, you know? So, we're gonna have a new manager no matter what." She ran a finger around her empty plate and picked up a few crumbs to lick.

"But why would you want *me* to stay? Me in particular?" Leah's image of herself as a hard-as-nails manager was crumbling in front of her. A spike of anxiety ran up her back.

"Ain't it obvious?" Dahlia cocked her head. "You're a *woman*. And you're smart and pretty and, well, don't take this the wrong way, but you're—" She leaned forward and whispered, "Tough. And that's what the hotel needs."

"It does?" Leah blinked. Did she say that out loud?

"Heckfire, yes. Lots of good people work at Charmant Forest, but some are kinda lazy. And plus, we need to grow. We need to get with the times, you know." Dahlia nodded knowingly. "Julius is the sweetest man ever, but he's not exactly modern. He doesn't even know how to send email attachments." She rolled her eyes. "I forever have to help him."

"Ah." Leah nodded. Now she understood. Sort of. But Julius Cranford, sweet? What universe was Dahlia living in?

Chapter 12

Ash ran up and down the stairwells in the bowels of the hotel until sweat ran down his back. At last, he felt ready for the task.

He drank a full bottle of water as he mopped his face and booted up his laptop. Checking the time, he knew it was a risk, but he hit Video Call before he could talk himself out of it.

A few seconds later, the stern face of his father's secretary, Joan, appeared on the screen.

"*Damn*," he mumbled under his breath.

"Your father's in a meeting," the older woman announced, as devoid of emotion as the man she worked for. Her tasteful pearl earrings seemed to meld with her colorless earlobes. Her silver pageboy was cemented in place, much like the protective shield she maintained around Simon Gerard.

Ash's grip on his water bottle tightened. "Interrupt him, Joanie."

Joan didn't bother smiling. "You know I can't do that, Mr. Gerard."

Dry old bat. "You can and you will." Ash looked at his watch.

"It's his weekly briefing with your brother," she explained unnecessarily.

Ash grimaced. "I'll give you thirty seconds before I call Miles, and you know what happens when anyone intrudes on his little show." Under other circumstances, he might enjoy poking his egocentric younger brother, but this wasn't the time. "Tell him it's urgent."

The secretary's nostrils flared. "Hold, please." Her image vanished.

Ash tapped his fingers on the desk. At last, his father's face appeared. "This had better be important." The older man looked away from the screen before Ash could respond and spoke to someone out of camera range. "I'll be right with you, son. As soon as I deal with this." A door slammed and he turned back. "So?"

Simmering anger and memories of a thousand past dismissals burned in Ash's throat. "Hello to you, too, Dad."

Simon Gerard's impatience was palpable. "Asher, what do you need? I'm in an important meeting. Joan said you were insistent that something was urgent."

Ash folded his arms. So this was how it was going to be. All right then, no beating around the bush. "Did you tell Cranford to put me in charge of the Charmant Forest renovation contracts?"

His father leaned back in his chair. "This is the urgent issue?" He chuffed. "Ash, I can't waste my time on this right now. It may have escaped your attention, but I'm trying to run a hotel conglomerate here."

"I need to know." Ash gripped the water bottle so he wouldn't punch the computer screen. "There are implications."

"Which are?"

He ignored the question. "*Did you or did you not* tell Cranford to put me in charge of those contracts?"

His father sighed with irritation. "I instructed Cranford to give you some higher responsibility. To allow you to prove your competence. Apparently, he chose to give you purview over those contracts." He studied his manicured fingernails. "It wouldn't have been my choice, to tell you the truth. But that's what he did."

Ash gritted his teeth. A low vibration had started under his ribs. "'An opportunity to prove my competence'?" He couldn't hide his derision. "Dad, you know I'm competent. Sure, I've made mistakes— and I own those. But I've never *not* been competent." His voice was rising. "And what do you mean, it wouldn't have been your choice? Why the hell not? These are the simplest, most straightforward kind of contracts. A first-year business student could manage them."

Simon Gerard's gaze was chilling. "Too much at stake. Too much to lose. If you *prove yourself* in the way you have in the past, we'd lose any chance of building a steady income stream from conference bookings at Charmant Forest." His lips pursed in distaste and he grunted. "Cranford was supposed to be discreet about this. He seems to have failed at that. But he will be dealt with soon enough." With that ominous proclamation, the older man raised an eyebrow. "Are we done?"

Ash shook his head. "This isn't over. And don't blame Cranford. He let it slip to Leah because she confronted him about it. I imagine he had little choice." An image of Leah in action almost made him smile. Almost, but not quite.

Gerard studied his son. "You call her Leah?"

"That's irrelevant."

His father leaned forward. "Hardly. It's disrespectful."

"*I don't call her Leah*. I was only referring to her that way." The top of his head was tingling with rage and his biceps tensed. He crushed the water bottle in his fist and tossed it across the room.

His father's voice was scolding. "See you don't. Your disrespect of women has gotten you into trouble too many times in the past."

That was rich. Philandering, patronizing old sod. "Dad, this isn't about what I call or don't call Ms. Leah Bellerose. This is about your going behind my back and testing me in some arbitrary way that has now impacted the way *Ms. Bellerose* views my performance."

Simon smirked. "So, she's not happy with you? Already? Is that what this is all about?"

"Christ." Ash leaned back in the chair and put a hand over his eyes. How had this conversation veered off into lunatic territory?

Neither man spoke for what seemed an eternity. Though risky, he wasn't going to dignify his father's question with a response. At last, Ash met his father's gaze. "Look, I'm doing my best here. Just let me do it. If that's not possible..." He paused, not sure where to go from there.

"Is that it?" His father looked at his watch, clearly done with the conversation.

Ash looked away, nodding. He snapped the laptop closed, but not before his father had signed off the call without so much as a good-bye.

***

The next week was a blur of staff reviews and financial reports, checking in on the ballroom, and trying to arrange catering for the mayors' meeting. After too many twelve-hour days in a row, Leah was ready to drop.

She stood and stretched and went to the converted minibar to find a snack. Nothing looked good so she'd have to wait for dinner, whenever that might happen. It was already getting dark outside. She settled on a ginger ale. Kicking off her high heels, she padded soundlessly across the carpet to the window, which overlooked the hotel pool.

"Ms. Bellerose?" Arthur Jones stood in the doorway and looked around uncertainly. "Wasn't sure I was in the right place."

She turned to the man and rolled her shoulders lightly to loosen them. "Come in, Mr. Jones. Sit where you like." She gestured to the couch and easy chairs.

Sharing an office with Cranford had become unbearable, so she'd had one of the guest rooms in the short hallway behind the management suite converted to an office. Being able to look out the window and even stretch out on the couch with her laptop between meetings was proving to be a godsend.

"This is right nice," Arthur said, surveying the room and settling in a cushioned chair. "Makes sense. These rooms don't rent very often now. Too close to the kitchens and the exercise room. Getting the bed out gives you lots o' room to work. Could fit two desks in here if you had a mind to."

Leah sat opposite him, computer in hand. "I agree. I'm considering converting this hallway to an extended conference room space."

Arthur's eyes widened. "I never thought of that. Guess that would mean more money for the hotel."

"That's the idea," she murmured, logging on to her computer.

"If you don't mind me asking, ma'am, how long do you expect this to take?" He glanced at the darkening window. "I can stay however long you need, o'course. It's that I try to get home in time to see my grandson before he goes to bed."

Leah didn't look up as she searched for the review document. "Shouldn't take more than a few minutes and you should be on your way home. I appreciate you staying late to meet with me. It's a crunch trying to get these reviews done for the corporate office."

Arthur nodded. "I can understand that and it ain't no trouble."

"Fine." She looked up. "So, Mr. Jones, let's review your job performance and talk about your goals."

Arthur chuckled. "Goals, miss? Don't know that I have goals beyond doing my job well and not getting myself in the obituaries until I'm good and ready."

She smiled wearily. "Well, let's see if we can expand on the 'doing the job well' part."

"Yes, ma'am." The man cleared his throat. "Ash says I'm doing okay, so I guess I shouldn't be too nervous."

Leah tried to ignore the zap of heat in her chest at the sound of Ash's name. She hadn't seen or heard from him since their conversation in the walk-in refrigerator, which was both a relief and a bewilderment to her. He invaded her thoughts constantly, much to her chagrin. How could she be so distracted by an uneducated, obstreperous maintenance man, even if he did smell good, make her come like a freight train, and— most bewildering of all— make her feel, well, safe? It was confounding. Their night together already seemed like a distant memory and she half wondered if it had been a fluke. Something she should mentally box up, label as nice but weird and not to be repeated. Maybe he wasn't even interested anymore. His silence certainly seemed to suggest that.

But somehow, she couldn't quite believe that was the case. It had felt too real.

Anyway, it didn't matter. She had to concentrate on work, which today consisted of performance reviews.

Arthur was staring at her, waiting, and she quickly refocused.

"You've been here a long time, Mr. Jones. No one doubts your basic skills or commitment to the job."

Arthur considered this. "Mr. Ash, he knows I love this hotel. It's been good to me. My wife done told him we don't know what woulda happened if the hotel wasn't hiring when the mill closed, years ago. And that Mr. Julius was a saint, the way he gave our William a job."

Leah paused. "Ash—Mr. Banks—spoke to your wife?"

"Oh, yes. He came to our house for supper the other day. After his electricity class. Asked *me* questions. Imagine that." The freckled face broke into a delighted grin. "I can teach that boy some things." He chuckled. "So, Mr. Ash says I'm doing good. He'll tell you that if you ask him."

Her voice sounded hollow, as if coming from a distance. "I have Mr. Banks's notes here, the ones he sent to Mr. Cranford. I'm basing this review on those."

Arthur twisted a handkerchief between gnarled fingers. "You haven't spoken to Mr. Ash?"

"Not lately, no." She hoped she sounded neutral and that her voice wasn't shaking as her heart seemed to be. Maybe it had been a mistake to meet with Arthur today.

"Well, I expect he's not wanting to bother you. Everybody knows you're busy as all get out." Arthur nodded to himself. "That's probably it. And he's busy, too. We all are."

Leah didn't have time to respond. An urgent knock at the door caused them both to turn. "Miss Bellers." William's voice came through the door. "You need to come."

Leah and Arthur glanced at each other in alarm.

When she opened the door, a smiling William grabbed her hand. "You come to the ballroom. Ash and Miss Hilda say."

Arthur held up a hand. "Now wait a minute, son. What's happening?"

"A party. Come on," William insisted, tugging at Leah.

"A party? What do you mean, William?" Leah tried to be gentle and hold her ground, but the disabled man was stronger than he looked.

"Because we got the ballroom *all clean*. And I was Ash's helper. We're having a party." William giggled and gestured to his father to follow them as he trundled Leah down the hallway.

Leah sighed. "Just for a minute, William. I need to meet with your father. It's important." What had happened to her management strategies, her graduate school knowledge, her iron maiden demeanor?

William nodded exaggeratedly at her as he pulled her along. "Yes. Very important. But first, you have to come to the party. It's for *you*."

Leah frowned as they rounded the corner. "For me?" she mumbled, still trying to absorb the statement as William pushed her through the tall double doors of the ballroom. She stood still for a long moment, stunned.

The ballroom *was* all clean, the walls scraped free of ancient wallpaper, patched, sanded, and wiped down. The floor was bare of moldering carpet, the subfloor smooth, ready for something new. The drapes were gone, out being cleaned. The entire room was bare and clean of dust and no longer smelled of mildew.

Antonio Duran's crew and at least ten other staff members milled around, talking and laughing. Someone had set up a portable stereo on a ladder in the corner and a Latin beat thrummed in the cavernous space. A large cooler sat on the floor, canned soda and beer visible above crushed ice.

"Miss Bellerose." Hilda scurried over. "We all agreed you needed to see this. The painting prep completed two days early, so Ash, I mean, Mr. Banks, said to have a little party."

Leah nodded, trying to decide if she should be horrified or elated. "I appreciate your...thoughtfulness, Hilda. Where is Mr. Banks?"

"He'll be right back. He went to—Oh. There he is." She turned and beamed at Ash, who had appeared at Leah's side.

"There she is. The woman of honor." His voice was right in her ear. Warmth radiated from him, drawing her in like a tractor beam.

She resisted the pull and scanned the smiling faces now turned in her direction, offering what she hoped was a pleasant expression. "I certainly appreciate this and the ballroom looks much better than I'd expected at this point. Amazing, actually. But I'm a little confused."

Hector stepped forward. "We've all been working long days and weekends to get ready for the mayors' meeting. And you're the reason. You know, trying to improve the hotel. So, Ash thought it would be good to celebrate a little bit."

"Ah. How kind. But," she hesitated, not wanting to sound like a wet blanket, "who is currently running the hotel and attending to the guests?"

Hilda laughed. "Oh, we're all off the clock." She gestured around the room. "Joey brought some drinks in and went right back to the bar." She put her hands on her hips. "You don't think we'd abandon our guests, do you?" She leaned toward Leah as if sharing a secret. "Antonio brought his karaoke machine in. My husband's coming to join since it's his favorite thing."

Leah was perplexed. What kind of employees stayed at work after they clocked out to have a party, particularly with the people they worked with all day? Everywhere she'd ever worked, she'd never met anyone she'd want to spend time with outside of the office.

Until now.

She rubbed a hand over her eyes. "I'm not sure what to think."

Ash held up a bottle of champagne. "Don't think anything. Take a break, Bellerose. You've been running a hundred miles an hour all week."

Tempting. But she still had deadlines. "I owe Mr. Jones his performance review, which—"

"I can come in early tomorrow for it, miss." Arthur was still behind her, taking in the scene with her. "You go on now and relax." He disappeared before she could argue.

Suddenly she and Ash were standing alone, as everyone else gathered around Antonio's karaoke machine. She felt him lean in, felt the warmth of his skin, his breath, as he spoke.

"I've missed you," he murmured, barely loud enough for her to hear.

She felt her stomach plummet with some unnamed emotion. "I can't do this here," she said quietly.

He nodded. "Champagne?"

Why the hell not? She seemed to have traveled through a wormhole into a different dimension lately. "Sure," she said on a sigh. "But Ash, this isn't entirely kosher from a management standpoint. You're providing alcohol for the staff, and it came from the hotel bar?"

He grinned. "It's all paid for. And everyone here has been told that this party is going to end early and no one who wants a job tomorrow better get sauced."

She had to give him credit. That's exactly how she would have handled it. "Wait. Paid for how?"

"Oh, uh, Cranford." Ash looked around as if searching for the old man. "He wanted to make sure everyone was motivated to keep working full steam and this was one way to ensure that." He turned back and winked at her. "Kind of brilliant, if you think about it."

"Uh-huh." Did she believe him? She had a sense that there was more to the story, but she was tired and he smelled wonderful and she was having a hard time not thinking about kissing him.

He handed her a plastic tumbler of champagne and toasted her with a can of seltzer. "To you. And this." He gestured around the room. "It's going to be spectacular. A mayors' meeting for the ages."

Leah sipped. "I certainly hope so. A lot is riding on it. Aren't you having any?" She indicated her cup.

"I'm better with this." He raised his can of seltzer and grabbed her hand. "Let's go karaoke."

Chapter 13

An hour later, everyone was breathless from laughter and dancing. Abba and Prince and Elvis blasted from the karaoke machine, which quickly devolved into a contest to see who the worst singer might be. Applause indicated that Dahlia Markley was the likely winner, with Karen Pembroke a close second.

Ash tried to pay attention to whoever was singing or doing the funkiest dance move, but he couldn't take his eyes off Leah. His body wanted to be pulled in her direction. Staying away from her for nearly a week had made him crazy. It irked him. She was a human magnet, her energy as intoxicating as anything he'd ever experienced.

Basic decency had prevented him from stalking her, but he'd been sorely tempted, especially when he smelled her perfume in the hallways and knew she was close by. It would have been easy enough to find ways to secretly watch her as she moved through her workdays, but he'd resisted. And now she was here, not ten feet away from him.

He could almost taste her mouth, almost feel the silk of her skin as he watched her dance, watched her body shimmy and turn, becoming looser with movement and laughter.

He had to get her alone. Tonight.

Now.

She danced with William, who was clearly smitten, as Hector tried to sing Rick James's "Super Freak." Her moves were sinuous, free. Seeing her in stocking feet, and without the signature veneer of high anxiety, heightened his wicked desire to feel her skin next to his again. As the music wound down and everyone clapped for Hector, Ash approached the dancing duo.

"William, I need to borrow Ms. Bellerose." He smiled mildly at the man.

"Why?" William's face fell in disappointment. "Is the party over?"

"I need to talk to her, but you can stay at the party for a while longer. Hilda will need you to help clean up in a few minutes."

"I can do that."

Ash clapped William on the shoulder, feeling only a little guilty about manipulating the innocent man, albeit in a harmless way. "Great. That's my man."

William laughed, high fived Ash, and went to find Hilda.

Leah was slightly out of breath, the camisole under her tailored suit jacket rising and falling silkily. Ash briefly closed his eyes, having a hard time not being aroused by even that.

I need to feel this woman in my arms soon or I'm going to lose my mind. He tried to sound matter of fact. "Someone was asking for some disco CDs to wrap up the party. Come help me choose some from my collection?"

Leah went very still. "In your apartment?" She glanced around to make sure no one was in hearing range. "I'm not sure that's a good idea."

"I'm not sure I can wait the few minutes it would take to follow you to your place." His eyes studied hers, green irises sparking in response to his words. "You know where it is." He turned, viscerally aware of the arc of electricity between them, and made his way out.

Ten minutes later, he heard a soft knock at his door, which he'd left open. She stood framed in the doorway, wild tendrils of hair escaping from her ponytail, cheeks still pink from dancing. Her high heels dangled from one hand, the other carried a bottle of Pellegrino, which she offered him.

He flicked the door closed and locked, accepted the bottle wordlessly, and placed it on the small dining table. As he turned back, her face tilted toward him curiously. "You don't have a disco collection, do you?"

He shook his head silently, feeling a tiny smile crook the edge of his mouth.

"And no one asked for disco CDs, did they?"

He carefully took her high heels and dropped them to the floor. "Of course not. Disco sucks." His arms went around her as her arms encircled his neck. Suddenly unable to hold back any longer, his mouth found hers. He felt her soften, felt the glow of heat against his body as she responded to his hunger for her. It was clear she was in this with him, clear she needed to be kissed and kissed well.

But he wanted more. After a week in the desert, his need to give and to take was near the breaking point.

She gasped as he pulled away briefly and lifted her into his arms to carry her across the room. He lowered his mouth to hers as he placed her gently on the bed. He stretched out next to her, caressing her as she pulled him closer. The only light was the small bulb over the sink in the kitchenette. The room was dim, shadows played on the walls. He stroked her cheek as he explored her mouth as if for the first time. He couldn't get enough.

"Ash," she whispered against his lips. "I want you."

Desire rolled through him like thunder as he responded, still kissing her. "That's convenient."

"*Now*," she insisted, moving to unzip his monkey suit. Damn. He'd forgotten he had that on. Now she was unbuttoning the shirt he had on underneath, threatening to make him lose it. "Slow down, little girl. This party's getting started."

"Oh, no." She sat up and pulled off her jacket, exposing the satiny slope of her breasts, still covered by the gray silk chemise. "I'm no good at waiting." Her skirt was slipped off and tossed across the room before he knew what was happening. She lay back wearing only the chemise and white lace panties and he sucked in a breath. This was going to be challenging.

After shrugging out of the coveralls, he lowered himself on top of her, bare chested, wearing only his jeans. "Let's teach you some patience," he murmured, angling his mouth into the hollow beneath her jaw. His tongue traced the pulse in her neck as she moaned against him. Her hand ran over his shoulders, down his arm to his abdomen, fingers following the hair that trailed down past his belly button. She rubbed the long bulge in his jeans, exploring his contours with insistence. She made a noise in her throat as her attentions intensified and his blood howled.

He hissed, biting against her neck.

He went back to her mouth and their tongues entwined as their breath synchronized. He nipped her bottom lip and she ran her hand back up his abdomen to his chest. Fingernails lightly scratched across his pecs, then her hand went back to his waistband and beyond, seeking and finding the hard evidence of his desire for her.

The palm of her hand rubbed against him mercilessly. The woman certainly knew what she wanted.

Arousal pounded through him, but he forced himself to concentrate on her.

He broke the kiss and moved lower, lips skimming her breasts through the chemise and landing on the line above her panties. Kissing and licking, he traced the delicate skin from one pelvic bone to the other, back and forth. Hands went under her bottom to pull her against him. He opened his mouth over the lace material to blow warm breath against her. She writhed, fingers curling into his hair.

"That's hot," she whispered, lifting toward him.

Her scent rose, curling around him, sending him to the brink. His erection was almost painful as he breathed again through the panties, heating her skin even more, driving her wild.

"Ash." Her voice was ragged. "I need you."

His response was to take the waistband of her panties in his mouth and pull, first one side, then the other. He simultaneously lifted her bottom and lowered the lace, tugging with his teeth like a feral animal. Slipping the panties off, he tossed them away and growled.

"This," he said, pushing her thighs apart. "This is what *I* want." Slowly, he ran his tongue up the inside of each thigh, ending at the apex. He felt her shiver in anticipation as he used his fingers to spread her open. "Now," he murmured. His tongue traced the delicate lips, the exquisitely sensitive inner labia. Applying pressure second by second, his ministrations continued like a drumbeat, matching the thundering of his heart. Her moisture, musky clean and inviting, dampened her cleft and his chin. She was an elixir, enticing, irresistible.

"Oh, God." Leah groped for his shoulders. "Don't torture me."

His fingers gripped her hips, pulling her hard against his mouth, tongue slipping down, deeper and deeper still into the sweet space above her opening. Her back arched as he flicked a faster rhythm, then he slowed, deliberately modulating the pace of her arousal. She groaned and thumped his shoulders with her fists. Her face flushed, eyes closed.

"You're beautiful," he murmured as he pushed her knees up to spread her open further. "I could spend all night doing this."

Her breath became ragged. "Ash, I need you. Don't make me wait."

He smiled, rose to kiss her lips, then trailed kisses down her body. "Believe me, waiting is a lot harder on me than it is on you." He bit her inner thigh gently and heard her moan again.

Her scent was pulling him in again, his lips and tongue couldn't get enough. She was sweet, spicy, and earthy, a tincture for what ailed him. He stroked the length of her vulva, tongue pushing progressively deeper inside with each pass. Tongue-stroking her most sensitive parts, he moved in tandem with the motion she had begun, a slow rocking that indicated she was close.

Only when she began to pant in earnest did he focus attention solely on her clit. His tongue swirled the erect bud on a staccato rhythm. As he did so, he slipped two long fingers inside her, pushing up and against her sensitive inner wall.

Leah gasped and rocked hard against him. Pumping his fingers, thrusting higher, he closed his mouth over her clit and sucked hard.

Leah's body went rigid and a slow cry rose from her. Fingers twisted in his hair as she convulsed against him. It went on and on, his arousal clawing at him until he couldn't stand it anymore.

He rose to kiss her glowing face as she continued to gasp. He pushed his jeans and boxers down with one hand and shrugged out of them.

Breathless, she opened her eyes, hazy with passion. "You," she whispered. "Now, you." She pulled his hips toward her, put her legs around his waist, and locked ankles behind his back. He'd never seen anything so provocative in his life.

Ash closed his eyes briefly to hold off the avalanche inside him as he rolled on a condom. When he felt her hand close around his erection, it took everything he had not to explode.

"Oh, baby, let's slow this down." He focused on her face, her mussed hair, her freckles. Then, heaving in a breath, he lowered himself.

He felt her take him in, slick and tight and impossibly hot. He held back, pulling out, then thrusting again, enough to tease her. He had more control now and was going to use it.

She arched. "More," she whispered.

His response was to kiss her, long and deep, as he held himself inside her. He withdrew, hearing her gasp, then penetrated again, this time a bit more. There were tears in her eyes.

Then, her hands on his butt, pulling him in, he thrust fully, hard, and deep. The sound she made was half moan, half cry. He gritted his teeth and pulled out, then began thrusting in earnest, pumping hard, pushing himself against her pubic bone, grinding her clit as he impaled her.

It was starting. The rumble of his climax came from deep within and rolled hard. As his eyes closed against the onslaught, he felt her rise against him, her own orgasm matching his.

They rocked together, breath hard, then slowly softening. As he came back to earth, he saw her smile in the dim light. She rolled against him, pressing her bottom against him in a spoon position. His arm enveloped her protectively.

He slept.

***

Leah tiptoed into her apartment and was met with a loud caterwaul from Prunella.

"Oh, my angel." She scooped up the cat and kissed her hairless head. "Your bad mommy abandoned you last night. Are you mad at me?"

Prune wriggled away and meowed her complaints as she danced over to her food bowl, long tail curling and swishing.

Leah poured kitty kibble and murmured her apologies. "I have to abandon you again, sweet pea. But I'll be home this evening." *Unless I get waylaid again by my own hormones.*

She showered fast, the pulse of the water soothing the dissonance of her thoughts. The heat of Ash's body was palpable on her skin, the memory of how he had looked at her— like he *saw her*—caused her breath to catch. His care for her felt real. Which was odd, in and of itself. He didn't know her well yet seemed to like what he knew. Whoever he was (and who *was* he?), she felt safe with him. And Leah Bellerose wasn't accustomed to feeling safe with anyone, least of all a man.

She sighed, closing her eyes under the stream of warm water. There was no denying it now, no matter how uncomfortable it made her or how many problems it might cause.

She was smitten with Asher Banks. The maintenance man.

Had she ever been smitten before? She didn't think so. Not like this. *Never* like this. It was equally thrilling and terrifying.

"Keep it in a box, Bellerose," she muttered as she dressed for work. "Can't let emotions—or lust—derail your mission."

As she waited in her office for Estelle Markley to arrive for her performance review, Ash invaded her thoughts repeatedly. Her skin hummed. Her stomach fluttered, for pity's sake. The scent of his body, his hair, his breath, was as real to her as if he were standing there with her.

"Honestly, you're going to have to join a support group if this keeps up." The bathroom mirror revealed cheeks a little too pink, eyes a bit too bright. She forced herself to take a long, slow, deep breath and replaced Ash's image with that of Mrs. Markley. She had too much to do, too many obligations and goals, to let herself get distracted. And there could be disastrous consequences if staff—or, God forbid, the corporate office—got a whiff of the relationship. Her life as she knew it, along with all her dreams, would be over.

That couldn't happen. She had to focus.

"Miss Bellerose?" Estelle marched into the room and plunked herself in a chair. "Let's get this done. I'm behind on my bread this morning." She whipped out a notepad and pencil from her apron pocket, ready to take notes.

Leah raised an eyebrow, grateful for the concrete task in front of her. "All business, Mrs. Markley. Excellent." She sat opposite the woman and opened her laptop. "You mentioned being behind on the bread. Tell me about your baking schedule. Then we'll move to overall review and goals."

Mrs. Markley withdrew a folded calendar page from her pocket. "Alright. Starting every Monday…"

Ten minutes later, Leah was shaking her head in amazement. "Estelle, I'm impressed. I wasn't aware of the extent of what you've been doing. You've essentially developed an additional funding stream here, one that could be scaled up and used to increase the hotel's recognition."

Mrs. Markley smiled modestly. "Well, I'm not sure about that, now. But I will admit, my bread *is* tasty, and folks seem to like it. The grocery's always asking me to deliver more. They always sell out. And lately, I'm doing more variety. You know, cornbread, muffins, and such."

"Hm." Leah's mind was racing. The tiny profit on selling through the grocery could be maximized by selling the produce in the hotel itself. There might be other possibilities as well. Charmant was a small town, one visited by those passing through or coming for annual events such as the azalea festival or the national fiddle contest. Finding a way to capitalize on local goods would be a great way to further develop the hotel brand.

"I'd like to put together a working group on this, Estelle, and you're going to be the chair." Leah held up a hand to silence Estelle's protests. "I'll give you some pointers, but you're the one who started this bread business, so you're the entrepreneur in the house." As she said it Leah realized it was entirely true. She'd assumed she'd have to hire someone new to work on expanding the hotel's reach and boutique visibility. But Estelle Markley knew the hotel, the town, and the region like the back of her hand. She was part of it.

Much as it irked her to admit it, Leah also knew small towns. Trust and familiarity were key. It was unlikely anyone better or more trusted than Estelle would be found. She might be older, but she was built like a Sherman tank and about as forceful.

Estelle considered. "Well, I suppose I could give it a try. With your help." She leaned forward, voice low. "Julius never did branch out the way he could have. I gave up trying to convince him of anything a long time ago. This hotel has potential, but he's never had much truck for anything new."

That's for sure, Leah thought. Even a new desk chair was anathema. "You and Mr. Cranford are very different." She smiled.

Estelle tut-tutted. "The day he showed up here, I thought we'd never get along. Don't get me wrong. He's not a bad man, but hindered by…well, his personality. Kind of nervous, I guess you'd say." She glanced down at her hands, clasped tight. "He's always been good to me, though. He surprised me. We're close, in our way." She stared out of the window.

Leah suddenly had the sense she knew precious little about the woman in front of her. Personal questions weren't allowed in a meeting such as this, but she found herself nonetheless intrigued.

"Mr. Cranford seems quite fond of you," she offered.

Estelle turned back to Leah and cleared her throat. "We have an understanding." She straightened. "So, my review?"

Chapter 14

Antonio Duran pointed toward the ceiling of the ballroom. "Our scaffolds don't extend up that high. We're waiting on some from Southport to get here early next week."

Ash frowned. "How far behind will that put you?"

The painting contractor made an effort to appear unconcerned and Ash was reminded again how young Antonio was. "It will be close, but we should make it, as long as nothing bizarre happens." He gestured to the walls, three of which were gleaming with fresh paint. "As you can see, we're making good progress."

"I can see that, but the ceiling is an issue. It won't go fast, and it has to be done before the new carpet can go in." Ash calculated in his head. It was going to be close. He'd have to keep pushing this guy, no matter how well-intentioned the kid was. "We have a contract, but we can't afford to not meet the deadline. I'll have to bring in another painter next week if the scaffolds don't get here."

Antonio's face paled. "I'll go to Southport myself and make sure they're here first thing Monday."

Ash clapped the young man's shoulder. "Sooner is better. Make it happen."

He tried to ignore the anxiety buzzing in his chest as he made his way out to the greenhouse. The stakes were higher than he liked to admit with this renovation. It was clear his father was using this as a litmus test of his management skills, so he couldn't afford to fail if his career with the Gerard Hospitality Group had any chance of salvation.

And then there was Leah. The project was her baby, her first chance to demonstrate her chops. He knew enough about her now to realize she had substantial drive. The ballroom renovation and successful mayors' meeting was something she was banking on. It was the kind of project that, if done well, could propel a manager upward relatively quickly.

Suddenly, the buzzing under his sternum turned to a leaden weight. Leah would be moving on, leaving Charmant Forest very soon.

The thought came unbidden, and he realized he'd had a distant awareness of this almost from the beginning but had refused to let himself think about it, being too much in the moment.

He might be a major screwup, but he was no fool, and no stranger to corporate politics. A successful young manager with ambition wouldn't stay long. She would be drafted quickly for bigger and more lucrative endeavors in the company before anyone knew what was happening. And that would be the end of whatever was going on between them.

He would lose her.

His vision blurred momentarily with the full realization of what that meant. Potential unexplored. Passion lost. No flash of green eyes hitting him in the gut. No annoying reactions to what he did. No vulnerability revealed beneath a bristling exterior.

Just when he'd begun to feel himself open up when an actual relationship seemed possible. They had something that might be true and lasting. It was the last thing he'd been expecting when he came to this place. When had they gone from "lovers" to something else? Something he couldn't—or wouldn't—name? He couldn't explain it to himself, much less anyone else.

Thoughts and emotions tumbled as he made his way through the manicured trees.

The sight of the greenhouse was welcome. He pushed away thoughts of his future, or lack of it, with Leah to focus on his present task.

Karen Pembroke waved at him from the back corner of the building. "Ash. What can I do for you? Looking for your best friend, William?" She chuckled.

Ash grinned. "You called that right," he admitted. "I'm thinking of hiring William as my personal coach and therapist." He approached and leaned against a wooden table laden with trays of colorful petunias and coleus. "But I'm not looking for him right now. I need to talk to you about the mayors' meeting and what we can do in-house to augment the current plantings and to decorate the ballroom."

Karen raised a bare foot to rest it on a nearby barrel. "Sure. I can see what we have and put together a plan. We've got lots of annuals to fill in the gaps"—she waved toward the table behind him—"and I can move some of the showier things from the back gardens to the front." Seeing Ash nod, she continued. "As for inside, maybe we can use the things that are still blooming in the back garden as cuttings for arrangements in the room. Even the ivy and some of the other ground covers would work."

"Perfect."

Karen's head cocked slightly. "Trying to save money?"

Ash gestured. "Yeah. But it has to be good. Has to be 'boutique level' in terms of appearance."

"Hm. 'Boutique'?"

He nodded. "Charmant Forest is an older hotel. Plenty of charm in the architecture, but needed updating, which it got, except for the ballroom. Boutique hotels are often renovations, unusual, upscale. They're destinations in and of themselves."

Karen's eyes widened. "How do you know all that?"

Ash realized he might have revealed too much. He shrugged. "Heard about it somewhere, I guess." He cast his eyes toward the greenhouse door and the back side of the hotel. "This place has a way to go before it qualifies as 'boutique,'" he muttered sarcastically.

Karen laughed and considered him closely. "I guess that's why Ms. Bellerose was hired."

The hum of anxiety returned. He stood, ready to get out of there before the conversation could progress any further. "I guess."

"She needs this thing to go well. I hear she started out kind of bitchy but hasn't been too bad in the staff reviews." Karen studied her dirt-caked fingernails. "Haven't had mine yet. Scheduled for tomorrow." She cleared her throat. "She's pretty hot, don't you think?"

This got his attention. He looked at Karen, who was studying him tentatively. He felt himself relax slightly. "You like her," he said.

The pink cheeks answered his question. The gardener's mouth twitched. "I know she doesn't play on my team, but yeah. I do. Like her."

Ash's smile was sympathetic. "How could you not?" He exhaled. "She is indeed hot." This was safe enough territory.

Karen returned his smile. "What about you?"

"What about me?"

She laughed. "You gonna go for it? Or is she out of your league?"

Ash was stymied, then gathered himself. "Actually, she *is* out of my league." He sighed. "Way out." Saying it out loud caused a burn of something, something akin to dread, to streak down his back.

Karen plunged on, unaware of his discomfort. "Oh, come on. Maybe a fling? And you could share all the graphic details with me." She watched him, then tilted her head, perhaps picking up on the way his grin froze on this face. "Seriously, she's kind of intimidating. A man-eater, I'll bet." She straightened and brushed her hands together. "Anyway, I'll get going on those arrangements. You can count on me. Oh, and William, my 'best helper.'"

Ash nodded, his voice sounding hollow to him. "Awesome. Tell William I'll be by to see him later."

***

Work was a welcome diversion. Distracting thoughts of Asher Banks barely made their way through and the morning passed quickly. By early afternoon, Leah was famished.

She passed Hilda on her way out. "Where you going, Miss Manager?" Hilda asked in her lilting accent. "The mayor, he may call again."

"Give him my cell number, Hilda." Leah waved as she left. "I'm taking a break."

Hilda nodded. "Go get you some pie, Miss Manager."

Leah had to smile to herself as she left the hotel grounds and crossed the street. Pie seemed to be the number one prescription for personal restoration around here. She considered this as she made her way down two uncrowded blocks to the Bluebell. There were things to be said for a place smaller than New York City.

The diner was nearly full, even at this time of the afternoon. Leah scanned the booths and tables for a free spot and was greeted by an enthusiastically waving hand. She approached the table where William and Arthur were sitting, finishing their pie.

The two men stood up and waited for her to sit. When had any man stood up for her in recent memory? Certainly no one in New York. She wondered idly if men did that in Singapore.

"Miss Bellers Lady," William said, spitting crumbs. "Are you gonna have some pie?"

Leah laughed as Arthur handed his son a napkin and William dutifully wiped his mouth. "William don't know there's anything on the menu here but pie." He winked at Leah.

"I think I *will* have pie, William. Since you recommend it." Her whole body felt lighter as William clapped and raised his hand for a high five.

Arthur turned to his son. "Now our break's about over. We need to let Miss Bellerose have her time to herself." He stood.

Leah quickly chimed in, noting the way William's face fell. "I'd be happy for you to stay and keep me company, William, if you'd like to."

William nodded vigorously. Arthur shook his head ruefully. "William has the charm, I see." He chuckled. "I ain't never had it. But he does." He waved good-bye. "Don't talk the lady's ear off, now, son."

William watched his father exit the diner and shook his head. "My dad," he said.

"Hm. What about your dad?"

"He doesn't think I should have a girlfriend like you."

Uh-oh. "Oh, William," Leah said gently. "I can't be your girlfriend."

His smile faded to confusion. "You can't?"

"No. I'm sorry."

The man struggled to absorb this information. "Why not? You don't like me?"

Leah grasped for words. "Of course I like you, William. My goodness, you're one of our best helpers at the hotel."

"Yes, I am." He beamed.

"Yes." She gestured to the waitress for pie, buying herself time to think. "It's that, well, I like you as a friend. A *good* friend."

"Oh. Okay."

Grateful that seemed to satisfy him, she went on. "And besides, it's not okay for me to date anyone I work with at the hotel." As she said it, the blatant irony caused her stomach to churn. Suddenly, the thought of pie was unwelcome.

William cogitated on this. "So you can't have a boyfriend at the hotel?"

"No, I can't. It's against the rules." Leah took a sip of water to keep from meeting the man's questioning gaze.

"So you can't date *anyone*? Not even Ash?"

Leah choked down her sip of water and took a few seconds to straighten her jacket. "No, not anyone."

"But Ash likes you."

Could this conversation get any worse? She regretted coming to the diner. Should have stuck to the hotel kitchen. "It doesn't matter if someone likes me, William. I can't date someone I work with."

William watched the waitress place the wedge of pie in front of Leah and nodded. "That looks like excellent pie."

"Yes," Leah murmured, wondering how she was going to force it down now. At least William seemed distracted from their topic.

"But"—the young man raised a finger into the air to emphasize his point—"you *can* date someone secretly."

Okay, now it was worse. She inhaled and wondered how to put this to rest once and for all, and how to get out of the diner. "No, I can't do that, William. I can't date anyone secretly."

William leaned forward across the table, stage-whispering. "Other people do it."

Her eyebrows rose.

"Is true. I've seen it." He sat back and nodded with satisfaction. "It was a long time ago. And they didn't know I saw them. I was very quiet and sneaky."

Now she was confused. "William, I'm not sure what you're talking about. I thought you were talking about me and...you." She felt silly saying it but couldn't bring herself to say Ash's name again.

William gestured impatiently. "You only like me as a friend, Miss Bellers. You can't be my girlfriend." He sounded incredulous that she would still be considering this possibility.

Leah ran a hand over her eyes. "So, who did you see? Who was secretly dating?"

He laughed. "It's a secret."

"Still?"

His nod was exaggerated. "I'm the only one who knows. And nobody knows that I know."

"Aw. Nobody knows that you know...the secret?"

"Yes. Except Julius." The moment the words were spoken, William slapped a hand over his mouth and he rolled his eyes to the ceiling. "Oh, no." He wailed and slapped a second hand over his mouth.

Leah reached across the table. "William, it's okay. Don't worry. You haven't told me anything." She wasn't entirely sure about that, but right now she had to comfort the distraught man in front of her.

William removed his hands from his face. "I haven't told you anything?"

"Nothing."

"I'm not in trouble?"

Leah exhaled. "You're not in trouble. And to prove it to you, I'm going to give you my pie." She pushed the plate across the table.

William's eyes lit up, and she was amazed, not for the first time, at the man's ability to recover from apparent distress and swing right back to joie de vivre.

She left William outside the Bluebell, telling him she had to take a walk, which was true. Her head was spinning.

The breeze on her face was calming and she was still amped up as she strode down Main Street. Wishing she'd brought her walking shoes, she turned at the end of the street to return to the hotel. A familiar silhouette, a loose masculine stride, caught her attention at the far end of the block. It was a man, walking toward her. Her heart leapt.

Was he looking for her? The thought came first as a zap of hope, a spring in her stomach, then an embarrassing awareness of *feelings*. Dumb, adolescent emotions. *Of course* he wasn't out looking for her. Why on earth would he do that? He had plenty of other things to do and had promised to stay away from her during the day. That was their agreement, such that it was.

She admonished herself. That was their rule. It had to be.

But there he was.

His smile was killer, his eyes bright as they crinkled with something like happiness at seeing her. When had anyone else looked at her like that recently— or ever?

"Hey." He stopped in front of her, hands in the pockets of his maintenance jumpsuit. "I was looking for you."

Chapter 15

"How did you find me?"

She looked bewildered and hopeful and terrified all at once. The mix of emotions on her face was too much to interpret. Ash rocked back and forth on his heels and wondered what had happened, wishing he could take her in his arms right there in the middle of Main Street.

"I ran into William. He said you gave him your pie." His mouth tipped up. "William has a way of talking people out of their pie."

She smiled wanly. "I wasn't hungry." They began to walk back in the direction of the hotel. "Why were you looking for me?"

He studied her, aware that she was avoiding looking at him. "Just wanted to check in, show you some progress in the ballroom." *Kiss you all over, feel your body next to mine, make love to you on the roof of the hotel.* He sucked in a breath and focused on the sidewalk ahead.

"Banks, you can come over tonight, but I'd rather not be seen with you in the hotel." She glanced over at him, then away.

He stopped and took her arm. "Leah."

The gesture surprised her. She stopped but kept her face averted. A spark of alarm in his heart was quickly shoved away. He continued. "Look, if we're never seen together, *that* will be odd. I think we can present a normal working relationship at the hotel." *Maybe.*

Leah sighed. "William says you like me."

"I do like you."

She closed her eyes briefly. "Ash, be serious. This could come back on both of us."

He grunted in frustration. "Okay. But Leah, because a man with Down syndrome says I like you doesn't mean that everyone is going to think something inappropriate is going on. I mean, come on. I love the guy, but William thinks that Disneyland is a real country.

He thinks that Dahlia is Julius's daughter." He almost jumped at her reaction.

"What?" Her gaze skewered him, eyebrows knitted while a small smile crooked her mouth.

"Yeah. He told me that once, then said it was a secret." Ash put his hands back in his pockets. "It can't be true." Though now that he said it, he realized it wasn't entirely impossible.

"Why can't it be true?" She was curious, which meant she was now facing him full-on and talking to him without worrying about being seen with him. Her gaze held him, that cursed magnetic field palpable. His every cell felt drawn toward her.

"Because Julius is gay. At least, I think so." Ash shrugged. "It's my theory, or supposition, based on observation."

"No kidding." Leah bit her lip thoughtfully, wheels turning. She stared, unseeing, into the window of a nearby shop. "That might make sense." She looked back at him and focused. "I'm suddenly hungry again. Want some pie?"

Five minutes later they were sitting in the diner, each with an enormous slice of pie in front of them. Leah told him about the conversation with William, which revealed both that William couldn't keep secrets, and that there was almost certainly something between Cranford and Mrs. Markley.

"So you've seen pictures of Julius as a young man? And he had curly red hair?" Leah forked a glossy slice of peach into her mouth.

Momentarily distracted by the image of her lips, glistening with peach juice, Ash told himself to pay attention. It was hard when he was so aroused every minute he was in her presence. He wanted to sweep the plates and glasses to the floor, pull her onto the table and...

He drew a breath. "Yeah. There are a few pictures in the basement, in a storage closet. Most of them are from before Julius's time, but there are some from around the time he came on board."

"And?"

He chewed pie. "That's it. Well, and there was a man with him."

"A man?"

"Yeah. Like, not a woman. You've heard of men." He winked at her.

She huffed. "Come on, Ash. You know what I mean."

He licked peach juice off his thumb. "Looked like a boyfriend or something."

"Based on?"

"The vibe. The way they were standing together."

"Hm." He could see her thinking. She nodded.

"When was this, do you think?"

He shrugged. "Thirty, forty years ago?"

She pushed her plate away. "So what happened to this boyfriend?"

Ash sat back. "Now that we're putting the pieces together, I'd say he might have been sick and probably passed away. In the photos, he was thin and frail-looking. And given the time frame…" He looked out the window of the diner. "It was a devastating period."

Leah was silent for the moment, considering. "So Julius is heartbroken. Bereft. His partner and friends are dying. He comes to Charmant, meets Estelle…?" A line appeared between her eyes. "But he's gay, perhaps bisexual. And wouldn't Estelle have been married at that time?"

Ash sipped water. "It's been known to happen."

Her reply was stony. "But Estelle? And Julius? It's kind of hard to picture." She grimaced. "I don't want to picture it. Although," she paused, trailing off. He waited.

And waited. "Although?"

"Well, it makes a kind of sense. Julius was mourning. Estelle we don't know about. Her situation could have been anything. But they must have meant something important to each other, somehow met each other's needs at the time. Sometimes people have temporary relationships— you know, based on their specific needs at a particular time."

Ash felt his chest clench as her words hung awkwardly in the air.

Sometimes people have temporary relationships…

She glanced away, then back, continuing. "Estelle mentioned to me that she and Julius are 'close' and 'have an understanding.'" She tapped the table with her butter knife. "At the time, I thought she was referring to getting along with him, the old sour puss. But maybe he wasn't always so sour."

"Or old."

She nodded slowly. "Or old."

Ash paid the bill and they stood on the sidewalk in front of the diner. "Want to make a detour to your place?" He placed a hand on her back gently. He felt her lean into him slightly before pulling away, which made his hopes soar. She wasn't so reactive, so defensive anymore.

"Probably shouldn't," she murmured. "But," she continued, looking up at him, "I wish we could." A small smile tugged at the corner of her mouth.

"I'm having a hard time waiting," he whispered as they walked down the street.

Her voice took on a tinge of irritation as she responded. "If you're that horny, feel free to take care of yourself. You don't need me."

He frowned and stepped in front of her to stop her. "Give me some credit, Bellerose. You know me better than that."

"Do I, though?"

"I hope you do." He reached up to touch her face. "Leah, I like being with you. You're amazing. I can't explain it, but I'm honestly not interested in other options right now." *Or maybe ever*. He pushed away the anxiety that clawed at him and turned to walk beside her again.

Her stride matched his as she responded. "It's scaring me, Banks." She sighed. "I *don't* know very much about you, practically nothing. But I do know you like being with me." She reached for his hand, squeezed it, then dropped it determinedly. "And I like being with you. Though I can't for the life of me figure out why." She laughed lightly and turned her face up to the sun. "Maybe because it seems like you're real."

He slowed his pace. They were nearing the hotel entrance. "It seems like I'm real?" This felt dangerous. He shouldn't delve into this territory with her right now.

She folded her arms, assuming her armored visage now that they were in range of hotel staff who might see them. "It seems like you are who you say you are," she said. "And I haven't had much experience of that with men." Her tiny smile was brief but dazzling— and heartbreaking. Ash's jaw tensed as he followed her into the lobby. He was an imposter of the worst kind. It didn't matter that he had to put on a pretense for the sake of his job. But with her, it meant something else altogether. How he would solve that, he had no idea.

And the longer he waited, the greater the chance was he'd lose her.

***

Leah sent Ash to work with Arthur since she wanted to deal with the ballroom's progress on her own. Having Ash standing next to her, smelling irresistible, and emanating erotic energy would be far too distracting. It had stretched the limits of her self-discipline to resist the temptation to drag him to her apartment midday, strip him naked, make him tell her everything about himself, and then shag him 'til nightfall.

It was bewildering. What kind of woman was she turning into?

She surveyed the ballroom and shook her head. "Antonio, we've got to get this ceiling done faster. The carpet is scheduled to go in at the end of next week. I'm afraid we'll have to find another painter."

The young contractor paled. "But Ms. Bellerose, I told Mr. Banks that I'm going to Southpoint myself to see to the scaffolding. We'll work over the weekend, double shifts."

"Ah." Leah crossed her arms. "What did Banks say about that?"

"He's the one who said I had to have it finished, otherwise he'd hire someone else." The young man leaned toward her. "He was forceful about it. Nice," he hurried to add. "But forceful." He shivered. "I promised him we would have it done."

Hm. This sounded exactly like Asher, but it also sounded like management skills that were not commonly found in maintenance men. Not for the first time, Leah wondered who the hell Ash was. Not his preferences or general interests, but who he was at his core. She felt like she knew him— at least, the part of him he revealed to her— but it was increasingly clear she didn't have the whole picture. This should bother her more than it did. She almost didn't care who he was, which in itself irked her. The guy had some juju to make her so lackadaisical.

"Alright, Mr. Duran. I'll give you until Friday to get the scaffolding and working the weekend sounds like the only way to meet the deadline." She tried to smile at him. "Make it happen."

He laughed. "That's what Mr. Banks said."

Leah considered this as she made her way back to the office. When Ash showed up in the open doorway a few minutes later, she was sitting on the couch, lost in thought.

"Arthur and I finished getting those laundry carts repaired..." He trailed off as he saw her. "What's up? You look zoned out."

She studied him. "I'm thinking."

"I can see that. Care to share?"

Her inner reaction was a resounding *No*. But a larger part of her wanted to let him know. Talking should wait until the evening, when they could have more privacy, but it felt immediate. "Close the door. Please." She waited to hear the automatic lock click, then pointed to the chair next to the couch. It would be too much to have him sit closer at this point.

She cleared her throat. "I'm thinking about my father."

This took him by surprise, she could see. He nodded as he sat, face expectant.

"I'm not sure why, but he keeps showing up in my head lately." She sighed. "It's weird. I go months, years even, hardly thinking about him at all." His eyes were on hers as she continued. "But lately, I wonder what kind of effect he had on me. And how that affects me now...with you." Her fingers tapped an uncertain rhythm against her thigh. "My father was, let's say, less than trustworthy. So, I'm not very trusting. Of anyone. Particularly men. That's not your fault. It's the way it is."

His tone was mild. "You haven't told me anything at all about your family, where you come from. I know nothing about you."

"Well." She crossed her legs and felt her rational brain kick in. "Then we're even. I know nothing about you either."

"Maybe that's the best way, for now." Did he sound relieved?

Her gut tightened, but she nodded. "I agree." She shouldn't have mentioned her father. It was a moment of weakness. The last thing she wanted to do was share anything about her upbringing, the poverty, the torrid family dramas, the way she couldn't get out fast enough. She'd promised herself a long time ago that her family was her private situation. Not a secret. Just private.

And why tell Asher Banks any of that? He was the maintenance man. Someone she was attracted to, but who would be in her past before she could blink. She had much greater concerns.

She rose, intending to usher Banks out of the room so she could get back to work, but somehow she was reaching for him, then tumbling back onto the couch, his arms catching her, pulling her into the strong, solid length of him. A long exhale escaped her, and his mouth was on hers, slaking a thirst she'd been unaware of ten seconds before. Her hands went into his hair. She was strafed by the afternoon roughness of his chin as he kissed her, his craving palpable.

He was murmuring as he kissed her. "This is all I need to know about you." His hands cradled her face, then moved to her shoulders, arms winding around her. "Just you. In this moment." He took her mouth, teeth nipping, tongue exploring. "This is enough. It's everything."

Her mind went blessedly blank. She wanted him more desperately than she'd ever wanted anything. It was painful. Her lungs filled with his breath, his scent, his overwhelming clean muskiness. He smelled of pure desire.

"Leah," he murmured, breaking into her thoughts, still kissing her. "Leah." His voice was full of wonder. He explored her mouth with his tongue, whispering, "You're magic. You're a drug."

She tightened her grip on him, pulling him closer. "I need you," she heard herself whisper. "Hurry." Not knowing what she expected, she was surprised to feel his hand make its way up her thigh, his intent clear. His teeth scraped at the skin on her neck, biting hard enough to make her gasp.

She arched against him, need and thrill and trepidation vying for dominance. The few men who'd done this with her had been entirely disinterested in the activity. They were eager to find their own pleasure and were impatient and unskilled.

This was not the case with Asher Banks.

Heat rose, her cheeks flushed. A rush of moisture between her legs met Ash's fingers as he pulled her panties down and off in one swift motion. She reached down to remove a spike heel but Ash's growled instruction, "Leave them on," had her lying back beside him.

His mouth covered hers again as he rubbed into her cleft, finding her clit, and stroking gently up and down, then harder. His voice was husky, commanding but tender. "God, you're wet. Open up for me now." She moaned into his mouth and he pushed her thighs wider apart, skirt raised almost to her waist.

He looked down at her, naked between the bunched skirt and high heels. "Christ," he muttered. "I could eat you alive." Her skin was on fire underneath his touch. A finger played at the edge of her opening, tempting her, dipping in, then out. His palm covered her clit and rubbed as the finger teased her.

"Ash." Her hands gripped his shoulders, willing him to take her, to make it happen. She needed to feel possessed, out of control. Free.

His mouth covered hers, breathing into her, pulling breath from her. One, then two fingers entered her with aching slowness as his thumb circled her clit. He pulled out, then penetrated again, deeper this time. Out, then in. She rocked her pelvis against his hand as he began to thrust in earnest.

"That's it," he whispered, biting down hard on her bottom lip. "Let it come."

It was happening too fast. Leah felt a torrent of energy building in her, rushing at her from all directions. "I need..." her voice trailed off in a tiny gasping choke.

Ash slowed his ministrations to her clit and reversed direction, building speed and pressure as his fingers pushed into her, harder and deeper. He pressed upward into the inner wall, where the sensation became electric. His palm pulsed against her clit as he pumped. Her internal muscles clenched rhythmically, pulling him in.

Suddenly it was on her. A great implosion gripped her, she arched into him, biting back on a scream as her body convulsed. Her hands clawed his back and she lost herself. Time slowed and revved back up, and still her body rocked. On and on it went, he slowed his stimulation but didn't stop, using the tempo of her movements to orchestrate his.

He was going to make her come again.

No, no, no. The words were silent, the thought fleeting. How was this possible? But her body knew.

"That's it." His tongue slid down her throat as she drew a deep breath. Then, unbelievably, she felt the circular motion between her legs become a different thing, a side to side motion. Her body levitated into the pressure of its own free will, pushing her hard against his hand. Somehow a third finger entered her, pushing in and up as his thumb continued its action, circling the labia, spinning against her clit. She was born away on a wave of pure ecstasy. A sense of splitting out of her skin, shedding her cocoon like a butterfly, caused her mouth to open in a silent wail. Tears spilled down her cheeks as every muscle in her body lit up, then relaxed into exquisite, alien liquidity.

Chapter 16

Ash sat in his truck outside her apartment, scanning the retro wrought iron railing, the turquoise doors with their stylized numbers. The sun was setting. He'd told himself he'd casually swing by after his plumbing class. That seemed innocent enough— though he'd showered and changed into decent clothes first. Now he was faced with a decision. His body and brain were tired, but all he could think about was her.

Seeing her face, hearing her voice, smelling her perfume. The softness of her skin, the taste of her most secret places, had him caught up in so many fantasies at once that his head spun.

"Man, you are a goner," he muttered as he flipped his water bottle open.

The afternoon replayed in his head over and over, the echo of words spoken causing fear to skitter under the surface.

Had they agreed not to know anything about each other? And if so, shouldn't he be relieved? It aligned with their original arrangement, such that it was, to be lovers and nothing else.

That had been his idea.

"You dumb shit," he said aloud.

Not knowing anything about each other worked as cover for him, of course. The problem was, he wanted to know more about her. Damn, he wanted to know *everything* about her. Wanted to be able to share things—good and bad—with her. Sticking to a "don't ask, don't tell" policy didn't only feel wrong, it bordered on spiritually obscene.

He snorted at himself in disgust. "You're becoming a philosopher. And a crappy one at that."

The light in Leah's kitchen window burned bright, but there was no evidence of movement there. She must be in her living room. He wondered what she was doing. Did she watch TV? What did she like? Did she read? If so, what kinds of books? What was she wearing? What was she thinking?

He rested his head against the back of the old vinyl seat and considered. He couldn't remember being this smitten with anyone, ever.

Well, there had been that time in middle school when he'd developed a crush on an exchange student named Katrina Ludovik, but that didn't count. He'd mooned around for so long, his mother had laughingly told his father about it, and there it had ended. Simon Gerard let his son know in no uncertain terms that his only acceptable options for future relationships would be ivy league graduates from prestigious families.

He'd continued to love Katrina from afar, until she returned to her own country, but the divide between what he felt and what he was allowed to express became hardened. It was an unquestioned understanding from there onward that he was only allowed certain feelings and certain actions. This almost certainly created a perfect opportunity for teenage rebellion to morph into adult rebellion. Indulgence. Escapism. Self-sabotage.

He grimaced. That he'd gotten out alive was a minor miracle.

And now, here he was, with a woman he'd never even hoped dream of only a few yards away, ensconced in her apartment, pulling him toward her with the force of a thousand Katrina Ludoviks.

***

Prunella sat contentedly on Leah's lap as she sipped tea and watched old television reruns. It was what she needed after the last few days. Mindless escape.

I Dream of Jeanie ended and *The Brady Bunch* came on. Leah clicked the TV off with a sigh. She didn't need a reminder of the kind of family life she'd never had. It had always bewildered her as a child that a family full of healthy, smiling people in a huge, clean house would have a housekeeper. Why would they need that? There was no mess. No one was sick or dragging an oxygen tank around. There were no money problems, they never had to move on a moment's notice. There was plenty of food, and most miraculously of all, no one ever yelled or threw punches or smashed things against walls.

She hated *The Brady Bunch*.

"Hop up, Prune," she said, lifting the complaining cat from her lap and depositing her on the coffee table. It was inky black outside the tiny kitchen window as she rinsed her mug. She stared into the darkness, the hollowness in her chest both uninvited and familiar.

Ever since the conversation with Ash that afternoon, memories of her childhood had been pushing at her from beyond the veil of consciousness, intruding, invading.

An image of a dingy shotgun house, the one they'd lived in when she was six or seven, blew into her mind like an ill wind. The dilapidated structure was on the edge of the tiny town in which she'd lived with her parents. No streetlights graced their dirt road, no glow emanated from other houses. It was isolated and desolate. She could still remember how scared she'd been those first few weeks. Having left their previous home in a trailer park full of children her age, her younger self suddenly had nowhere to go if her parents began screaming at each other. The dark was her enemy. It epitomized her vulnerability, the knowledge that no one was going to take care of her but her.

Leah shook herself and turned back to her apartment, every light on bright. Prunella meowed and bumped against her leg, demanding attention. "I know, I know," she murmured, picking the cat up to nuzzle her. "Well, Prune. It's time. It can't be avoided any longer." She sighed and sat, picking up her phone while Prunella began kneading into her sweatpants.

The phone rang several times and was finally answered. "Well, lookie who's calling me?" Cecelia Bellerose crowed. "My baby girl."

Leah smiled ruefully. "How are you, Mama?"

"Can't complain. 'Course if I did, no one would care." Her mother inhaled and blew out a heavy, smoke-filled breath. "What's happening?" The implication was clear. Leah didn't call her mother unless there was something significant to report.

"Just thought I'd check in." Leah studied her fingernails, her preferred method of distraction whenever she spoke to the indomitable Cecelia.

Her mother snorted. "That's rich. You never call to 'check in.'" She coughed for several seconds, then continued. "Something going on? You in trouble?"

Her chest tightened. "No. No trouble." She couldn't even convince herself. How could she possibly fool her mother?

Cecelia grunted, but her voice softened. "Now, Maggie, I want you to come out here and visit real soon. We've got a holiday weekend coming up."

Leah closed her eyes. She had no energy to correct her mother's use of her forsaken name. Some things were too entrenched to worry about.

She considered her mother's suggestion with a mix of dread and unwanted nostalgia. What would it be like to go back now? Her grandmother's old house in town, where she'd lived with her mother in high school. Stone steps crumbling, front porch sagging. Sheets tacked up over windows. Cigarette smoke. Piles of yellowing newspapers.

Her eyes opened and she scanned her living room, reminding herself she was in the present moment. Clean apartment. New Venetian blinds on the windows. Food in the cupboard. "I'm not sure, Mama."

Her mother tsk-tsked. "Well, my lands. Don't those people ever give you a day off?" The snick of a lighter punctuated her comment. "Aunt Sugar's been asking after you. She's doing right poorly lately."

Leah wavered. She almost regretted calling her mother, but something about visiting felt potentially helpful. It might be good to get an injection of Cecelia's ability to be emotionally independent and self-reliant. Anyone who lived in the circumstances she did and was able to bulldoze through her days with an intact sense of self could be a source of inspiration.

She *had* been a source of inspiration in an odd way. The old iron maiden, from whom Leah got her strength, if not her capacity to embrace hardship.

"I'll see what I can arrange. But no promises." They said their matter-of-fact good-byes and hung up. Leah sat still for a long moment, wondering what she'd done.

"It will be good, Prune," she declared with determination, stroking the cat's hairless body. "And I'll talk to Dahlia about coming over to take care of you. She likes cats." The feline offered a disdainful meow and jumped to the floor.

Her phone chirped. A text appeared on the screen. Ash: *I'm outside your door.* A tiny zip of happiness tipped her mouth into a smile as she texted back a winking smiley face.

Ash's grin was huge and his eyes crinkled as she opened the door. "Sweatpants. You know I can't resist." He took her in his arms and picked her up, kicking the door closed behind him.

She laughed, surprised by how glad she was to see him. "Where's the monkey suit? This casual stud look is de rigueur."

It was his turn to laugh as he adopted a heavy accent. "Ah, pardon. *C'est naturel.*"

He carried her into the kitchen and deposited her on the little dining table. She leaned away from him as he moved in to kiss her, placing a hand on his broad chest. "Since when do maintenance men speak French? Or," she continued, taking in the cut of his shirt, "wear custom tailored shirts?"

He stilled for a second, then plucked her hand from his chest. His mouth hovered over hers. "Didn't we agree to no personal questions outside the office, Bellerose?"

She narrowed her eyes at him. "I'm not sure that was the agreement."

He shrugged. "Maintenance men go to high school," he murmured. "At least, this one did." His lips skimmed her mouth, then her cheeks, eyelids, and each ear. "And I know all the best thrift stores."

"Uh-huh." She closed her eyes as his lips touched hers. If they had any kind of real agreement, it was to keep things in the moment, and that's what she needed to do. In this moment, it was nearly impossible to think of anything except the way he smelled, the flame of his tongue as it moved against hers, the gentle bite of his teeth against her neck.

The drumbeat of desire became louder, more insistent. She pulled him closer. "Up for round two?"

His groan was answer enough.

"I'm not coming without you this time." She moved to unbutton his shirt, holding back from ripping it open.

He whispered in her ear, "I won't argue with you. Hey." He pulled back abruptly as Prunella jumped onto the table and stared at him accusingly.

Leah rolled her eyes. "She's jealous. She wants all my attention." The cat meowed loudly as if to verify this. Her gaze went back to Ash, his tousled dark hair, amber-flecked eyes, and sultry five-o'clock shadow. The picture of male seductiveness.

He kissed her again, slowly, then stood, shirt flapping open to reveal his muscled torso. Leah was breathless with wanting as he swept her into his arms. "Miss Kitty will get all our attention in a few minutes." He carried her into the bedroom and shut the door in Prune's face. Leah was dropped onto the bed sideways with a small bounce.

She looked at him in wonder. "You said '*our* attention.' Miss Kitty will get *our* attention."

Ash fell on top of her, his weight feeling like certainty and safety. "Yeah?"

"So, that means not only *my* attention. Yours, too."

He blinked. "Yes, I believe that's what I meant." An eyebrow rose.

Her hand went to his face. "You mean that."

He rolled to her side and placed a hand on her shoulder, stroking down her arm to her hand. "Leah Bellerose, I mean that. Prunella is a beautiful feline goddess, and she is deserving of my attention." He raised her hand to his lips and kissed each fingertip slowly, lingeringly. His eyes rose to hers, skewering her with a lustful gaze. "After I give you some of my exceptional, Leah-only attention."

She didn't remember shimmying out of her clothes, or Ash shrugging out of his. Heat rose like a shimmering swell between them and then he was inside her, rocking into her, making her gasp. Her nails raked his back as he hooked one of her legs over his arm. His cock seemed to expand, and she was stretched full and wanting more. Her cries intensified as his hand found its way between them, rubbing into her as he continued to thrust.

Their breaths harmonized and became more urgent as they each reached the peak together. Leah felt the irresistible pull as the drumbeat became deafening, reverberating throughout her entire body. She clutched him, holding on for all she was worth as the waves crashed into her. He rode her in a frenzy, then froze in climax. They were silent except for their gasps, unmoving save for the rise and fall of their heaving breaths.

Several minutes passed. The sound of crickets floated through the window. At last, Ash raised himself above her again and kissed her softly, then more passionately. Not for the first time, Leah was struck with the near miraculous eroticism of the way he used his mouth.

Then he was grinning mildly at her, eyebrow cocked.

"What?" she asked.

The grin became a full smile. "Time to rescue the goddess," he said. As if on cue, Prunella, outside the door, issued a stupendous yowl.

***

Ash was supposed to be surveying the ballroom ceiling, but standing next to Leah, it was hard to concentrate. She was wearing an actual dress today, a deep V-neck, body-hugging cobalt number that fell over her curves like liquid. High heeled sandals completed what he considered to be the most unfairly seductive outfit imaginable.

It almost made him angry at her. How was he supposed to work?

"Mr. Banks?" Antonio broke into his thoughts.

"Ah." Ash came back to the moment. "Looks good, Antonio. Thanks for stepping on the gas." He glanced at Leah, who was looking resolutely away from him and continued. "Carpet installers will be here first thing in the morning. Your team will be cleaned up and out of here by then?"

"If it takes us all night. Which it won't." Antonio tapped the calendar on his clipboard. "I've personally coordinated with the installers. We're heading out so they can come in. Carpeting a room this size will take a few days."

Leah straightened at this. "I'll need confirmation of the transition from painting to carpeting, Mr. Duran. Please inform Mr. Cranford and me every step of the way. I'll be out of town over the weekend, so I'll expect you to communicate with me immediately if there are any issues."

This was news to Ash. Why hadn't she mentioned her plans? She still wasn't looking at him but he could feel her nervous energy. He lowered his voice. "You're going away?"

Leah gestured dismissively. "Just for a day or two. I have some personal business to conduct." She directed her comments to

Antonio. "I'll be in contact with Mr. Cranford at all times. I'll expect all renovations to continue on our aggressive timeline."

She left Antonio nodding into thin air. Ash considered following her but decided against it. Whatever she had to do, it was none of his business.

Except his stomach clenched, wondering. Could Leah be interviewing for another position somewhere? He'd become convinced she would be leaving Charmant at any moment and braced for it like he would a blow to the gut. As armored as she was, the compelling force of her personality was irresistible. Maybe the armor was even part of the draw.

He drew a hard breath as he left Antonio to finish his work. There was a task weighing on him that he couldn't put off any longer.

Ten minutes later, he was in his apartment, in front of his computer. His father's secretary and gatekeeper, Joan, answered the video call.

"Your father isn't expecting a call from you." She made it sound like it had been written on stone tablets.

"Just send me through, Joanie." He knew she hated the nickname, but his tolerance for protocol was draining away with every passing day.

She pursed her lips but said nothing. Several seconds later, Simon Gerard appeared. The older man's face and voice were impassive. "Asher. What do you need?"

Ash schooled his expression, trying not to convey frustration. "Thought I'd check in early, let you know things are rolling along well with the ballroom renovation." He stopped, unsure how to approach the topic of Leah. He wanted to make sure his father knew she was doing an excellent job, solving problems, making things more efficient. If his agenda was also about wanting her to stay at Charmant Forest as long as possible, fine.

His father didn't blink. "Is that it?"

He took a moment to consider his reply. "It's significant, Dad. Our timeline is seriously compressed. Ms. Bellerose has gotten all the contractors moving faster than anyone I've ever seen. She's going to pull this off, and it's going to be great for the hotel." Saying it, he felt a swell of pride in Leah's ability to get things done in the face of difficult odds.

Simon shifted in his desk chair. "That's her job."

"Right, I know, and—"

"And I put you in charge of managing the contracts. Are you telling me she had to do this for you? That's below her pay grade."

"No." Ash felt his fists clench. "I *have* been managing them. But she's overseeing everything. We've been working…together."

That was true. Hearing it out loud made it even more real. And it felt good, like he was getting his management feet under him again, no matter how slowly. He realized he'd become more optimistic lately about his prospects, without explicitly thinking about it. Working with Leah— and William, Arthur, Karen, Antonio, and the others— he felt more himself than he had in a long time.

His father was studying him sharply. "You're maintaining appropriate professional boundaries with her? Not being offensive or flirtatious?"

"Oh, Jesus," Ash muttered, looking at the ceiling, then back. He didn't want to go down this road right now, but at some point, he would. If Leah didn't leave him, he'd have to face his father regarding his relationship with her. Because *he* wasn't going to leave *her*. He knew that now, somehow, in this moment.

Simon pointed a finger in the direction of the computer screen. "I know you, Ash. I know your weaknesses. You've coasted through life on your charm and family connections."

"That's not fair—"

"But you're not coasting anymore. Not on my dime." His father grinned a small, cold, crocodile grin. "If I find out you've been anything but entirely professional with anyone at Charmant Forest, you'll be unceremoniously ushered out of this company once and for all." He tapped his wristwatch. "Are we done?"

Ash slammed the laptop shut and pounded a fist on the desk. "Impossible to have a conversation like this." He stood and the realization hit him. He would have to go see his father in person, to reiterate the progress that Leah had made with the staff, the renovation, everything. Even the branding ideas she had were something Simon couldn't know about as yet, and he had to let his father know. In person and soon. This weekend would make a good time. Everything was on track with the renovations and Leah would be gone. He could afford one night away.

He popped the computer back open to look for last minute flights.

Chapter 17

Leah navigated the road between Charmant and her hometown with a sense of impending doom, mixed with what felt like foolish optimism. She dreaded what were certain to be painful reminders of where she'd come from and yet still had vague hopes of making some kind of peace with her origins. It seemed remote, but these days she was inclined to think anything was possible.

She had a two-hour drive ahead of her, which she intended to use to full advantage to get work done. She commanded her phone. "Call Gerard corporate office."

A moment later, Joan connected her to Simon Gerard.

"Ms. Bellerose. I look forward to your update." He was all business, as usual. A great boss, she told herself. Never emotional. Not driven by anything but logic and good business sense.

He was a real mentor, albeit a bit remote.

"Sir, I have reports on the staff I've been reviewing. I emailed you the draft document a few minutes ago." She reached over to shuffle through papers on the passenger's seat. "The high-level assessment is that most of the staff are efficient and performing well. My opinion is that they need to be kept on. Only a few, mostly in temporary or part-time positions, would be prudent to let go."

She heard the click of the keyboard as Gerard scrolled through her report. His silence was palpable.

"I know what you're thinking and I'd like to give you my rationale." Trying to head off his concerns, she plunged on. "The current departmental managers are modestly compensated and loyal to the hotel. Hiring new employees would almost certainly cost more, would take time to train, and we'd be losing the sense of community that exists now."

She paused. There was still silence.

"When I first arrived in Charmant, you asked me about Hector Duran, head of housekeeping. You said it's unusual to have a man in that position, and it is. Hector is unusual. He's one of the hardest working staff members we have. His housekeepers are almost all personally known to him—family and friends and friends of friends. That might sound like nepotism, but it's typical in a small town." She switched on the air conditioner, realizing she was suddenly feeling warm.

"If a housekeeper needs disciplinary action, Hector does it himself. The turnover rate is extremely low, despite modest, industry-standard pay rates. If we reorganized that department, we'd almost certainly be paying as much or more for a less reliable, less well-managed group of workers."

"All right, I'm going to stop you right there." Simon's voice was low but firm. "Leah, I respect your opinion, but you're a rookie when it comes to reorganizing a large structure for greater profitability." He cleared his throat and she could almost see him sitting behind his enormous oak desk, twisting the class ring he wore on his right pinkie. "My directive was to cut costs, not to maintain a sense of family or loyalty within the staff. I went against my better judgement and allowed you a budget for the ballroom renovation. That was based on my confidence that you would bring in this reorg to save us big dollars."

He paused briefly for effect. "Now I'm skimming this report, I can tell you this is unacceptable. I'm surprised and frankly disappointed."

Leah's hands went cold on the steering wheel. She forced herself to breathe and pay attention to the road as Simon continued, his words hitting her like arrows.

"What happened to that steely young woman I sent down to Charmant Forest to clean it up? The one as tough as nails and hungry to climb the ladder?"

She swallowed at the description, which was far too reminiscent of her childhood nickname. And accurate. "I...I'm still that woman, sir." But was she? What had happened to that woman, so often described in terms of cold, unyielding metal? Uncertainty clawed at her, even as she reminded herself she had confidence in her work. That much was sure. "With respect, sir, solid management principles undergird these recommendations—"

He cut her off. "We need to regroup on this situation as soon as possible. The board is hounding me. When can you get up here?"

"Sir?"

His voice was clipped, impatient. "To *New York*. I need you here in person. We're going to have to bring this reorganization to the senior leadership committee."

Shock jolted through her like ice water. He was taking her out of the top role, going up the chain because he thought she was handling things the wrong way. *Inhale. Exhale.* Her fingers were white on the wheel. *Steady going, Bellerose.* "I don't think that's necessary, sir. I'm happy to send you the detailed financial calculations in my plan, and, if needed, propose some potential compromises." Even as she said it, her stomach plummeted. Her mind was racing. If she had to let someone go, who would it be? William? Julius? Arthur?

Her boss wasn't listening. "Can you get here Tuesday of next week?"

Her business instincts took over. "The mayors' meeting is in ten days, sir. I can't be available before then. We've invested too much in the renovation and meeting planning for me to leave before it happens. But I'll book my flight for the day after." She held her breath.

She could hear his anger, barely contained, in the silence that followed and wondered what it would be like to be in the room with it. She shivered.

"Ms. Bellerose, I'm displeased. You've been given a lot of latitude because we thought you were a rising star in our company." He cleared his throat to emphasize his use of the past tense. "Book that flight."

"Yes, sir." Leah exhaled slowly. "And I'll send you the detailed report in advance, so you and the board can consider all the angles."

His response was to hang up. Leah stared at the phone, then at the road ahead, the concrete divider blurring as the miles flew by.

***

"Toothbrush, toothpaste, razor..." Ash threw a few other items in a backpack along with a book and one of Estelle's cranberry muffins. That left enough room to bring back a small souvenir for William.

He picked up his phone as he headed for the stairs. "Antonio, fill me in." He listened to the man's update and nodded. "Great. I'll take a look on my way out when I check in with the carpet guys."

Everything was on track. It will all be fine, he told himself. He'd be gone for less than twenty-four hours. What could possibly go wrong?

"Never ask that question," he muttered to himself as he jogged up the three flights to the hotel's main floor.

Oscar Valdez, Hector's friend and owner of Oscar's Fantastico Flooring, met Ash at the ballroom door. "Ready to install, Mr. Banks," he said, gesturing broadly toward the towering rolls of deep green carpet. "The pad is laid. My men will have this done by the end of the weekend."

Ash tried to quell the uneasy feeling that things were going too well. He'd never been the paranoid type, but a lot was riding on this project. "I'll be available by phone and back late tomorrow. Call me if anything comes up."

Oscar grinned. "Nothing will come up. This is what we do. We are happy to work on the weekend— and a holiday, at that." An eyebrow rose to confirm this.

"Yes, your men will get holiday pay rates. That's in the contract." Ash shook the man's hand. "Call me." He waved and headed to the office to confer with Cranford.

Cranford was sitting at his desk, staring blankly at his computer. He looked older than Ash remembered him. When Ash stopped in the doorway, the man looked up, rheumy eyes blinking to orient himself. "Mr. Banks."

Ash shifted his backpack to the opposite shoulder. "I'm heading out until tomorrow evening. Arthur and William and Hector will cover for me. I spoke to Oscar and everything looks good for the carpet to be installed this weekend." He paused and studied Cranford's face, then stepped into the office and took a seat. "Is there anything I can do for you before I leave? It's been an intense few weeks and we're all..." He searched for something to say that wouldn't offend the man. "Well, we're all tired."

Cranford's face went slack, then he seemed to collect himself. "Thank you, Mr. Banks. I do appreciate it. But," he said, head tilting toward his computer screen, "it appears that Ms. Bellerose has taken care of everything." He steepled his hands and gazed at them. "She seems to have everything under control."

Ash placed a hand on the desk. "She is extraordinary, I'll give you that. A force of nature." He exhaled and tried a light tone. "And I know she values what you've done here over the years, sir."

Cranford glanced up. "She said that?"

"She did." He hoped he wasn't giving too much away.

"That means a lot." The older man sighed and toyed with a small flash drive, which was sitting on the blotter. "She's trying to allow me to stay on, when it's long past time for me to retire."

Ash inclined his head.

"This," Cranford said, indicating the drive, "is her report to the corporate office. The long-term plan, with budgets and expenditure projections. She proposes giving me two more years to 'assist with the full transition' to boutique status." He smiled. "I doubt she thinks I'm necessary. I'm not sure why that's part of her plan."

Ash sat back and regarded Cranford. "Ms. Bellerose is impressed with the way this hotel has become a family for so many of the staff. It may not align with high-end business concepts, but you've demonstrated that it's worked here, in this place."

Cranford's hangdog expression perked up. "It is like a family, in its way," he agreed. "I didn't intend that. At least, not consciously." His eyes were far away. "But it is a small town, after all— and that's what I suppose I needed."

Ash nodded. "I know."

Cranford's focus returned and he met Ash's gaze for a silent moment. "You know." It was a statement and question both.

"I think I do. There are lots of old photos in the basement. When William and I were organizing the storage rooms..."

"Ah." Cranford pursed his lips. "I see. Yes. Well." He tapped his fingers together. "I'd forgotten those were there. Suppose I should throw some of those old things out."

Ash's chin tilted. "Why not bring some things back up here, into the office? Or take them home with you?"

Cranford sat still for a moment, then shrugged. "I'll think about it." He allowed himself the smallest smile. "I haven't thought of that time in many years. Easier not to."

Ash stood. "Understandable." He offered Cranford a wave. "See you tomorrow."

Cranford's voice stopped him as he got to the door. "Take this," the older man said, extending the flash drive.

"Sir?"

Cranford offered Ash a shrewd gaze. "It appears that you and I share suspicions about each other. Suspicions that may be well-founded." He dropped the flash drive into Ash's hand. "I think I know where you're going. This might make a difference."

***

"Damn." The gravel driveway was mostly mud puddles and Leah's wedges were the exact wrong thing to be wearing. And why had she worn dress jeans and a designer top to her mother's house?

Nothing had changed. A pile of old tires still sat at the corner of the dirt yard, next to a rusting oil drum. An ancient pickup truck was propped on cinder blocks at the side of the house, its bed filled with years' worth of junk.

She sighed, reached into the back seat, and grabbed her running shoes, changing into them in time for the front door of the house to fling open and four Pomeranians to come rushing out, yapping at the top of their tiny lungs.

"Elvis. Reba. Dolly. Patsy." Her mother stood in the doorway and hollered, cigarette waving.

Patience. Leah drew a deep breath and opened the car door, prepared for the onslaught. All four dogs jumped into the car. Ten minutes later, after chasing various pairs of canines around the yard, everyone was corralled in the living room. Leah dropped onto the afghan-covered sofa and pushed one dog after another off her lap. Her dress jeans were now covered in fur and dusty paw prints.

Cecelia Bellerose cackled as she settled back into her threadbare recliner. "They remember you. Been missing you, I guess." She lit a fresh cigarette and swigged from a bottle of neon yellow soda.

Missing Prunella, Leah tried to smile. "I wish you'd train them better, Mama. They're so…enthusiastic." Grimacing inwardly, she remembered her promise to herself to make this visit short and friendly. *No need to get into arguments or bring up subjects that might enflame Mama's famous temper.*

"Elvis is my only problem," Cecelia said, pointing at the tan-colored offender. "He's the leader of the pack and pure trouble." She drew on her cigarette and blew smoke at the ceiling. "Typical man. Even neutered he can't control himself."

There was nothing to say to that. Leah uncapped her water bottle.

"Can I get you a soda, Maggie? Or iced tea?" Her mother heaved herself out of the recliner. "Or a beer?"

"It's eleven in the morning." Leah stood up to prevent the dogs from climbing on her. "And *please* call me Leah."

Her mother waved dismissively as she made her way into the kitchen. "Hard to teach this old dog new tricks." She hooted, which turned into a coughing fit. "Your Great Aunt Sugar'll be over any minute. Gonna get the iced tea."

Leah followed her mother, taking in the faded wallpaper and ancient linoleum kitchen table where she'd eaten her childhood meals. The speckled plastic chairs were cracked and peeling. Acrid smoke hung in the air. Suddenly her chest and legs felt numb. Nausea rolled through her stomach. She closed her eyes briefly.

I don't live here anymore. I'm grown up. This *is the present. I am Managing Director of Charmant Forest.*

An image of Ash came to her unbidden. The way his eyes crinkled when he smiled at her. His strength when he carried her across the room. The weight of his body against hers, making her feel safe.

She inhaled. "Can I help you, Mama?"

Cecelia handed her a pitcher. "Just put this on the table there. We're not going to stand on formality today." She pulled a package of cookies out of the cupboard, shooing away the dogs as they clambered for a forbidden treat. "Git back."

A knock at the door was followed by a "Yoo-hoo." and before she knew it, Leah was being enveloped by the rail-thin arms of Aunt Sugar. The tiny woman was wizened and gray but wore a bright pink track suit and fire engine red lipstick, smeared outside the lines. "Look at you, I swear." She stood back and took Leah in, shaking her head. "You look like a model, honey." She dragged Leah back to the living room and plunked onto the sofa with her.

"Now, tell us everything about big city life," Sugar said. "And all the men you've gotten to know since you gave Barry the boot." She turned to Cecelia. "I never liked that boy. You remember I said that?"

Cecelia nodded, swigging her soda. "Well, he's a man, so that's the problem. Can't trust a one of 'em."

Sugar nodded. "It's a right shame. But once I had Doogie and Tiffany, I was done with men."

"Your Wayne was a real piece a work," Cecelia agreed. "Only interested in one thing."

"Sperm donors. That's all they're good for." Sugar howled. "But seriously, Maggie. Tell us. Any new men?" Her eyes were bright.

Leah steeled herself. She'd prepared for this. "I don't have time to date."

Cecelia snorted. "Since when has that ever stopped you? Though you spent so long with that loser, Barry, I lost hope you'd ever come to your senses."

Leah bit her tongue on a sharp rejoinder.

"O'course, you were always susceptible to any boy who sniffed around, bein' that you were not an easy child to like, at times. So moody. Always reading." Her mother tapped her cigarette into an overflowing ashtray. "Even as a baby, your father said you were hard to love."

Sugar waved the words away. "Oh, go on, Cecelia. Maggie's not hard to love, just...well, a bit prickly sometimes." She turned to her niece. "'Fess up, Maggie. A beautiful girl like you must get all kinds of attention. I bet some handsome lady killer has set his sights on you."

Leah closed her eyes briefly and Sugar crowed. "I knew it. There *is* someone."

Cecelia rolled her eyes. "I sure as hell hope not. My child don't need anyone. 'Specially not no man who's gonna lie and cheat and treat her like dirt. I raised her to take care of herself." She pointed her cigarette at Leah. "Mark my words, you stay away from men. You want a baby, go to one of them sperm banks for lesbians. It's expensive, but you've got that big management job now."

Sugar clapped her hands. "She's right, Maggie. Sorry to say. But still, us women can get kinda distracted by, how should I say it, our *needs*?"

Cecelia guffawed. "Needs." She stage-whispered, "You know you can buy a dildo on the internet now? Marla Perkins has one. Got it right off the computer."

Leah felt the situation careening completely out of control. "I thought you wanted to know about my job."

"We do," Sugar exclaimed. "Tell us all about it." Both women leaned forward eagerly.

Hallelujah.

"It's not *that* big a job." *And I might not have it week after next.* She pushed the thought away. "But it's okay. Just a lot of work." She glanced at her watch. How much longer did she have to stay?

Cecelia wasn't satisfied. "Well, how hard could it be? You're telling other people what to do." She sucked her teeth.

Irritation crept up Leah's back, a familiar feeling, one she'd experienced too many times in this house as she'd gotten older. Typical Cecelia, not listening to Leah at all, dogged in her own perceptions. "It's not that easy to tell other people what to do. Sometimes they aren't used to doing things the right way. And they often don't like what you tell them."

"Ah." Sugar jumped on this. "So you have to make them change?"

Leah shifted on the couch and shoved Dolly off her lap. "Sometimes. But," she admitted, "in this case, most of the staff are working pretty efficiently."

"Like I said," Cecelia declared. "It doesn't sound that hard."

Sugar was still curious. "So what *do* you do, then? If everybody's doing their job already?"

This she could deal with, a safe topic that could take up a few minutes. "There's a regional meeting of mayors happening at the hotel next week, and it's a big opportunity for the hotel. And for me." She filled her mother and aunt in on the details. "If all goes well, it'll be good for everyone on staff." *And I'll recover some credibility with Simon Gerard,* she thought. *Maybe enough to save my job.*

She arranged her face into a smile and lifted Reba off her lap. "So that's why I can't stay long today. Just a short visit." She sipped her water and gingerly accepted a cookie from the tray that Sugar offered her.

"You're not staying overnight?" Sugar sounded disappointed. "Your mother's been getting your old room ready."

Leah's heart sank. The last thing she wanted to do was spend the night in her old bedroom, with its cracked window and gray walls. There were ghosts in that room. "I can't," she said. "It's important I get right back to oversee the meeting preparations." She nibbled a tiny corner of cookie and pushed Patsy away with her foot.

Cecelia beamed. "See, I knew you were doing big things. That's my baby. You'll come back soon." She nodded, agreeing with herself. "You've made it. *And* you got rid of Barry, so you can concentrate on you and not being some man's fool. Best thing you ever did. You finally learned from my example."

That did it. Words were tumbling out of her mouth before she had time to stop herself. "You know, Mama, not all men are duplicitous monsters. Some are even kind of amazing." She stopped, feeling the vibration of her mother's surprise.

Cecelia threw her head back. "Lord, help me. She *has* got a new man."

Sugar's attention swiveled from Leah to Cecelia and back again.

"Mama, I'm only saying that not all men are like Daddy. I know you got hurt badly and..." *And so did I.* She swallowed. "You decided all men are bad. But that's not fair— or true."

Her mother's mouth twisted sourly. "You're young and innocent, Maggie. You know I'm right. And so help me, if you come back here all brokenhearted from some man's mess, don't look to me for comfort."

Leah rubbed a hand over her eyes. "When have I ever come here for comfort, Mama? And give me some credit. I'm thirty-eight years old and I have excellent people sense." She sat up straighter on the sofa. It was true. She *could* trust her radar with people, even with men. *With Ash.*

Cecelia snorted and looked at Sugar. "Thinks she's got good sense. That takes the cake, don't it, Sugar? Pride goeth before a fall, Maggie. Like I said, don't come back here crying to your mama when you get burned again. You've been warned."

The red tip of her mother's cigarette was all Leah could see for a moment. It glowed, expanding in her vision like a small sun, consuming all thoughts. Her whole body went numb. The cookie in her mouth was cardboard.

Sugar broke into her reverie. "We're so proud of you, honey. I was telling Doogie this morning that I was coming to see you. He'd be here himself but..."

The voice droned on, but Leah barely heard her. Why had she come home? What possible inspiration had she hoped to gain from Cecelia? The iron maiden was exactly that. Iron. Implacable. Hard.

Alone.

Not only that, her mother's inability to trust had cut her off from others, even from her daughter. Leah had always known, in an intellectual sense, that she was loved— but she had never *felt* loved.

In fact, feeling loved was something she'd only now experienced, for the first time in her life, in the last month with Ash.

Suddenly, her mother seemed impossibly old. Bitter. Waving her cigarette, propped up in a decaying chair in a crumbling house, surrounded by the detritus of a life of disappointment. Armored in her righteous anger at men and what had been done to her by an unfair world.

Ultimately, that was Cecelia's legacy gift to Leah. Except for anger and its variants, feelings were always dangerous things. Better avoided, dismissed, or denied.

But I can't deny my feelings anymore. And I don't want to. Sitting there, the previously unquestioned lessons of her childhood echoing around her, Leah shivered. Her legs and arms tingled and her chest rose and fell on a deep, rolling breath. She felt a veil lift, a lightening, and her eyes refocused on her mother and aunt.

"I have to leave," she declared, rising and sending the dogs into a new frenzy of barking and jumping.

Cecelia's eyes widened. "*Magnolia Evangeline Sebastian Bellerose*, what are you talking about? You just got here."

Leah leaned over to kiss Aunt Sugar, then reached to take her mother's hand. "I have to go back to my life, Mama. Lots to do." She kissed her mother's cheek. At the door, she turned. "And once and for all, for the record, I'm not Magnolia anymore. I'm not 'Steel Magnolia' or the 'junior iron maiden.' I'm Leah. Leah Bellerose."

Chapter 18

Ash sat under a portrait of his mother, feeling like a schoolboy waiting to see the principal. It was one of his favorite paintings of the woman he still missed every day. The others were all hanging in the family home, which he'd not visited in years. He wondered if anyone was taking care of them.

The image on the canvas gave him a sense of solidity here in the inner sanctum of the Gerard Hospitality Group. His father's offices had been places of mystery when he was growing up, a competitive battleground as he'd gotten older.

It was not his favorite place.

Joan stared at him from behind her desk. She didn't bother to hide her disapproval of his backpack, jeans, and rolled-up sleeves. He shifted, crossed his legs, and met her gaze steadily. She looked away.

A moment later, an intercom buzzed on the desk. "Send him in," Simon's voice commanded his secretary. Joan glanced back at Ash and waved him toward the inner office door.

Simon didn't rise as his son entered. "Sit." He gestured toward a chair, effectively distancing himself behind the large oak desk that had been Ash's grandfather's, in the early days of the company.

"Thanks for finding time for me," Ash murmured, hoping his father didn't hear the sarcasm in his voice. Pissing his father off wouldn't help him get what he wanted today.

The older man rifled through files on his desk and didn't look up. "Might as well get this done. Though we could have done it virtually."

"It felt important to be here in person."

"Hm. Well, then. I'll let you begin." His father sat back and assessed him.

Ash opened his backpack and withdrew the flash drive. He handed it to his father.

"And this is...?" Simon didn't take the proffered object.

Ash placed it on the desk, next to the computer. "It's a copy of Leah's staff report and plan for reorganization."

Simon Gerard frowned. "I already have that. You flew up here for this? I'm not reimbursing that expense."

Ash forcefully relaxed his posture. "You don't have the full draft. Leah believed that the preliminary staff recommendations you asked for would be sufficient. That you had enough faith in her abilities to know that her final plan would make good sense for the company."

Gerard grunted. "Leah?"

"Ms. Bellerose."

His father tapped the desktop with irritation. "I've already spoken to Ms. Bellerose and let her know that her recommendations are completely unacceptable. Whatever that is"—he waved at the flash drive—"isn't going to change that fact."

Ash felt his fists clench and he flexed his fingers. "What did you tell her?" The hardness in his father's face was sending off alarm bells. He hadn't spoken to Leah since the day before, and now anxiety over what his father might have done spiked. An impulse to call her, to check on her, was almost overwhelming. He forced himself to stay in the seat and focus on why he'd come.

His father's tone was dismissive. "The details aren't important for you to know. You stick to doing your job, maintenance man, and let Ms. Bellerose face the consequences for her own management decisions." He scrutinized his son with barely masked condescension. "I thought you were coming here to campaign for your release from penury. To convince me you're a reformed man."

Ash shook his head impatiently. "This isn't about me. I'm serving out my time. Though," he admitted, "I did add a document here, a proposal I worked up to expand the physical plant management at the hotel over the next five years."

Simon frowned. "To what end?"

"Efficiency." Ash tapped the flash drive. "The hotel is going to be busier than ever under Ms. Bellerose's plan. We need to be proactive."

His father's expression was disinterested. "Drafting organizational proposals is not your job. Stick to plumbing."

"I'm doing the job you sent me to do. But I can't turn off the business side of my brain, no matter what so-called 'menial' tasks I'm involved in." Ash thought of William and almost smiled. "Surprisingly, I haven't minded the maintenance work lately. Honestly, it's turned out to be kind of refreshing."

Simon snorted. "Forgive me if I find that hard to believe."

Ash eyes closed briefly to try to wrest control of his anger, then nudged the flash drive closer to the computer. "Take a look. You owe it to her. She worked incredibly hard to come up with a comprehensive plan that works on both financial and personnel levels. It's brilliant. And I would know."

His father stood up and turned toward his bar. The scotch made a delicious sound as it poured from bottle to tumbler, but Ash wasn't tempted. Not now.

Gerard faced his son, eyes narrowed, while he sipped his whiskey. "Why are you defending her?"

Ash didn't flinch from his father's gaze. "She's a woman of intelligence and integrity. I respect her."

A gray eyebrow rose. "It's not like you to respect a woman."

Silence. A distant horn honked. The clock ticked on the mantelpiece. His father grunted. "Are you sleeping with her?" Silence again. Simon continued, voice derisive. "She's way out of your league, you know."

Ash didn't react, except to pick up the flash drive and extend it to his father. "Dad. Please."

For a long moment, neither of them moved. Ash felt rooted to the floor. Finally, Simon placed his tumbler of scotch on the desk with a *clink*. He accepted the flash drive and gave a brief jerk of his head toward to office door. "Dismissed," he muttered, turning away from his son.

Ash made to leave. Hand on the doorknob, he turned. "You're lucky to have her working for you, you know," he said. "If you let her go, she'll be snapped up by a competitor and I guarantee she'll be a force to contend with." A warm swell of pride filled him. Leah *was* a force to contend with. And he hoped to be around to see what she did next, even if that meant breaking with the company. One day soon, he would come back to this office and place a resignation letter on the desk.

It felt so real to imagine it, so spectacularly liberating, he almost shouted the words aloud. But he resisted. He couldn't put Leah's job in jeopardy now.

He'd have to wait a little bit longer.

**

Leah told herself to focus on work. Only a few more days before the mayors' meeting, then she would fix things with Simon Gerard. Then and only then could she see what might happen with Ash.

As she scratched out a list of tasks to be done, she repeated her instructions to herself. *Work. Focus. Concentrate.*

Don't think about Ash.

The list stared back at her. *Call caterer to confirm menu and food delivery for mayors' meeting. Confirm chandelier cleaning for tomorrow. Call party rental to ensure enough tables and chairs for ballroom.* Etcetera, etcetera. Details and more details.

She thunked her head on the desk and rested for a moment, eyes closed. This felt surprisingly good.

"Miss Bellerose?" Dahlia Markley knocked softly on the doorjamb. "Are you okay?"

"Yep. Good." Leah sat up and gestured for Dahlia to enter the office. "Just reviewing some last-minute things for the meeting. What's up?"

The woman's red curls bounced as she sat. "Mama wants to know exactly how much you want her to bake for the showcase. Like, how many full loaves, mini-loaves, muffins, and all?"

The showcase was Leah's idea to introduce the branding of the hotel as an iconic small-town boutique meeting place. It wouldn't simply be a hotel, but a meeting venue, upscale but locally sourced restaurant, and craft market. The mayors' meeting would be the launching event, and would include Estelle's baked goods, local artwork, and a special, gourmet dinner buffet featuring produce from local farms.

"As many as we can reasonably get done without anything going stale. We want everything as 'fresh baked' as possible." Leah moved to her printer and handed a page to Dahlia. "I'll email this to your mother after I finalize some details with the print shop making the package labels, but this will get her started."

Dahlia nodded and took the paper. "How was your day off? You didn't stay gone long."

Leah grimaced. "Sometimes visits to family need to be short." She lightened her tone. "But I'm glad to be back. There's lots to do in the next few days." That was all true. And it was good to be back. Good to see Dahlia and finish preparations for the project she hoped would make her career. If she could hang on that long.

She went to the window and stared out toward the hotel's back gardens, scanning the area by the greenhouse. Was she looking for Ash? She hadn't seen him since getting back and had no idea what he was doing. Multiple impulses to call him or ask Julius what he was doing had been thwarted by her management brain, her determination to remain focused and efficient.

Still. Was he out there, helping William or Karen to prune the hedges or replant flowers for the showcase? Her fingers gripped the windowsill.

She sighed. "Get back to work, Bellerose. Time for romance later." Her phone chirped and she jumped. "I asked not to be interrupted," she muttered, picking up the phone and reading the screen.

Ash: *I have a confession to make. Come to room 425.*

She stared at the screen, heart thumping. Her stomach flipped as the words danced in front of her. *I have a confession to make.* That sounded ominous. Trepidation and desire to see him had her immobilized for a long moment.

I have a confession to make.

What could it be? A sudden image of Ash's face was so real, she blinked in surprise. Her breath caught, imagining herself touching him, feeling the solid warmth of him next to her.

She could almost hear her voice in response. *I have a confession to make, too. I think I'm in love with you.*

She was still staring at the phone. Room 425.

The Honeymoon Suite.

She only knew this from the budget she'd been working on. It was the one special guest room in the hotel, one that was not often booked. Judging from the size and cost of the room, it had to be lavish, but she'd never seen it.

What was Ash doing, asking her to meet him there? Her mind refused to speculate, preferring to freeze up, along with her limbs.

She swallowed and flexed her fingers and toes, then shook her shoulders to loosen them. On a determined exhale, she typed a response.

Be there in five.

The corridors were empty as she made her way upstairs, only the sound of the carpet installers in the ballroom echoed as she entered the elevator and hit four. Room 425 was at the far end of the hall, facing the back of the hotel. She knocked, feeling her heart thunder in her chest.

The door swung open and Ash was there, a small smile crinkling his eyes. He was stunning in fitted jeans and dress shirt with the sleeves rolled up. Dark hair curled at the open neck of his shirt. His feet were bare.

Apparently, he wasn't the maintenance man right now. A shiver ran down her back.

He didn't say anything, took a step toward her, scooped her up in his arms, and swept her into the room, kicking the door shut behind him.

He placed her gently on her feet at the entrance to the large room. Her back was against the wall, her arms still around his neck. His hands framed her face and he gazed at her silently. "Your confess—" she began, only to be silenced as his mouth lowered to hers, hungrily pulling her into him.

Pressed to the wall, Leah gasped, every cell lighting up as she responded in kind to his wordless demand. All thoughts of what might be appropriate left her, any concerns about propriety or what she *should* be doing were entirely gone.

There was only him. And her, trembling against him.

They exchanged breath, lips fused. Her body went liquid as Ash breathed for her, through her, her lungs rising and falling effortlessly on the oxygen he gave her. Heat rose in a wave, enveloping and entwining them. She shivered again.

His tongue lashed at hers. Broad hands framed her face. The kiss went unbroken as he pulled the elastic from her ponytail and ran his hands through her hair, groaning into her mouth. The passion he radiated trembled in the air, drawing her into him. It hit her in the solar plexus, then lower in her belly. She went dizzy and teetered, feeling him catching her, cradling her in his arms. She steadied.

The kiss went on, and if it were only this, it would almost be enough, Leah thought. He was so big, so solid and safe. But the heat was consuming, the connection between them unbearably arousing.

Something was different. The air was charged with energy, organic and volatile. They were animals. Human animals whose only need was each other.

An overwhelming need shuddered outward from her core. She kicked off her shoes and began unbuttoning his shirt. She had to feel the hair on his chest, had to feel his skin against hers. Nothing else mattered.

Ash's hands moved to her suit jacket. Leah gasped as he held the lapels and yanked, scattering buttons. The message was clear. *You are mine.*

He tossed the jacket away and moved from her mouth to her neck, his teeth scraping the sensitive skin, strafing her, marking her. She arched into him, her hands on his back, nails scratching through the fabric of his shirt. Her return message was straightforward. *And you are mine.*

Desire rolled through her, a craving so keen she could have cried out. She moaned, a sigh in her throat that echoed in their kiss. *Desperate. I'm desperate for you.* There was so much to say, yet no words were needed. Talking would come later.

Ash pulled away slightly, dipped and lifted her again, carrying her to the enormous bed. He pulled his shirt off in one swift motion and dropped on top of her, his weight pressing her deliciously into the softness of the bed. She reached for him as his mouth found hers again, this time punishingly passionate, brutal in its insistence. A cry escaped her as she felt the bulge of his arousal against her thigh.

He lifted her skirt and hooked a finger around the elastic of her panties. He pulled and flung them across the room. His fingers went to her cleft and she pushed him away. "Later," she gasped. "This." Her hand rubbed him hard, then unsnapped his jeans as he swore under his breath.

"You come first." His voice was husky as he kissed her and stroked her face. "You will always come first, Ms. Bellerose." He unhooked her skirt and tossed it aside.

Leah arched against him and yanked his zipper down. "This," she repeated, reaching in and wrapping her hand around his enormous erection. A rhythmic squeeze had him groaning, a guttural gasp, and he shimmied reluctantly out of his jeans. She could smell him, the clean, aromatic scent of flesh usually kept confined in clothing, his cologne, his breath. His scent alone was going to make her come.

"Bossy woman," he murmured, rolling her onto her side. She felt him behind her, his erection against her bottom. His mouth was on the back of her neck, biting, licking into the slope of her shoulder. Moving down, he kissed down her back, biting at the skin under her shoulder blade. She moaned. A hand found her breasts through the silk chemise she still wore and pinched her nipples as his teeth scraped her scapula. She arched against the erotic assault on both sides of her body, wondering if she might die of wanting right then and there. Moisture slicked her thighs and she bucked back, rubbing against his arousal as he pulled her to lie on her back on top of him.

His whiskers scraped her neck as he drew her thighs apart and plunged his hands between her legs. The substantial pressure of his cock against her bottom was demanding and she rubbed her whole body up and down on it. He bit her shoulder and spread her labia, using one hand to hold her open while the other began a rhythmic motion there, readying her.

Leah bucked against his manual assault. Her body hurdled toward a climax at breakneck speed. "Ash," she whispered, "I can't wait but don't want this to end so fast."

His response was to pull her right leg up, draping it over his arm and thereby increasing the exquisite pressure on her clitoris as his fingers continued their dance. "This isn't ending any time soon, I assure you." His voice was a low rumble against her ear. "This is a first course."

He rolled her back to her side, this time in front of him, while he circled her clit in earnest. She began to moan, a drumbeat beginning at the base of her spine. Then the head of his erection was there, at the opening, teasing her, offering her sweet relief.

She reached back to grip his lean hips and pull him forward. "Yes," she gasped. "Now."

Instead of impaling her, as she desperately wanted, he rolled her onto her back underneath him, then moved between her open legs. "Later," he murmured. "First, this." He lowered himself, his dark curls brushing her stomach, then her thighs. His hands spread her open again and she arched, feeling her muscles clench in need.

His tongue was on her then, licking into the depths of her. Her body felt like it floated above the bed, hovering against the worshiping mouth of the man she loved. He sucked at her center of pleasure and she came apart.

His tongue and mouth continued to assault her. His fingers invaded her as she came. Her low cry became a wail. As the spasms continued, then slowly diminished, he continued, slowing his movements but not stopping.

"More," he whispered against her wet thigh, biting the flesh there and tugging slightly for emphasis. "I want more of this." Fingers withdrew from her slowly, slickened with her moisture, and his hands gripped her thighs, pushing them apart. His tongue went to her vagina and lapped eagerly, plunging inside, exploring her contours while his fingers held her open. His thumbs began a maddening circling of her clit, swollen with arousal, and Leah felt tears spring to her eyes.

"Oh, god. Please." She fisted her hands in his hair. "Give me your cock." Just saying it almost sent her over the edge. If she didn't get him inside her soon, she would go mad. "I can't come again without you."

He was determined to prove her wrong. He pushed his tongue inside her as far as it would go and sucked at her clit. She felt a surge of moisture as her internal muscles seized again and her legs clamped Ash's head between her thighs. Her mind was blank as she rode the wave, aware only of his tongue, which had become her center of awareness. If she made a sound, she didn't hear it.

Again, he continued his maddening stimulation, only more slowly as her shuddering diminished. When her breath had returned almost to normal, he rose over her, lifted her hips, and placed a pillow underneath. His cock was enormous, bursting, as he played her like an instrument. He wrapped his hand around the head of his arousal and rubbed against her slick and swollen folds, then circled her clit again and again, keeping her on edge.

He pushed her knees up, nearly to her shoulders, offering him the deepest access possible. "Now," he whispered. "Now." He fingered her swollen bud as he entered her, inch by inch, finally filling her. He thrust and withdrew, thrust and withdrew, pushing her to the edge and over.

Her back arched and she rose, the wave that rolled through her exquisite and painful and blinding. From a distance, she heard Ash's groans as he reached his peak, his body pounding into her, stretching the orgasm to timelessness. Tears rolled down her face as she gasped for breath. Her legs shook. Slowly, their rhythm became less urgent, and they rocked together, her sobbing and his gasps creating a sensuous music, echoing in the room, lulling them into sleep.

Chapter 19

Early evening light slanted across the enormous bed, tousled sheets, and tangled limbs. Ash propped up on an elbow and twirled a lock of Leah's hair around his index finger. He surveyed her face, placid with contentment. The dusting of light freckles across her nose and relaxed visage made her look younger, more real than when she was buttoned up and on the job. A small smile crooked the edge of his mouth. She was adorable.

He felt weightless, like he might levitate right off the bed. The sensation was odd, wonderful, something he'd felt for the first time in his life over the last few weeks, first in tiny sparks, now in full flame. The visceral awareness of this was followed by an unwelcome whisper of fear. As the silk of Leah's skin next to his created a shimmering warmth, the fear became louder, insistent, vying for acknowledgement.

You're in love with her.

He realized he'd known it long before this moment but had not admitted it to himself. The implications were almost too much to contemplate. But even as he pushed the disastrous consequences out of his mind, the truth of his feeling rang like a bell through every cell in his body. He, Asher Banks Gerard, was in love with Leah Bellerose.

And there his thoughts ran into an impenetrable brick wall. There was no way this could end well.

The internal voice ratcheted up. *You have to tell her. Tell her who you are.*

That was the whole point of getting her up to the Honeymoon Suite. To confess, to beg her forgiveness, and hope against hope she wouldn't kick him out of her life on the spot.

But that was before he realized he was in love with her. Somehow, allowing those words to reverberate in his head changed everything. He felt like he was teetering at the edge of a cliff.

Leah was smiling at him drowsily. "What are you thinking about?"

He paused too long before answering. "Not much...You kind of blew my mind earlier."

Coward. She didn't deserve him. His father was right. She was way out of his league.

A slender eyebrow arched. She didn't buy it. He cleared his throat and leaned over to kiss her lightly. "Honestly..." His voice trailed off and thoughts raced. Maybe he could distract her. "I was thinking that you've needed a break, working as hard as you've been the last few weeks. How about a massage?"

Leah hitched over in bed and faced him square on. "Banks." Kind, but Leah-firm. No-nonsense. She placed a hand on his arm. "What were you going to confess to me?"

Again, stymied. But quicker on the uptake this time. He winked at her. "Just that I couldn't go another day without seeing you. Even an hour felt like too long."

She studied his face and he was suddenly afraid his statement had been too close to the truth. Her expression was serious as she spoke, her words catching him entirely off guard.

"I felt the same way." She bit her lip, an uncharacteristically anxious smile flashing across her face. "Banks, I don't know what this is...between us. But whatever it is, I wasn't expecting it." A laugh, more like a hiccup, erupted from her and she stared at the ceiling and blew out a breath. "I pride myself on knowing what's going on, on being in control in my life. You might have noticed that about me."

He had to smile at that. Tension softened and the glow returned to his chest. "Just a bit," he admitted.

She traced his lips with the tip of a finger. "I'm not in control of this. But," she continued, eyes widening slightly, "I have to trust you, at least a little. And I have to trust my own feelings. It's ridiculous how hard that is. But I'm ready to try."

Ash felt the glow in his chest dissolve, but he refused to let the cold spike of fear take its place. He'd find a way to make this right, somehow. He had to. Losing Leah was not an option.

Then the hammer fell.

"Ash," she whispered, voice halting. "I think I'm in love with you."

***

They were sitting in Ash's pickup truck, parked at the edge of the hill overlooking the town square. Behind them was darkness, trees thickly shrouded by mist rising from the nearby Charmant River. In front of them, visible through the cracked windshield, were the lights of the town, streetlamps glowing, the clock in the courthouse tower chiming the hour.

Leah wished she'd changed into more comfortable clothing, but Ash hadn't given her time. After her confession, to which he'd not responded, he'd grabbed her hand, hauled her from the bed, and told her they were getting out of the hotel.

Now she was nervous. Had she been too impulsive in her declaration of love? She hadn't planned it, it had emerged. She wasn't sorry she'd said it—even felt a bit of a relief. But his lack of response left her wondering if she'd put him in an awkward spot. He'd hardly looked at her or spoken to her since that moment, though he hadn't run screaming from the room either.

Remember, he said he wasn't interested in a great romance.

She drew breath, kicked off her heels, and curled up on the seat next to him. "Nice view. This town is…well, it's kind of grown on me. Which is bizarre, to say the least." It was true. She felt like she was in a parallel universe, where all the rules were broken or didn't exist in the first place.

Beside her, Ash nodded in the dark. "I know." He put his arm around her and pulled her into him. "If anything has surprised me about being here, it's that I actually kind of like this place. The town. The people." He chuckled. "Even Cranford, who, despite his crusty exterior, is a pretty straight-up kind of guy."

Leah felt herself smile. "Unsuspected depth."

"Exactly." She felt his breath on her cheek as he leaned and turned her face toward his. "The only thing that's surprised me more is…" He hesitated, more serious than she'd ever seen him, and she felt herself go very still. The air in the cab of the truck vibrated with unnamed energy as he spoke at last.

"I'm in love with you." He exhaled slowly. "I can't believe I'm saying this out loud, but I love you, Leah Bellerose. God help me. I didn't mean for it to happen. *How* it happened, I'll never understand. And I know it's a problem. But it's the truth."

Leah's heart thundered, her skin hummed. She wasn't sure if she could breathe. "Ash." She swallowed. "Was that actually what you were going to confess to me this afternoon?"

He glanced away from her. "I lost my chutzpah. Afraid of what it would mean for us."

She frowned. "But after I confessed..."

His jaw tightened. "I didn't want it to be a problem for you." Long pause. His tone lightened, trying to ease the tension. "Being in love with me is something I'm sure you can manage—because you seem to be able to manage anything. But"—he took her hand—"me being in love with you? That makes it a lot more complicated." He leaned in and rested his forehead against hers. "But I can't deny it. Not to you, or to myself. And believe me, I've tried."

Leah felt tears sting her eyes as his lips touched hers and then she was lost, all the responses, all the questions, momentarily forgotten.

The windows of the truck quickly fogged, creating a private world, away from everything. Leah wished it would never end.

"I'm in love with you, Leah Bellerose," Ash murmured as he kissed her over and over. "I have no idea what will happen next. I will lose my job, I may even lose you, but none of that will change the fact that I'm in love with you."

Leah pulled back from him and framed his face—that gorgeous face—with her hands. "Shut up, Banks. For now, let's ignore the rest of the world and give ourselves this moment." She kissed him briefly, then became serious. "Reality will intrude soon enough, and when it does, we'll deal with it. But right now, here, in this decrepit old truck, at the edge of this strange little town, it's you and me."

He smiled. "That's my girl." His teeth nipped her bottom lip playfully and his eyes twinkled. "How long has it been since you've made love in a parked vehicle?"

She laughed and shook her head. "Never."

That got his attention. "Never?"

"Nope. I've had sex in a car once or twice. But"—she began unbuttoning his shirt and leaned forward to kiss his collarbone—"I've never *made love* in one."

***

"You sound rather cheery today." Julius Cranford barely glanced up from his desk as Ash strode into the office. As was often the case, his declaration sounded like an accusation.

Ash settled into a chair opposite the older man and gave him a lazy grin. "Why do you say that?"

Cranford trained a watery eye on him. "Because you were whistling as you came down the hallway."

"Ah." He hadn't realized. "Well, it's a beautiful morning." *And I'm in love. And my body's buzzing from doin' the wild thang all night.* He forced himself to focus. "Things are on track for the mayors' meeting. You and I are reviewing the final details. What's not to be cheery about?"

"Indeed." Cranford's mouth twitched into what could have been a smile or a grimace. It was hard to tell. He handed Ash a list of items with checkmarks next to them. "Please go over this and see if any details are outstanding. I've left things up to you, as requested. I'm trusting the event will be a success for all of us."

Ash tipped his head. "I trust it will be, too, Julius." He considered, then continued. "This project is critical to me and everyone involved. And, since you mention it..." He hesitated, not sure the time was right to play detective. However, given the situation, the more information he had, the better. If his life were a puzzle, a few pieces were missing, or at least out of place, at the moment. And some of those pieces felt like potential threats.

Julius was waiting.

"What prompted you to give me that flash drive last week, when I took a day off? I didn't say anything about where I was going or what I was doing."

Julius regarded him coolly. "What prompted you to accept it?"

Touché. Ash leaned back in his chair. "Listen, it feels like you and I may be making assumptions about each other, but I'm not sure we're making assumptions about the same thing."

"I don't make assumptions."

"Educated guesses, then."

Cranford steepled his hands and suddenly looked very weary. "Banks, I only know what I see, and what I'm told, which, these days, isn't much." He paused to blow his nose noisily. Ash waited, impatient.

Cranford continued. "I suppose there's no point in keeping it secret. Just before you arrived here at Charmant Forest, I received a call from someone at Gerard Hospitality corporate offices. She indicated that they were sending a new maintenance manager who was going to be on probationary status and to keep an eye on your performance."

Ash froze. *She?*

"I thought nothing of it at the time. The Gerard Group has told me to jump so many times in the last six months that I no longer bother to ask questions." The expression of fatigue couldn't hide the frustration in the other man's voice. "And I didn't question the probationary status. That's a big company standard policy, isn't it? No one is considered permanent until they've worked a certain amount of time and proven themselves."

Ash murmured agreement. The tension in his chest was mounting.

Cranford continued. "But then I got follow-up calls every couple of weeks— calls in which specific questions were asked. How was Mr. Banks doing? Was he honest? Was he working hard?" He studied the blotter, then looked up at Ash. "Was he behaving professionally? Had I received any complaints about him from women or bartenders?"

Ash blew out the breath he hadn't known he was holding and glanced at the ceiling. "Jesus."

"Young man," Cranford said, tapping the desk for emphasis. His tone became serious. "I have no idea who you are. And I don't care. What I do know is that you've done whatever you came here to do. With a few early hiccups, such as basic plumbing." He paused and allowed a flicker of a smile to cross his face. "You've proven yourself to be an exemplary employee, popular with everyone, and reliable. Mostly." Again, the small smile. "Your biggest fan seems to be William Jones. And while William likes most everyone, he is nobody's fool. His instincts are better than most." Julius chuckled, which came out as a wheezy growl. "We had a sous-chef here years ago who was stealing from the pantry. Not sure we would have noticed if it weren't for William. Told his dad that the guy was 'like the snake in *The Jungle Book*,' trying to get people to trust him. Just didn't feel right to the boy."

Ash blinked in surprise. "Glad I passed The William Test, then."

Julius nodded. "So, Mr. Banks. I have no idea who you report to. I don't need to know or even want to know. But last week I had a feeling you were going to report to whatever minions the corporate office has in charge of little projects like this hotel. And that the plan on the flash drive might help them know that things are going well here." His lip curled slightly. "Since no one seems to believe anything I say anymore."

Ash drew a breath. "Thank you, Julius. I appreciate you being honest with me." At least, he hoped the man was honest. There was no way to know. But for now, it was the best he had. "One thing. Who was the woman who called from the head office, the one who initially told you I was being sent to Charmant?" He composed himself despite the dread in his gut.

Please, don't let it be Leah. Please.

Julius shook his head. "I've no idea. She said she was calling from the corporate office, that's all. An older woman. Quite stern."

Joan. Ash felt his chest relax. "I see. Well, the agency that sent me here must have gone through the corporate folks." He stopped. *That's enough subterfuge for now.* He rose to leave and indicated the list Cranford had given him. "I'll get on this. I don't want to tempt the gods, but I think we're ready. The chandelier is being cleaned this afternoon and the tables are being brought in this evening. Tomorrow, showtime."

Julius gestured agreement.

"One more thing." Ash stopped in the doorway and turned back. "You said you don't know who I report to. As far as I'm concerned, I report to you, Mr. Cranford. And Ms. Bellerose."

The older man's eyes widened slightly. "Much appreciated, Mr. Banks. Though that situation will likely change shortly."

Ash's eyebrow rose. "Sir?"

"I don't expect I'll be here much longer, which will leave Ms. Bellerose. And, as we all know, it is strictly against policy for a manager to be in a romantic relationship with a direct report."

Ash felt his mouth go slack before he regained composure. "Julius?"

The older man waved him toward the door. "Go do your job, Banks. But I will give you this piece of personal advice." His gaze went to a framed photo on the corner of the desk, one that Ash suddenly recognized from the closet in the basement. "Life is short.

If you are lucky enough to find love, hang onto it. You may never be that lucky again."

Chapter 20

Leah sat down heavily on a folding chair in the staff meeting room. She'd been on her feet all morning, reviewing preparations, making final phone calls, and troubleshooting minor glitches.

Everything was in order. The arrangements, the staff, the ballroom.

Her love life. It felt like she was living in a fantasy, a fairy tale of her imagining.

Strike that. *Beyond* anything she'd ever imagined.

And if the future was unknown that would have to be okay for now. She and Ash had agreed. No analyzing until after the mayors' meeting was over. There was plenty of time for reality. Later.

She rubbed her eyes. "It feels like this is all going too well, Estelle. I must be missing something." Mrs. Markley clucked her tongue at Leah as she bustled around her, shuttling trays of mini-loaves and muffins into place for wrapping. At the table next to Leah, several kitchen and housekeeping staff were busy hand-packaging and labeling the baked goods. From there, they were stacked on towering trolleys, awaiting transport to the enormous rented party tent in the back garden. This was the focal point of the "local market," where crafts, food items, and local music would be on display starting the next morning.

Estelle patted Leah's shoulder as she trundled by. "Nonsense. This is what a good ol' fashioned organization does. The mayors are all set for a big meetin', and the town is all set for the food and craft fair. The Charmant Clarion did a front-page story on us yesterday." She turned from Leah and hollered over her shoulder. "Dahlia Where are the extra muffin labels? Look smart, girl." She sighed. "My stars, that child lives in her own world."

Leah smiled wearily. She hadn't slept much the night before. "Have I told you lately how amazing you are, Estelle?"

The older woman chuckled. "You're a bit of a whirlwind yo'self, miss. This place is right lucky to have you." She regarded Leah. "Why, you're positively glowing this morning. Being busy must agree with you." She didn't notice Leah's astonished expression as she trotted away, kitchen clogs thumping.

The vibration of her cell phone caused Leah to jump slightly. "Calm down," she muttered. "Don't want everyone commenting on your 'glow.'" *Jeez.* Did multiple orgasms show on her face?

After talking to the catering company that was helping with servers for the mayors' meeting, she made her way out to the greenhouse to check on the flower arrangements. On the way, she stopped in to see the party tent set-up.

"Oh, my," she breathed, entering the vast white space. Display tables with clean, white linen tablecloths lined the room. Ceramic pots of various sizes were placed in artistic arrangements between the tables, filled with brilliant flowers and trailing vines. Fairy lights hung around the perimeter. A small stage was set up at one end of the tent, while two wide side flaps were open to create an airy, open feel.

"It's magical, ain't it?" Karen Pembroke appeared at her side. "Me and Arthur and William've been working our tails off to get all these plantings right. Turned out pretty good, if I do say so myself. Doing the same thing for inside, in the ballroom."

Leah shook her head in wonderment. "I'm stunned, Ms. Pembroke. It's all done. And it's truly gorgeous."

Karen's cheeks went pink. "I'm glad you like it. We did it for you. Well," she quickly amended, "obviously we did it for everyone. But, you know, we especially wanted it to be nice for you. Because of, uh, all the ways you want to make the hotel better and all."

Leah touched Karen's shoulder in thanks. "I appreciate that, Ms. Pembroke."

"Please call me Karen. I mean, if it's okay." She cleared her throat awkwardly. "If you want to."

That got a chuckle from Leah. "I tend to default to formality. But I'll work on it. Karen." Surveying the space, she nodded. "The vendors will be thrilled. This will be good for them and the hotel. Everybody wins."

Her words reverberated in her head. Not exactly the cutthroat attitude she'd absorbed in business school. Her internship mentor, a man who took no prisoners and was a billionaire twice over, would be astonished, maybe even horrified. An echo of chagrin ran through her. What on earth had happened to her?

Charmant. Charmant happened to me. And Asher Banks happened to me.

She wasn't the same woman she'd been a month ago. Over the past few weeks, she'd met or talked to at least twenty local artisans, specialty food vendors, and musicians. She would never have guessed this little town held so many creative people. And all of them wanted to be part of the hotel's endeavor. The Leah Bellerose who had arrived in Charmant came carrying assumptions she didn't even know she had, assumptions that had been upended one by one. She'd been surprised by people over and over until she felt she was living in a different world.

A few weeks ago, she'd thought of herself as hard as iron, dismissive, and contemptuous of inconvenient emotions, of human vulnerability. It had rarely occurred to her to wonder about other people's experiences, maybe because to do so would have opened up the very feelings she denied.

Most transformative of all, she had allowed herself to share at least some of her true self with another person, and she'd begun to trust him. Ash's care for her felt real, and it created a feeling of safety that was entirely new.

The chagrin disappeared, replaced by a sensation of solidity and ease.

She turned to Karen with a smile. "I'm off to see the ballroom. Come along?"

***

Dark green carpet with floral edging set off creamy vanilla walls. Newly laundered, dove-gray drapes, tied back from tall, and sparkling clean windows set the tone for a welcoming meeting place. Except for one thing.

Ash frowned. "Why isn't this chandelier finished?" He regarded the dusty, yellowed glass monstrosity that hung, incongruously filthy, from the high ceiling. A scaffolding ladder, empty of workers, sat under the enormous light, which hung askew.

Antonio Duran shook his head. "We put the tarps down." He pointed to the layers of plastic protecting the new carpet. "But the lighting guys said they had to go get another ladder or something. They wanted more people working at the same time to finish. That's all I know."

"Why is it hanging like that?"

Antonio shrugged, indicating ignorance. "They were working, then said they had to go get some other equipment. I came in to check everything one last time. That's the only reason I saw them at all." He looked like he wanted to bolt from the room.

Ash sighed. "Alright. Thanks, Antonio. You can go." He turned to Arthur Jones, who was rolling in round tables and stacking them against the walls. "We may have to delay setting some of the tables out until the damn chandelier gets fixed. When are the floral arrangements coming in?"

Arthur looked at his watch. "Any minute, Mr. Banks. I'll call Karen and tell her to hold off 'til she hears from me."

Ash turned and nearly bumped into William, who was pulling a large cart stacked with folding chairs into the room. "Ash. Look. Me and Hector are—"

His words were cut off by the ear-splitting screech of metal against metal, followed by a splintering crash. Glass fragments exploded in all directions.

Simultaneously, Ash threw himself at William and covered him. The two of them fell to the ground with a grunt.

Glass shards tinkled, dust rose. Then there was silence.

"Ash." He heard Leah's voice, then felt her hand on his shoulder as she knelt next to him. "Are you hurt?" Her voice broke.

Ash inhaled carefully and took stock of himself. No broken bones, no missing limbs. "I'm fine." He rolled off William, who was stunned into wide-eyed silence. "William, buddy. Sorry I knocked you over like that." He accepted Leah's hand and felt her squeeze it reassuringly. The emerald green eyes were still worried, but he nodded to her that he was all right. He turned back to William. "Hey, my man. You okay?"

Arthur materialized at William's side, blood trickling from a small cut on his forehead. "Son. You're all right now. The light fell, but we're all fine." He looked over his shoulder at the pile of broken glass and twisted metal. "No one got hurt."

William looked slowly from his father to Ash and back again. Satisfied at last, he sat up. "Wow, did you hear that?" He chuckled as Ash and his father helped him to his feet. "That was scary."

"Yes, it was," Ash heard Leah murmur next to him. "When I quit shaking, someone's head is going to roll."

That was true. The lighting company hired to clean the chandelier would pay dearly. Ash would make sure of that. He would get to them first, to spare them the guillotine of Leah's anger.

He brushed off his coveralls and surveyed the damage. "Guys, we have work to do here. I'm going to make some calls. This mess has to be out of here *now*." He pulled his phone from his pocket and turned to Hector, who'd entered the room seconds after Leah. "Mr. Duran, please call Antonio and his crew. See if they're willing to come back and pitch in on the cleanup. It'll take more than the lighting crew to get this out of here in time. That chandelier was as big as a Buick." He noted the glittering mess on the floor. "And get your industrial vacuums up here pronto."

He gestured to Karen. "Ms. Pembroke, line up your flowering planters in the hall, ready to move in when we're done with clean up. Arthur, get the first aid kit and have Estelle or Hilda help you bandage that cut. It doesn't look serious but make sure. Just as soon as this mess is out of here, you and William resume setting up tables and chairs. Grab some of the housekeepers to help. We need to get tables set asap this evening." He drew a breath and thought quickly. *What else?*

Beside him, Leah was watching and listening. A small smile tipped that luscious mouth. "What?" he said.

She ran a tongue over her bottom lip, a motion he was sure wasn't designed to be provocative but was. "Just nice to watch someone else taking care of things. Even as all hell breaks loose." Aware that others were watching, she turned from him to scan the room. "Well, this is a disaster. No light in the room and evening falling fast." She folded her arms and began striding the perimeter of the vast space, avoiding the occasional chunk of dusty glass that littered the carpet. "We're going to need multiple lights in here," she said, tapping a finger against her lips. "But the arrangement can't look like a poor substitute for a chandelier."

Ash watched her, sparks practically flying off the top of her head as she went into problem-solving mode. Her green eyes flashed and she snapped her fingers. "Hector, get a couple of guys with trucks and head to Southport. The home improvement store there is huge. Buy—let me see—twenty lampposts. Make sure you get bulbs—bright ones." She spoke to the open-mouthed group now watching and listening. "We're going to turn this ballroom into the streets of a little southern town."

***

Mayor Philpott leaned back in his chair and raised his glass. "Ms. Bellerose, darlin', here's to you. I admit I wasn't sure you could pull this off, but nuts be damned, you did." He issued a gelatinous chuckle and sipped his third whiskey of the evening.

Leah offered what she hoped was a natural-looking smile and raised her water glass. "Thank you, Mayor. It was a great day. And I had a lot of help." She sent a knowing look to Julius Cranford, who sat opposite her. He nodded almost imperceptibly.

They were nearly the only ones left in the ballroom at the end of a marathon day. Caterers moved silently around the room, removing the last of the dirty dishes, soiled tablecloths, and discarded meeting programs. Small tables around the room's perimeter that had served as proxy town spaces, such as the bakery, the library, and the toy shop, were being dismantled by the vendors.

"Love the lampposts," the mayor continued. "Never would have thought of that myself." He slapped the table. "Shows those big city boys what's what. It's the smaller towns that are the lifeblood of this state. And the market outside: pure genius. Really showed off Charmant in particular." He sipped again. "Yessir. Fine day. Wouldn't be surprised if the committee of mayors wouldn't ask to meet here again next year."

Leah felt a zap of satisfaction. "We'd be glad to host, Mr. Mayor. And I can tell you that our plans for additional breakout meeting spaces are in the works." This wasn't one hundred percent true, but after the day's success, she intended to push for an expansion budget.

If she still had a job tomorrow.

"Capital." The mayor rose. "That'll make Charmant more attractive for regional meetings, county meetings, what have you. Why, the sky's the limit." He shook hands with Cranford and turned to Leah. "Sweetheart, pleasure to meet you in person. A *real pleasure*." He leered at her as he planted a moist kiss on her cheek. He didn't hide his appreciation of her cleavage as his eyes traveled up and down her curves, which were accentuated by a fitted azure dress and black heels.

Leah suppressed her recoil reflex and shook his hand with purpose. "Thank you, sir. I'm sure we'll be in touch." She waved as he trundled out of the room like a rooster leaving the hen house.

Leah turned to Cranford and wiped her cheek with a napkin. "Julius, tell me today was worth doing business with that old coot."

Julius snickered. "He is, it has to be said, a royal ass. But yes, my dear. It was well worth it." He gestured around the room. "I would never have thought the old ballroom could be transformed like this. It truly is amazing. And the business potential is hard to overestimate. This puts Charmant Forest in a whole different class than I could ever have imagined." The faded eyes met her gaze squarely. "This hotel is fortunate to have you."

She leaned over and touched his boney arm through the old suit. "Thank you, Julius. That means a lot to me."

"Now, shall we go and ask Joey for a bottle of champagne?"

She smiled as she followed Cranford out of the room. "I'll take a rain check. Too much to do tonight."

Cranford sounded surprised. "It's late. You sent everyone else home an hour ago. Surely you need to rest."

"I will." She paused, then continued. "I'm on an early flight to New York for a meeting at the corporate office, which I'll ask you to keep confidential. My guess is I'll only be gone for a day."

Unless I get fired. Or called onto the carpet in front of the board.

"Well," Cranford said lightly, "then I'll keep the champagne on ice, awaiting your return."

They parted and Leah headed home, trying to suppress an urge to call Ash. She hadn't seen him since early that morning and was almost dizzy with wanting to hear his voice. But it was nearly midnight, far too late for a phone call.

She rounded the corner to her apartment and was surprised to see him leaning against her door. He wore boots, jeans, and a forest-green flannel shirt, open over a white T-shirt. Off-duty. Very comfortable and small-town.

A rush of relief and joy filled her like a sunburst.

"You aren't supposed to be here," she chided as she approached, though her voice betrayed her happiness.

His mouth twitched. "I missed Prunella."

"I believe that."

"Do. It's the truth. We have a relationship, Prune and I."

She fell into his arms. "Mmm, you smell good," she mumbled against his chest.

He was warm, solid, and safe. His voice was a rumble against her ear. "And you look stunning. I love this dress. It makes you look edible." He pulled back to gaze at her and planted a light kiss on her forehead. "I don't have to hang out. Just wanted to see Prune. Okay, *and* to congratulate you on today."

She laughed and unlocked the door. "Alright, but only for a minute. I'm exhausted and have a meeting tomorrow I need to prep for." She stopped. No one could know the details of what tomorrow was about. Cranford was the only one who knew she would be gone, and that's the way it was going to stay. Avoiding questions was the best way to handle this until she knew the outcome.

They flopped on the couch and Leah kicked off her heels. Prunella leapt up and across her to Ash's lap. Her motor was on full throttle as she bumped against the hand that stroked her. The long tail curled around his wrist. Leah grinned with fatigue and tenderness, watching the domestic scene. It was sweet— and a little frightening.

He seemed to read her thoughts.

"Now that we're past the mayors' meeting, we need to talk." He continued petting the cat with one hand and reached for Leah with the other. Fingers entwined with hers, he went on. "I know you're exhausted tonight, with good reason. But we— *I*— need to say some things. Important things."

She felt the heat and energy of him, the intense vibration that emanated from him, and suddenly felt terribly anxious. It was an effort to steady her voice. "I know. But not tonight. And not tomorrow."

"When?"

Her breath was jittery. "Soon. Day after tomorrow. I need time to take care of some business and get my thoughts in order." That was an understatement. She needed to figure out *everything*.

Ash squeezed her hand. "I can wait. But not long."

She nodded wordlessly.

He pushed Prunella away gently and turned to her. "That was quite a feat you pulled off today, Manager Lady. I might have peeked in a time or two, and I heard all the backroom reports."

"It was a team effort." She reached for his other hand. "Much as I hate to admit it, I honestly could not have done it without you."

Ash's eyes crinkled. Leaning in, his mouth touched hers and for a moment, her mind went blissfully blank. It would be so easy to give in to her primal needs and rip his shirt off, or at least curl up on his lap and go to sleep. But neither of those was possible tonight.

She sighed. "Tell Prunella good night. This girl's turning into a pumpkin."

Ash chuckled. "Only if you agree to have breakfast with me the day after tomorrow. We'll meet first thing at the Bluebell. Seven a.m.?"

Leah pushed the nagging fear away and nodded. "It's a date."

Chapter 21

Ash hit video call. A moment later, his old friend's face appeared. "Asher Gerard, you bastard, it's the crack of dawn. When you texted earlier, I thought I was hallucinating."

Ash rolled his eyes and grinned at the familiar banter. "Great to see you, too, Wasserman, you wanker. And it's not exactly the crack of dawn. You *are* in your office."

"You're looking way too good these days, Gerard. Healthy and, dare I say, happy? What the hell's happened to you?"

Ash waved dismissively. "Taking care of myself for once in my life." *And it might not hurt that I'm madly in love.*

Zack Wasserman, one of Ash's oldest friends in the world, clearly had lots more questions. "I'm impressed. And skeptical. When have you ever taken care of yourself? And *why*?"

Ash snickered. "I'd tell you to go screw yourself, but I need you, Wasserman. Superior though I am to you in nearly all ways, you are the greater wizard with investments."

Zack nodded sagely. "Indisputable. What do you need?"

Ash briefly explained, trying to be as vague as possible about his motives.

"I don't get it, Gerard. Why would you be interested in this kind of diversifying? Isn't most of your stock with the family company?"

Ash shook his head. "Trust me. I need to move some assets around and free up a small amount of capital. What are my options?"

Zack frowned. "Ash, you in trouble again? And where *are* you? Is that a cinder block wall?"

"I can't say. Doesn't matter."

His friend's eyes widened. "I haven't heard from you in a year and now you call out of the blue asking for help. You're kind of freaking me out, buddy."

Ash blew out a breath. "Listen, Zack. I'm not in trouble, but I need to know my options and I trust you. By this time next week, you'll have the full story. No details spared. Promise."

Zack nodded, picking up on Ash's seriousness. "Down to business, then. Okay, let's talk money." When the laptop was finally shut half an hour later, Ash stretched and felt a weight lift from his chest. He rose, grabbed his wallet, and headed into town.

***

Leah tried to slow her breath as she raced across the deep-pile carpet. "My flight was delayed," she muttered in the direction of the reception desk. It had been a rush from the airport, New York traffic causing her to grit her teeth in frustration. The last thing she needed now was to irritate her boss.

Joan waved Leah toward Simon Gerard's open office door. "He's been waiting for you," the woman said primly.

Simon's poker face did nothing to calm her nerves. Her skin felt like it was buzzing as she withdrew a file folder and laptop from her briefcase. *Keep it together, Bellerose*, she chided herself. *You won't get a second chance.*

"Sir, I have a full report here, including updated plans, budgets, staff reviews, and a draft summary of the mayors' meeting. As you may have already heard from Julius Cranford, the meeting was a success. While we've not tallied all the evaluation forms, in-person feedback yesterday was entirely positive." She paused but no response was forthcoming from the man sitting stonily behind his desk. "The mayors are already talking about meeting at Charmant Forest again, for both quarterly and annual meetings."

Another pause. She cleared her throat. "I suggest you first take a look at the expanded budget and personnel plans." She pointed to a printed spreadsheet. "Please let me know what questions you have as you go. I'm happy to answer and discuss any aspects of the organization." She stopped and tried to breathe normally as she accepted a glass of water from Joan, who entered and exited the office like a censorious ghost.

The older man spent what seemed like an eternity studying the printed reports, spreadsheets, and notes Leah had offered him. The tick of the clock on the mantle thundered in the room. She felt sweat break out under her suit jacket and shifted in her seat. "Everything you're looking at is also on a portable hard drive." She pulled the small drive from her purse and laid it on the desk. "This is for you, sir. Take as much time as you need." Her inward grimace was barely contained. Of course he'd take as much time as he needed. She tried to quell her mounting panic at Gerard's silence.

The man looked up at last, folded his arms, and leaned back in his chair. After a moment, he rose and poured himself a small measure of whiskey. Sitting, he sipped, winced in appreciation of the liquor, and placed his glass carefully on the blotter. "Ms. Bellerose, I have to say..." He paused and tapped the desktop, thinking.

Leah drew herself up.

Gerard regarded her coolly. "I have to say, I'm impressed. Your hard work and organizational skills are quite evident here. Quite evident." He motioned toward the papers in front of him. "It may be that I was...well, not fully aware of what was happening on the ground in Charmant."

His words hung in the air for a long moment while Leah absorbed the meaning. Gerard was saying she'd done a good job. Her hands pressed together in her lap to keep them from shaking. "I greatly appreciate that, sir."

"Yes. Well." He sucked his teeth and considered. "I'll need more time to go through each item more carefully—"

"Of course."

"—but I don't see any outstanding problems on the first review. I'm reassured. And pleased."

Leah's stomach unclenched. She wasn't being fired.

"I'd still like to see some fat trimmed from the budget but given the increase in income from the mayors' meeting—even after the expenditures on the ballroom—I believe the board will be less inclined to demand any immediate terminations." Gerard studied Leah's face for her reaction. "From what I gather, you've grown rather fond of some of the staff, so I'm sure you'll be relieved about that."

"Sir?" Anxiety flamed in her gut.

"Your ongoing insistence that the older staff members stay on has suggested a personal liking for these people." He said it as if recounting one of her worst faults.

This she could handle. "My fondness, which I don't deny, is based on the professionalism and dedication I've witnessed, sir."

"Ah." The man's eyebrows twitched. "Entirely?"

That gave her pause. "Not entirely, no." She met his hawkish gaze. "They are good people, sir." *And you would know if you bothered to get to know them, instead of sitting here, far away in your tower of privilege.*

"I'm sure they are." Gerard's smile was chilly. "Of course, they're provincial. Many are poorly educated or attended second rate schools. But I'm sure they're decent folks. Salt of the earth, as they say."

Leah stifled an impulse to lob a biting retort at the man. Overly empowered, entitled son of a bitch. She'd known far too many of those in her life.

Of course, her attitude hadn't been that different when she'd first landed at Charmant.

"They *are* decent, sir. And kind. And hard working. They value their jobs and each other." Leah thought of William, of Estelle, Hector, and the others. Her smile was genuine as she continued. "I feel very fortunate to have had the opportunity to work with them."

"Alright, then." Gerard gathered the files together and sat up, clearly concluding the meeting. "I'll share this with the board and we'll hold off on any further personnel decisions until the next quarter. That will give us all time to calculate the recent activity and see what our bottom line looks like." He gestured for her to stand with him and shook her hand briefly. "You'll stay at Charmant Forest in the near term and we'll revisit things by the end of the year. I anticipate that, barring any further issues, your continued success with the company will be assured."

Leah felt herself relax for the first time in days. "Thank you, sir. I'm grateful for your time and for the opportunities." She made her way out to reception, trying not to raise a triumphant fist into the air as she went.

***

"I can't decide." Ash held the blue velvet board in front of him, upon which several sparkling rings were displayed. "They're all so different."

"They are. They each have their own personality." The jeweler behind the glass counter straightened his shirt cuff and gestured to a chair. "Feel free to take your time and consider. Which one will best fit the personality of the woman for whom it's intended?" When Ash didn't immediately respond, the jeweler cleared his throat awkwardly. "Or...whomever the ring is intended for."

Ash remained standing, staring at the twinkling diamonds, emeralds, gold, platinum, and silver creations. "Oh, she's a woman all right. No question." He smiled briefly at the jeweler. "The personality is the tricky part."

That was an understatement. Buying a ring for Leah Bellerose was beginning to feel like one of the most challenging tasks he'd ever undertaken. He must have looked at thirty or forty rings before narrowing it down to these few.

The doorbell tinkled and a familiar voice rang out. "Ash." William strode to the counter. "Hi, Mr. Jackson. This is my friend, Ash. He knows me because I work with him."

The jeweler smiled. "Hello, William. How's your family?"

"Good. My sister's going to have another baby."

"Is she now? Why, I remember when your sister was born. Seems like yesterday." The man shook his head. "'Time flies, never to be recalled.' Virgil," he concluded, giving the disabled man a fond look.

Ash slapped William lightly on the shoulder, grateful for a moment's distraction. "Hey, my man. You surprised me. What are you doing here?"

"Walking home for lunch today. I saw you through the window." William gestured. "What are *you* doing here?" He looked down at the display board. "You're buying a ring?"

"I'm thinking about it." A split second's hesitation disappeared. Subterfuge with William was nearly impossible anyway. "Yes, I'm buying a ring. I'm not sure which one to get."

William nodded sagely. "I had a ring once. I won it at the fair. But it kept getting dirty in the greenhouse, so I had to throw it away. If you get a ring, you have to keep it clean when you do your work. Or else take it off— but don't lose it."

Ash nodded. "This ring isn't for me, William, so I don't need to worry about getting it dirty. Or losing it."

"Who's it for?"

"Miss Bellerose."

William looked from Ash to the jeweler, then whooped and clapped. "You're buying her a ring? So, you like her and want to date her?"

Ash felt the jeweler's smile as he responded. "Yes, I like her, William."

"I knew it. I could tell."

If that were true, it meant that everyone else could tell, too. Well, there were worse things. Everyone would officially know very soon anyway. And with his divestiture plan, if his father canned him as a result, so be it. He'd have what he wanted—Leah.

"But listen, William, you have to keep this a secret. I mean it." Ash became serious. "You can't tell *anyone* until I give Miss Bellerose the ring."

William was solemn. "I promise, Ash. I promise." He looked at the jeweler. "Do you promise, too, Mr. Jackson?"

"I certainly do. I'm very good at keeping promises—and secrets."

Ash pointed to the display board. "Alright, William. I'm having a little trouble deciding. What do you think? This big diamond, all by itself? Or maybe this diamond and emerald swirl? Or"—he turned the board so William could see it better—"this emerald with diamonds all around?"

William's eyes widened. "They are *all* pretty. Just like Miss Bellers."

Ash smiled at William's version of Leah's name. "They are."

William pointed to another ring, sitting in the corner of the blue velvet, set apart from the others. "What's that one?"

Ash picked it up. The gleaming sterling silver, studded with tiny pearls, winked at him under the bright lights of the jewelry store. "This one," he said, "is to give to Leah—Ms. Bellerose—if she decides she doesn't want to date me." As he said it, the heaviness of that distinct possibility cast a shadow over his excitement. It was a reality he had to consider. But he couldn't get sucked into that fear right now. "I want to give her something, no matter what she decides." His index finger caressed the pearls, smooth and lustrous as silk.

William shook his head solemnly. "She will want to date you."

"I hope so." Ash handed the blue velvet board back to the jeweler. "Mr. Jackson, I'll take this one." He pointed to the selected ring and William clapped again.

Jackson nodded. "Very well, Mr. Banks. I'll wrap it right up. And this one"—he pointed to the silver and pearls—"you will take with you, as well. A handshake is all I need for it. A gentleman's agreement. Bring one of the rings back to me after you ask the lady." He gave Ash a knowing and sympathetic smile. "I sincerely hope you'll bring back the pearls."

Ash shook the man's hand. "I hope so, too, Mr. Jackson. I hope so, too."

Chapter 22

Leah was ebullient as she exited Simon's inner office. The weight of the last few weeks had built up more than she'd realized. The sudden liberation from worry made her giddy. Simon was happy with her work and the plans she'd worked on so hard would be given a chance to develop fully. The meeting could not have gone better. She couldn't wait to tell Ash—and Julius, and everyone.

Strange. Little more than a month ago she would never have thought she'd be eager to get back to the town or the people at the hotel. Now it was all she could think about.

Joan gave Leah a sour wave. "Have a good trip back," the woman said, barely looking up from her desk.

Leah adjusted her briefcase strap on her shoulder. "Thank you, I will," she chimed, enjoying the look of surprise flashing across Joan's face. She turned to leave the reception area when something caught her attention.

It was a painting of a woman, a formal portrait, hanging inside the office vestibule. Something about the image had snagged her.

Those eyes. The woman's eyes were arresting, a rich, flecked topaz, set in an angular patrician face that could have been cut from crystal.

Leah froze as she stared at the painting. For a long moment, her brain refused to compute anything. Her arms and legs were immobilized.

There was a low buzzing in her head as an enormous weight settled, drifting down and over her, leaden rain, pinning her in one spot. She tried to swallow but her throat felt like stone.

From a distance came Joan's voice, tinged with concern. "Ms. Bellerose. Did you forget something?"

Leah was riveted in place barely aware she needed to answer the woman. Her shoulders hunched, her body curling in on itself. The room seemed to sway.

Breathe. Breathe, dammit. There was no air. She was going to suffocate.

"Ms. Bellerose?" Joan's voice was more concerned now. The sound of a chair creaking and footsteps approaching seemed to stretch across a great chasm to reach Leah.

"Who...who is this?" A whisper, coming out on a stutter, her breath choked. She managed to move one foot forward toward the painting and saw a small brass plaque affixed to the bottom of the frame.

A. Banks Gerard

Joan's reply words echoed around her in a deadly wave. "That's Mr. Gerard's wife. She passed away, oh, I suppose around fifteen years ago."

Leah continued to stare. The woman was beautiful. Stunning. She would have had beautiful children. Children with speckled brown eyes. Children with precise, aristocratic facial structure.

She'd known that, hadn't she? That his face was aristocratic?

A sudden recollection of words and images flooded into her mind. Inconsistencies. Disparate pieces of information she'd heard but not heard, noticed but not noticed. He spoke French and brought her Parisian truffles. He wore custom-tailored shirts and knew business terms not commensurate with his job as a maintenance man.

Because he was no mere maintenance man. He was a Gerard.

A cacophony of disbelief, of self-blame, of utter, gut-wrenching despair caused her fists to clench as she tried to wrest control of herself.

And through it all, one word echoed over and over in her head.

How?

How could she have been so blind?

It was inconceivable. How could he have fooled her? How could she have been blindsided like this when she was committed to never being duped again? It couldn't be coincidence. It had to be something she had allowed. What had she, Leah Bellerose, done to invite another deceitful man to take complete advantage of her trust?

And not just any deceitful man.

Ash.

The thought of his name caused a stab of pain so sharp she pressed a hand over her mouth. She tore her eyes from the painting and turned to Joan. A scream lurked behind her strangled whisper. "What does the 'A' stand for? What was her first name?"

"I believe it was Ashlyn. That's right. Ashlyn Banks. She came from an old family, quite patrician. Beautiful, wasn't she?" Joan frowned. "Are you quite all right? You look pale."

Leah forced herself not to look back at the painting. She sucked in air by sheer will and felt something inside her click into action. "I need to talk to Mr. Gerard." Before Joan could protest, she strode back to Simon's office, entering without preamble.

The man looked up abruptly from a phone call and took in Leah's expression. "I'll call you back," he said hastily, and hung up. He opened his mouth, but Leah spoke first, words shot like arrows.

"What kind of game have you been playing with me?" Her voice rose as her breath returned, though her chest felt crushed under a concrete weight. "And what were *his* instructions?" She couldn't bear to say his name aloud. "Did you send him to *spy* on me?" She sputtered with fury, which was far preferable to the deafening roar of grief at her back. "Did you think I'd never notice that painting? Or put the pieces together?" It was hard to stay upright, and she leaned on the desk for support. "*Unbelievable.* Completely unbelievable. Well, you underestimated me, Mr. Gerard. *Both* of you underestimated me."

Simon's brow furrowed. Then light dawned. "Ah. I see." He gestured to a chair. "Please sit, Miss Bellerose. Let me explain."

Her chest was imploding. She was going to have a stroke or a heart attack. Tears streaked down her face and were swiped away. "Oh, no. No more explanations from lying men. *Ever.*" She took the files from her briefcase and threw them onto the desk.

Drawing herself up, she squared her shoulders and met her former boss's gaze head on.

"I quit."

***

Ash slid into the booth at the Bluebell Diner at ten minutes to seven. Rain threatened, but an early morning sun shone brilliantly through the window, illuminating the scratches in the old linoleum tabletop. He smiled to himself. No five-star restaurant could compete with the charm of this place.

In place of his maintenance uniform, he wore jeans, dress shirt, and casual jacket, having decided against a formal suit situation. Too stuffy. He patted the tiny velvet box in his pocket and tried to calm his pulse. He'd never proposed to a woman before—in fact, he'd always tried to avoid commitments of all kinds—and it was hard not to feel like a fish out of water. He'd rehearsed his lines a hundred times but now, somehow, couldn't remember the first word.

It will be all right. You'll tell her you love her, set the box on the table, and ask her.

The waitress broke his reverie. "What'll you have?" Crystal chewed her gum loudly, studied her nails, and waited, pencil poised.

Ash beamed at her. "I'm expecting someone. Coffee for now."

Crystal left with a thumbs-up.

His fingers drummed on the tabletop. It was hard not to look out the window, down the street, anticipating Leah. He wondered what she would be wearing. Maybe the blue dress. That would be a fantasy. His romanticism almost made him laugh out loud. *Look what she's done to me.* Ash grinned. *She'll probably be wearing one of her stodgy gray suits and still look stunning.*

Leah would look smokin' hot in almost anything.

Twenty minutes later, he looked at his watch. Crystal came by with the coffeepot and he shook his head. He patted the tiny box in his pocket. His heart thrummed.

Chill out. She'll be here.

The sun disappeared behind a gray cloud, throwing shadows inside the diner. He sipped his water and began staring from the second hand on his watch to the window and back again. Now he knew what women felt, he mused, waiting on men all the time. His stomach rumbled, but he didn't feel hungry.

Another fifteen minutes went by. Ash gave in and texted Leah, attention shifting to his phone as he waited for a response. His hand gripped the box in his pocket, hanging onto it for reassurance.

His gaze was directed out the window, down the street, when his phone finally chirped. The relief he felt was sharp and short-lived.

The message was from Julius. *Call me.*

He dialed, bracing himself for the usual maintenance emergency, rehearsing excuses he could use to buy time this morning. Cranford's voice was solemn and didn't give time for alarm before he got straight to the point. "Ash, Ms. Bellerose has left."

Confusion. "What?"

"She's gone. She's not coming back to Charmant."

It took him a long moment to absorb what Cranford was saying. He went very still, staring ahead and not seeing. "Wait, wait. *What? I don't understand.*" His mind raced, scrambling to make sense of what he was hearing. "What happened?"

Cranford was apologetic. "I honestly don't know, Ash. I received a brief call from Mr. Gerard, informing me that I would be temporarily reinstated as managing director until a new director is identified. He didn't say much more than that."

Ash ran a hand over his face. "But what…How could…Julius, what were Mr. Gerard's *exact* words?" Desperation clawed at him, frantic to understand what was happening.

Julius sighed. "He said, 'Ms. Bellerose is leaving her position at Charmant Forest as of today.' I'm to resume the role of managing director until a replacement is appointed. He said, 'Nothing will change. All operations are to continue as is.' That was it. He hung up without waiting for my response."

That certainly sounded like Simon. Coffee churned in Ash's stomach and he was afraid he might vomit. "So, you haven't talked to Leah?"

"No. I haven't heard from her, and she's not answering her phone. She went to a meeting—a confidential meeting, though I guess it can't hurt to tell you now—in New York yesterday. I'm assuming she met with Mr. Gerard and—"

That's all Ash needed to hear. He jumped up, threw some cash on the table, and raced out of the diner, still talking. "Julius, I need the day off. Give my apologies to Arthur and Hector." Whatever had transpired while Leah was in New York had to be his father's fault, and he'd be damned if he let the old tyrant destroy the best thing that had ever happened to him.

He barely heard Cranford's response. "Take whatever time you need, Ash." There was a pause. "And, son? Good luck."

Thunderheads on the horizon were ominous as he ran back to the hotel. He redialed Leah's number over and over as he raced to his apartment, grabbed his backpack and wallet, and ordered a taxi to the airport. Nothing but voicemail. Message after message went into the ether. He texted repeatedly.

Where are you? What happened?

Please answer.

Are you all right? Please let me know me you're safe.

Call me.

Finally, as he jumped into a cab, his text failed to go through. Instead, he received a notification.

Number blocked.

His heart sank. She had cut him out, and he had no idea where she was, or what was wrong. The worried eyes of the cab driver were on him in the rearview mirror.

"Is there a problem, sir?"

Ash waved away the man's concern as he swallowed the bile that rose in his throat. "Get me to the airport. And hurry."

***

Lists. Lists were what had pulled her through more times than she could count. Going through tasks and marking them off were evidence that you were still alive and functioning, that you had control.

No matter how much the world felt like it was spinning off its axis.

Lists are what would get her through this. Along with her iron will, a legacy from the iron maiden. Leah had been a fool to think she could let that go and she was glad she had it now. Wasn't she?

Of course she was.

She couldn't get out of the city fast enough. She raced back to her hotel room, barely making it into the bathroom before the meager contents of her stomach were lost. For what seemed like an eternity, she sat on the floor, hugging herself, rocking back and forth, eyes blank with shock. Finally, she vomited again, heaving and keening, the sounds echoing off the tiles.

The final purge seemed to snap her back to reality.

Irritated, she washed out her mouth and sat on the edge of the tub with her tablet. After making notes, she picked up her phone.

"Dahlia, it's Leah. I need you to help me with Prune for a few days. Can you do that?"

Dahlia was clearly surprised to hear her voice. "Miss Bellerose. Where are you? Mr. Cranford said you're gone."

She pressed a hand to her eyes. "I can't explain right now, Dahlia, but I need your help. Please listen." Her instructions were clear, a bulleted list. The young woman listened silently as Leah went through everything. "I'll send you all this in an email but want to make sure you understand exactly what to do."

"Yes, ma'am." Dahlia's tone was somber. "But why take Prune to your mother's house? I'm happy to stay with her at your apartment until you come back to pack or say good-bye?"

No. I can't ever go back to that place. She steadied herself against the wall. "Just do as I'm asking, Dahlia. It's very important. My mother lives only two hours from Charmant, and I'll send you compensation for your time and travel expenses. The cat carrier is in my pantry. Can you do this for me?"

"Okay. Yes." Clearly confused, Dahlia's tone was soft. "I thought you liked it here in Charmant."

Shut the gates, Bellerose. No room for emotions today.

"I enjoyed many things about working at the hotel, and I appreciate all you've done to help me." She refocused. "Now, Dahlia. One more thing." She paused. This wasn't on the list. "When you get to my mother's, don't be...well, don't be surprised by the house. It's pretty old. And not as clean or well-maintained as it could be." Or should be, according to the laws of decency and reason. "Anyway, my mother will be expecting your call. I'm sure she'll try to make you feel welcome." Her lips twisted into a grimace on this last statement. She could only imagine how Cecelia would receive Dahlia.

"I'm sure she's as nice as can be," Dahlia offered.

Leah's foot tapped the tile floor in a disjointed rhythm. "She's a bit of a personality. Don't be surprised by that either." She closed her eyes on the images flooding her. "She and I are very different people." *In some ways. Though we may be more alike than I realized.* Her foot stilled as she felt her stomach lurch again. Luckily, it was empty, so nothing was forthcoming.

Nothing like dry heaves to keep you humble, she thought morosely. Of course, she'd brought it all on herself. "Dahlia, I have to get to the airport. Is all of this clear?"

"I think so. But I still don't understand why you have to go so suddenly." The hurt in the young woman's voice was undeniable and seeped through the tenuous iron shield.

"It's something I have to do, Dahlia. Just trust me on this." She ticked the phone call off her list. "I'll write to you as soon as I can." *Tell everyone I'm sorry.* Tears welled, and her throat thickened. Choking out a good-bye, she hit End and slid to the bathroom floor.

Chapter 23

Joan looked up in alarm as the vestibule door banged open. Ash didn't acknowledge her or the security guard who struggled to catch up with him as he strode through reception toward his father's office.

"Mr. Gerard, your father is in a meeting." She stood and tried to block his way.

He feinted and was around her in a second. The security guard hustled through the vestibule, yelling for Ash to halt.

The office door was locked, confirming what he'd suspected when the guard had tried to stop him downstairs. His father knew he would show up here and had tried to prevent him even getting into the building.

He drew back and rammed his shoulder into the door, which flew open. Simon, behind his desk, blinked but didn't move.

Ash was in front of the desk in an instant. "Where is she?" he demanded.

The security guard ran into the office a second later, taser at the ready. He looked at Simon.

His father's gaze didn't waver from his son as he addressed the guard with a snicker. "Thank you for your *vigilance*, Bernie. I won't be needing you or your little toy there." He waved the man out and regarded Ash with a tilt of his head. "I have a Sig Sauer nine millimeter in my desk drawer."

Ash placed both hands on the desk and leaned forward, nearly closing the space between them. "Are you threatening to shoot me?" he said through clenched teeth.

His father smiled, the crocodile's smile. "That would be a waste of a bullet. Besides, I can't wait to hear what you have to say." He gestured for Ash to sit.

Ash remained standing, hands balled into fists on the desk. "I have nothing to say to you. All I want to know is where Leah went, and what happened to send her away." He could feel his blood pounding, biceps bunching, wanting to beat the information from his father. Adrenaline flooded every muscle fiber. He'd never been so angry in his life.

Simon leaned back in his chair. "Why don't you ask her?"

"She won't answer my calls."

The reptilian smile again. "Strange. Sounds like she's angry at you. I wonder why."

Ash stared at the ceiling and felt his scalp prickle with the effort of not reaching across the desk and strangling his father. But blowing a gasket wouldn't get him what he wanted, and he had no time to waste. He blew out a breath and faced the older man. "All right. You seem to have figured out that Leah and I have a personal relationship. I won't deny that anymore."

"How special for you. You've never been an easy person to love, Ash."

He ignored the comment, which was something he'd heard repeatedly from his father throughout his lifetime. "It wasn't my intention or hers. It was something that happened despite both of us fighting it." That was an understatement if there ever was one.

"Isn't that romantic?" Simon smirked. "You realize this puts you in violation of our most basic agreement. You've effectively written your death sentence with this company. Not to mention implicating Ms. Bellerose in the same crime. Consorting with inferiors is grounds for immediate termination."

Ash shook his head. "*No*. No, no, no. It was my fault that it started. Don't blame Leah. I pushed. I was trying…" He faltered. "I was trying to manipulate her, but"—he sucked in a breath as shame caused bile to rise in his throat—"somehow, I couldn't stay away from her."

Simon's lip curled in disgust. "All this despite the simple directive to *do your job* and be professional, to save your place in this company."

Ash flung his hands into the air. "Christ, I *did* my job. I *was* professional. Well, mostly. More than I ever have been. You and I both know I earned my way back into the company's good graces ages ago. You've been punishing me since then." He was about to pull his hair out in frustration. "Dad. *Where is Leah?* Something terrible must have happened to make her block my calls. I'm worried about her." His voice wavered on the last statement. He *was* worried. Nearly frantic.

Something flickered in Simon's eyes. "You're worried about another human being? And a woman at that? That sounds nothing like you."

Ash pounded on the desk, causing his father to frown. "Dad, I'm in love with her. I don't—" He paused to wrest control over himself because it felt like he might disintegrate, right here, right now. "I don't want to live without her. I have to know what happened and where she went."

The older man sat up straight. "You're *in love* with her?" His tone was incredulous.

"Completely. Madly." Firm now and confident, Ash pulled an airplane cocktail napkin from his back pocket. Scribbled writing was visible on one side. He placed it on the desk.

Simon didn't move to pick it up. "What is this?"

"It's my resignation. I'll type it up later and submit it formally." Ash pushed the napkin toward his father. "This will free me up to have the life I want with Leah. I intend to ask her to marry me."

His father was staring at him, a tiny line between his eyebrows betraying his disbelief. He seemed to be pondering something, but Ash didn't have time for processing.

He rounded the desk and stood over the older man, using his height to full advantage. His voice was a steely whisper. *"Where. Is. Leah?"*

The elder Gerard was silent for several beats, then seemed to come to a decision. "Changi," he said

Ash's brow furrowed. "Changi? Where the hell is that?"

"Singapore."

***

From the air, the Singapore airport was surrounded by forest. Huge and sprawling, and busy, but set in a sea of lush green vegetation and surrounded on three sides by azure ocean. *See, this is beautiful*, Leah told herself. *I'm going to like it here.* She pinched the bridge of her nose to staunch the flow of tears that had uncontrollably plagued her the entire trip.

Once on the ground, she made her way through the sprawling terminal and across to the connecting train station. The push of crowds, ringing thrum of voices, and roar of planes was blessedly numbing.

Like New York, she mused determinedly. *I feel right at home.*

The aroma of food wafted toward her, but her stomach protested at the thought of eating. Other than a protein shake, she hadn't managed to keep anything down for the past two days.

High-end retail shops, local vendors, and kiosks vied for her attention, but she managed to stay focused on getting to the correct train terminal. The crush of people and noise was a blur as she pulled her rolling suitcase down the long corridor. Nearing her destination, she slowed and read the numbers on the signs written in multiple languages. "Station 8…" she murmured aloud, scanning placards.

At last, she found the spot and settled onto a row of attached seats broken up with charging stations. She plugged in her phone and dialed Dahlia. The young woman confirmed that Prunella was perfectly fine and would be delivered to Leah's mother the following day. "I can't thank you enough, Dahlia," she said, relief washing through her. She missed Prune more than she'd thought possible. The little feline had been with her through thick and thin for over five years, through four moves and countless difficult days. Not having her now was almost unbearable.

But dwelling on that was a luxury she couldn't afford. Emotions were unceremoniously shoved aside to be dealt with later.

She sat back and closed her eyes. Fatigue and the stress of the last few days quickly descended, and she was nearly comatose when a creaky voice interrupted her.

"Miss? You want charm?"

She didn't open her eyes. Her hand waved wearily, directing the person away.

"Miss? *Miss.* You need charm."

"I don't need anything. Leave me alone." She pulled her jacket around her and hugged her purse against her body.

The intruder was not so easily dissuaded. There was a thump as a small body sat down next to her, along with the scent of ginger and something else. Maybe cardamom.

"Oh, God," Leah groaned, opening her eyes. Beside her was the oldest person she'd ever seen. Possibly the oldest person on the planet.

The woman's face was wizened almost beyond recognition. Her eyes were twinkling dots in her wrinkled face, and her mouth, entirely toothless, was split into a wide grin. "You need charm." She leaned toward Leah and gripped her arm with a bony hand.

"I don't." Leah forced herself to sit up and face the tiny creature.

"You have pain"—the woman thumped her own torso—"here. Love hurt."

You have no idea. Leah's chest seized up and she admonished herself to close the gates and throw up the iron shields.

The old woman patted Leah's arm and shook her head. "Much pain."

Was it written on her forehead? Leah sighed and plucked the ancient claw from her arm. "I'm fine. I need—"

She stopped. What did she need?

"I need to be alone." Her breath left her on the last word, and she faltered, appalled to feel the sting of tears. She pushed ahead, too stubborn to stop. "I need you and everyone else to leave me alone. I can take care of myself." After swiping at her face with a tissue, she rummaged in her purse. "Okay, give me whatever you're selling and move on." She proffered a wad of cash. "I'm sure you can exchange this somewhere."

The old woman pushed the money away and shook her head. "No, no. *Charm*. Will help remember."

Leah was puzzled. "I'm not sure—"

The crone reached into a patchwork carpetbag she'd been dragging with her and extracted a small amulet. "You need." Pressing the object into Leah's hand, she patted her again. "Remember." The ancient woman rose and bowed repeatedly. "You keep." She gestured toward the charm in Leah's palm.

Nothing will help. The words echoed in her head as she nodded. "Fine, okay. Thanks." She closed her eyes again.

"You remember. *Real love*," the creaky voice said urgently, "does not lie."

Her eyes flew open.

"Keep. You." The woman waved, bowed again, and was gone, disappearing into the crowd.

Leah sighed and blew out a breath. Unfurling her palm, she gazed down at the little charm, which was cheap and probably made out of some kind of toxic metal.

It was a cat. A sleek, golden-colored feline with a long, curling tail.

***

"Singapore?" Ash's heart sank as he stared at his father. Leah was on the other side of the planet. "What in God's name is she doing there?"

Simon sat up and waved Ash back, away from him. "When she was here yesterday, she saw the portrait of your mother—"

"Oh, Jesus." Ash turned and ran a hand over his face. "This is a disaster."

"—and she quit. On the spot." His father pursed his lips. "Rather impulsive. And overly emotional, like so many females. Never pegged her that way before. Disappointing." He tut-tutted in annoyance. "But she's a determined young woman, I'll give her that. Stubborn. Took me a good hour to convince her to stay on with the company. We'd talked about Singapore as her next move, and that seemed far enough away to persuade her."

"Christ, Dad, what did you tell her? How did you explain the situation?"

"I didn't. I said only that your directives and hers were entirely separate, which they were. Anything that happened between the two of you was entirely your doing." He adjusted a cufflink. "She had her suspicions about motives on all sides. Nothing I said was going to change her mind, and as you know, I'm not a man who feels the impulse to offer needless justifications."

Ash made his way back around the desk and slumped into a chair. "I can't believe this," he muttered to himself, at the same time making quick calculations. "I'm going to need my passport. And enough cash to exchange when I get there."

"Good lord, you're not intending to fly to Singapore?" His father was dismayed.

Ash jumped up and grabbed his backpack. "Damn right I am." He shook his head. "You still don't get it. *I love her.* I'm not letting her get away." His laugh was bitter. "You wouldn't understand, though, would you? You never felt that way about Mom. You didn't deserve her." He turned to go and was stopped by his father's voice.

"Asher, you realize I was going to fire you when you came in here, if you hadn't resigned first." His tone was dispassionate.

"Is that supposed to make me feel better?"

"Certainly not. Simply informing you." His father regarded him carefully. "And on the subject of your mother and me, I'll remind you that you don't know everything about us. Or me. As, apparently, I don't know everything about you." Uninterested in a response, he gestured toward the door dismissively.

Ash frowned and went out to reception, mind churning. He had to try to talk to Leah, to make sure she was all right. There was no telling what suspicions she had or conclusions she'd drawn from the disastrous meeting with Simon.

"Joanie, let me use your phone." Without waiting for an answer, he pulled the landline toward him and began dialing.

"Mr. Gerard, you are not permitted—"

He held up a hand to silence the woman as the call went through.

Answer, answer, he prayed. Seeing the corporate office number on the phone should be enough to at least get her to pick up.

After three rings, his prayers were answered.

"Leah Bellerose." Her voice was businesslike, but exhausted. His heart clenched. She sounded miserable.

"Leah, it's me. Don't hang up. We have to talk—"

The sound of a click and disconnection felt like an amputation. He cursed and dialed again, using a different line on the phone. Hoping against hope that she'd risk answering at least once more, he planned what to say in the shortest time possible.

"Leah Bellerose." Wary this time, but still professional.

"Whatever you're thinking, I love you. Nothing changes that—"

Click.

"Shit." He hung up and turned to Joan, who was watching him warily.

He grabbed the older woman's hand. "Leah and I were…are…in a relationship and my father has chosen to sabotage it." Joan's eyes widened. "I'm pretty sure she won't call here, and she may not take any more calls from this office, but on the off chance…" He looked at her imploringly. "Joanie, please tell her I love her and I'm not letting her go. Will you do that for me?" The secretary's mouth was open in shock as she nodded, speechless.

"Thank you." Ash leaned over the desk and kissed the papery cheek. "Wish me luck."

Five minutes later he was in a cab on the way back to the airport, mind still racing, strategizing on the fly. He pulled out his phone and dialed.

"Arthur, it's me. Quick question. Does William have a passport?"

Chapter 24

Leah stared at her phone in numb bewilderment. Hearing Ash's voice had started a shuddering in her solar plexus that moved outward to her limbs. She hugged her briefcase against her chest to quell the keening grief that suffused her. The train bulleted ahead toward downtown. Her gaze went, unseeing, out the window at the setting sun and lights of Singapore city.

That voice, his words, echoed even as she tried to vanquish them.

"I love you. Nothing changes that."

Could that be true? The possibility was almost too painfully impossible, yet...

She straightened in her seat and refocused, self-recrimination kicking in.

Jesus, Bellerose. Are you that desperate? To believe a man who lied to you each and every day since you met?

The truth was it didn't matter how he felt about her. He had lied. Purposely concealed his true identity from her. That by itself meant that their relationship was built on something false and would never be something she could trust.

Still, she could hear his voice, as clearly if he were sitting next to her.

"I love you. Nothing changes that."

And then, another voice, one creaky with age. *"Real love does not lie."*

Did she say "lie" or "die"? The old woman's scratchy voice and thick accent had made it hard to decipher her message.

Did it matter?

Her hands curled in, fingernails digging into her palms as she struggled to gain some scrap of control. *You're not living in some romance novel, Bellerose. This is real life.* He lied. He lied. He lied.

On top of that, he'd agreed to the deception and used it for his professional gain, not considering for a moment how it would affect her, or anyone else. He truly had taken her for a fool—and she'd been a fool, for a short period.

She would never forgive him. She would get over this and move on with her life, as before. Cecelia Bellerose's daughter wasn't going to crumble because she loved a man who had betrayed her.

The trembling in her chest intensified with the thought. She *did* love him. The indisputable truth of it slammed into her, knocking the breath out of her, crushing her.

"I love you. Nothing changes that."

This time the voice in her head was her own. *I love you, too.*

Her nose began to run and she pressed a hand to her eyes. *Damn.*

At that moment, a robotic voice announced her stop. The distraction was welcome. She rose and gathered her bags, ignoring the stares of other travelers.

***

Dahlia Markley's eyes bugged out. "What kinda car *is* this?"

Ash shifted hard and skirted an eighteen-wheeler, swinging ahead of the speeding traffic. The force pressed them both back in their seats. "Porsche Taycan." He squinted into the distance to calculate his passing strategy.

"I thought you drove an old pickup."

"I do. I keep this in storage."

Dahlia gripped Prunella's carrier tightly to her chest. "Ain't we goin' sorta fast?"

He glanced over at her. "I'm in a hurry." He let up on the accelerator slightly. It wouldn't help to get pulled over in a speed trap.

The red curls bounced as Dahlia nodded. "I figured that out." She relaxed her hold on the carrier. "Tell me again why you're comin' with me?"

Ash sighed. The fear he'd been keeping at bay felt like a tidal wave at his back. *Just hang on, man. Do what's right in front of you.* "I need to talk to Leah's mother. When I see Leah in Singapore, I need to know as much about her as I can. To make my case."

It had hit him like a thunderbolt when he'd gotten back to Charmant to grab his passport and coordinate his plan with William and Arthur. Dahlia had been heading out to deliver Prune to Cecelia and the pieces had fallen into place in his mind. Finding out more about Leah and her story could be the key to getting her back.

Dahlia shook her head. "I don't understand none of this." Prunella meowed then, a glowering yowl that seemed to amplify Dahlia's statement.

"That makes two of us," Ash muttered, stomping on the accelerator to pass another semi. The car rocketed ahead.

An hour later they pulled up in front of Cecilia Bellerose's house. Dahlia peered at the sagging porch steps, the faded sheets tacked over the front windows, the dirt yard. "Are you sure this is it?"

Ash shut off the soundless Porsche. "You tell me. You're the one Leah gave the address to."

Dahlia stared at her phone to verify the information. At the same moment, the front door of the house swung open and four tiny brown blurs raced at them, yapping at the tops of their lungs.

The woman on the porch waved a cigarette in their direction as they gingerly exited the car, trying to avoid the canine security patrol.

"You must be Dahlia," the woman called. "I'm Cecelia. Come on in."

Ash scooped a yapping dog into his arms and nodded at Dahlia. "Looks like the right place."

The young woman's expression was unsure, cradling the cat carrier in her arms. "I guess." She followed Ash and the swirl of dogs into the house.

Ash preceded Dahlia into the darkened living room, stepping around dogs, piles of magazines and newspapers. He deposited the furball he was carrying on the floor and brushed himself off.

"Ma'am," he said, extending his hand toward Cecelia.

Before he could introduce himself, he found the woman's faded green eyes assessing him closely. "And who might *you* be?" she rasped.

"Oh, this is Ash," Dahlia chimed in breathlessly. "He drove me here. He's the maintenance man at the hotel."

"Is that right, now?" Cecelia looked from Dahlia to Ash and back again. "Well, let's get Miss Kitty put up in Maggie's room and then"—she flicked a suspicious gaze at Ash—"we can get to know each other a bit better."

Dahlia followed Cecelia down a hallway. "Who's Maggie?" Ash heard the young woman ask.

A sound from outside caught Ash's attention. "Yoo-hoo." An older woman in a purple jogging suit and a middle-aged man wearing a baseball cap and a bewildered expression clomped into the house.

"Well, hi howdy. I'm Sugar and this here's Doogie. Say hello, Doogie. And who are you? Are you a friend of Maggie's? That must be your car outside. Fancy. Must be foreign. My Wayne would never have a foreign car, but then, he didn't know much." The woman didn't wait for a response before heading into the kitchen. "Where's Cecelia? Doogie, get me that pitcher, will you? Mountain Dew or iced tea, do you think?"

Ash stood in the living room, surrounded by threadbare furniture and dogs trying to climb his leg. He didn't know whether to laugh or cry. *This* is where Leah came from?

"Well, that's done." Cecelia and Dahlia emerged from the hall. "That is one strange looking cat, I tell you. Never seen nuthin' like it. What does she eat?"

Dahlia headed toward the door. "I'll get her stuff out of the car." She threw a significant glance at Ash. "I have to tell you something," she hissed under her breath as she passed him.

Cecelia waved Ash toward the couch and lowered herself into an easy chair adorned with duct tape. She lit a fresh cigarette as Sugar and Doogie came in with iced tea and a package of Nutter Butters. Ash accepted a glass of tea, then handed one to Dahlia, who sat down next to him with the box of cat supplies.

Cecelia surveyed the group. "Alrighty now you two, tell us what's happening with Maggie and why I'm now saddled with a hairless cat." She pointed her cigarette at Ash. "You first, maintenance man."

Sugar turned to Ash, wrinkled face alight. "Are you a maintenance man? Well, ain't that a coincidence. That's what Doogie's been doing, down at the TruValue."

Doogie's slack face perked up, realizing he and Ash had something in common. "That's cool, man," he offered.

Ash struggled to orient himself. "Yeah, cool," he murmured in Doogie's direction. "Uh, Ms. Bellerose, I'm a bit confused. Who is Maggie?"

Dahlia vibrated next to him. *"That's what I was gonna tell you,"* she whispered.

The woman blew out smoke. "Honey, call me Cecelia. I don't truck with the name Bellerose, though I'm too cheap to change it." She chuckled. "Maggie's my daughter. She went and changed her name to Leah, but she'll always be Maggie to us."

Before Ash could absorb this, Sugar nodded and added, "Christened Magnolia Evangeline Sebastian Bellerose. Ain't that the prettiest name you ever heard? I'll never understand why she would want to change it."

"Ah." Ash nodded. The sliver of understanding regarding Leah's reticence to share her past was growing. "I see." He nodded at Dahlia, who still looked perplexed.

"So," Cecelia continued. *"Who are you?* What gives?"

She was clearly a no-nonsense woman, like her daughter. Ash drew a breath. He had no idea what the relationship between Leah and her mother was, but it was a fair guess that it was less than ideal. How much he shared with Cecelia would be a judgment call, but given the reason he was here, he'd have to hope Leah could forgive him for any mistakes he was about to make.

"Well, you see…" he began.

Ten minutes later, having left out a thousand details, he stopped. "So," he concluded to his rapt audience, "you can understand why I came here with Dahlia, to learn as much as I can about Leah—*Maggie*—so I can convince her to forgive me." He waited, feeling the thick tension in the air, the steely gaze of Cecelia, the laserlike attention of Sugar, and the confused aura of Doogie and Dahlia.

Then Sugar threw back her head. "God help me, Cecelia. I think I believe him."

Leah's mother crushed her cigarette out in an ashtray brimming with butts and gave Ash a long, cool, assessing look. Her mouth worked, her eyes glittered.

Ash felt his whole body go stiff with anxiety. What would he do if Cecelia threw him out of the house, as it would be her right to do, given everything he'd confessed?

The woman stared at him for another long moment, then sighed. "Men are no good. Lying men are worse than no good. And all the men I've ever met have been unrepentant liars." She paused.

"But"—she glanced at Sugar then back at Ash—"I think I believe you, too."

Ash heard a relieved exhalation from Dahlia.

Cecelia continued. "O'course, you did lie. You lied for selfish reasons. Like all men."

Ash nodded wretchedly, waiting for the hammer to fall.

"Then, later, you lied to protect Maggie. And you didn't know how to get out of it without hurting her even more." The woman lit a fresh cigarette and slowly took a drag. "I can understand that."

He realized he was holding his breath.

"Young man, I don't know what you're gonna do about this mess. And no idea what Maggie will do. She's stubborn and unforgiving." Cecelia took a sip of tea. "A hard child to love. Always was. But"—her tone softened—"worth the effort." When she spoke again, she was matter of fact. "So, what do you want to know about Maggie?"

***

Fifteen minutes after leaving the train station, Leah was in her new apartment on the eighteenth floor of a slick glass building next to the Gerard Hospitality Group's newest acquisition, an enormous resort-style hotel and casino.

"This is nice." She swallowed, dropped her suitcase, and took in the enormous space.

There was not an item out of place. No water stains to be seen. Not a speck of dust. A massive living room with sleek furniture and a plate glass wall facing the bay was more than she would ever need. A sliding glass patio door in the gleaming, modern kitchen looked out on the resort, its three swimming pools and multiple fountains sparkling in the evening air, roving klieg lights, and towering palm trees.

She kicked off her shoes and padded into the spacious bedroom, replete with a king-sized bed and marble en suite bath. Without undressing, she lay on the bed, curled up and fell asleep.

***

The next morning dawned bright and hot. Sun poured through every window as she hurried to shower and make herself presentable. At last, she hurried across the manicured lawn of the apartment building, wondering if jet lag could kill a person. She still couldn't eat, and fatigue pulled at her limbs.

As she entered the hotel and made her way to the office level, her face automatically arranged itself into a pleasantly professional expression. Through the exhaustion of the last few days, anxiety crept up her spine. There would be people taking her measure, evaluating her competence for the role she was stepping into. First impressions were critical. Today was about survival.

You can do this, Bellerose, she coached herself. *You could do this in your sleep.*

The unreality of what had happened and where Leah found herself was like walking through a dream world, or more like a nightmare dressed up in shiny, happy packaging.

She exited the elevator into a large reception area with two administrative assistants. One of them greeted her. "Ms. Bellerose, Ms. Dennis is ready for you." She was ushered into a bright office where an attractive woman in her fifties sat behind a glass desk.

Leah braced herself. *Why is everything here made of glass?*

"Ms. Bellerose." The woman extended a manicured hand. "I'm Margo Dennis, executive director of the hotel. You'll be meeting the two other associate directors tomorrow. For now, let's get acquainted." She gestured for Leah to sit, pulled up a file on her computer, and plunged in.

The next few hours were a blur. Leah's head was pounding by the time they broke for a late working lunch at one of the five restaurants in the hotel.

The press of people, kitchen noise, and loud music, even in the quieter corners of the main dining room, felt like an assault as Leah struggled to keep up with Ms. Dennis's fire-hose delivery of expectations and instructions.

At last, exhausted, Leah interrupted the woman. "Ms. Dennis, I'm afraid I've got terrible jet lag and I don't want to miss anything. I wonder if we could take a brief break and meet later this afternoon?"

The woman regarded Leah with a tilt of her head. "Of course. Forgive me. I'm eager to onboard you, and I wasn't thinking. You'll be starting at the junior level here, as you know, and that position—well, it's competitive. The other two associate directors are each quite ambitious in their way, so I wanted to give you the best chance to walk into tomorrow's meeting well prepared." She smiled, but it didn't quite reach her eyes.

She was not pleased.

Leah backpedaled quickly. "I appreciate that so much, and I'm fine. Really. I'll make sure to turn in early and be on point in the morning. Shall we continue?"

Chapter 25

Ash walked up the gangway from the plane to the terminal and sucked in the fresh air. It smelled different here, but he had a hard time identifying what the difference was. Something floral underneath the airport fumes.

The two men walking beside him were agonizingly unhurried and he had to slow his steps as he entered the building.

"Where are we?" William asked loudly, causing several nearby heads to turn.

"Singapore." Ash tried to smile but was distracted by his sense of urgency. He was beginning to regret his plan to include the disabled man.

Through the crowd of people outside security, a line of drivers was visible. One caught his attention. It was a black-suited local gentleman in a livery cap, holding a hand-lettered sign.

Gerard.

He stopped, momentarily confused. He hadn't ordered a driver.

Arthur stepped up beside him. "Is that for us?" he murmured. While he hadn't gone into detail, Ash had shared the basic outline of what was going on with Arthur during the long flight.

"I'm not sure." Ash approached the livery driver. "You're here for...?"

The man bowed slightly and consulted a note on the back of the sign. "Mr. Asher Gerard. A-One Limousine," he said in heavily accented English.

Ash chewed his lip, considering. There was only one person who could have done this, but it seemed impossible. "Who arranged this transportation?"

The man shook his head. "Ask office," he said apologetically.

Ash sighed. He'd figure it out later. "Come on," he said to his companions. "We have a ride."

As they headed to baggage claim, William waved at a wizened little person standing inside the broad doorway. It was a woman, wrapped in a red robe and carrying a threadbare carpet bag. The ancient face broke into a beaming smile and she waved back at William, pointed at Ash and began clapping. William veered in her direction.

Ash's eyebrows rose. There were odd people everywhere, he thought in bemusement.

"Come along, son," Arthur instructed, taking his William's arm. "We're going in a limousine to see Ms. Bellerose."

William whooped. "A limzeen. Okay." He paused. "What's a limzeen?"

As they sped into the city, William was glued to the window with excitement. Lush green landscape whizzed by. An early morning sun was blinding against glass skyscrapers as the limo flew down the freeway. "I like this place. It's pretty."

Ash tried to smile. "It is."

The younger man opened a bag of pretzels and munched loudly. "But I like Charmant better. That's where I live."

The lump in Ash's throat was painful as he nodded. Arthur patted him on the shoulder briefly. "We'll be back home soon, son," he said, and Ash wondered which of them he was addressing.

The hotel lobby was enormous, radiant as a diamond, and filled with brilliant, tropical flowers. Loud music bounced off glass walls.

"Miss Bellers won't like this," William announced, holding his hands over his ears as they walked to reception. "Those flowers hurt my eyes."

Ash silently agreed with him. Leah might be able to fit herself in and be brilliant in whatever job she was given, but he knew she wouldn't be happy here.

A stab of guilt hit him in the gut. It was his fault she was here. His fault she was miserable. He had lied to her in the worst way. And even though, as it turned out, she hadn't been entirely honest with him either, he intended to take her home and make sure she was happy for the rest of her life.

He looked at his watch. "Let's get upstairs and get ready," he said to his companions.

***

Leah straightened her pencil skirt and inhaled as she marched determinedly down the hall to the conference room. *You're going to slay this, Bellerose. This is your world. What you've always wanted.*

She ignored the cramp in her belly. It was probably due to the fact she'd only eaten a banana and a granola bar in the last forty-eight hours. She didn't feel at all like vomiting, which was an improvement.

The door to the conference room was open and she walked through, head high, professional smile at the ready. A couple of people were milling about talking, while others were already seated. Margo Dennis turned from the coffee urn. "Ah, Ms. Bellerose, please come in and sit. We're ready to start." She closed the door firmly behind Leah.

"Thank you." Leah sat and poured herself some water. Her mouth felt like sandpaper.

"Now, everyone, please introduce yourselves to Ms. Bellerose. State your name, position, how long you've been here, and something about yourself." She looked toward the younger woman on her left. "Sloane."

"Right." The woman, dressed in severe blue with a tight ponytail and understated gold jewelry, offered Leah a frosty smile. "Sloane Harrington, associate director for operations. I've been here about eight months. And something about me..." She pretended to think. "I'm a graduate of Wharton and one day hope to run my own enterprise."

She sounds like the person I used to be. Leah nodded at the woman, damp hands pressing into her skirt.

Ms. Dennis smiled at Sloane. "We have no doubt you'll do that, Sloane, unless you take over here when I retire."

Sloane demurred. "That was a joke, Margo."

Ms. Dennis laughed without humor and gestured to the young man sitting next to her. "Charles?"

"Charles Wickham," announced the kid, who looked barely old enough to drive. "Proud graduate of..."

Leah's mind went blank as she listened, one after another, to her new colleagues, a mild smile pasted on her face. She nodded occasionally, noting their names on a legal pad, but all she could think was, *these people are boring.* All their ambitions were the same and they were all clearly willing to claw ahead of each other for every promotion, every bonus dollar.

She knew these people. Knew them in her bones because she'd been one of them. Willing—even eager—to throw anyone under the bus if they got in her way.

Her stomach churned. That wasn't her anymore.

Taking notes was forgotten. She clasped her hands in her lap so hard the knuckles went white. *What the hell am I doing here?*

Her eyes closed briefly. *Because I have nowhere else to go.*

Her attention went back to Margo Dennis. She was remarkably attractive for her age, but underneath expert makeup, she looked worn. Even the subtle signs of expensive cosmetic surgery couldn't hide the price of sixteen-hour workdays that Leah knew would be part of the job in this place.

That would be her life, too.

Thoughts and emotions ping-ponged and she felt like she might jump out of her skin.

It's my fault I'm here. I fell for his con.

Her gaze went to Margo's left hand. No ring. Probably liked to say she was married to her job. It's what Leah herself had often said. It's what she would have to say again.

This isn't a nightmare. This is reality.

She had to make it work here in Singapore. Had to fit in, keep marching ahead. It was survival at all costs.

Her stomach heaved dangerously, and she swallowed hard.

He lied. I believed him. It all felt so real.

But it wasn't.

"Ms. Bellerose?" A voice broke into her thoughts. "We're waiting on you." Ms. Dennis was perplexed and mildly annoyed.

"I'm sorry. I…" She took a sip of water and cleared her throat.

Before she could speak, there was a loud knock on the conference room door, which banged opened unceremoniously.

"What…" Ms. Dennis frowned as her voice trailed off.

William Jones walked in, dressed in an ill-fitting suit and beaming from ear to ear.

Leah's lips parted and she blinked in confusion. Time slowed. She couldn't register what she was seeing.

"Hear ye, hear ye," William intoned, one stubby hand raised, commanding attention, the other hand holding a paper from which he read.

Everyone in the room swiveled around, gaping and looking at one another in bewilderment.

"I am here to requess that Miss Leah Bellers—" He stopped and pointed, grinning hugely, at Leah. "That's you." He consulted his script again. "I am here to requess that Miss Leah Bellers give Ash a chance. To hear him out." He stepped back and gestured to the doorway with a flourish.

Leah's entire body froze as Ash walked through the door, dressed in a Gucci tux. She barely heard the murmurs of her colleagues around the table as he walked toward her. He nodded slightly in the direction of the head of the table as he passed. "Margo."

Ms. Dennis looked poleaxed. "Mr. Gerard," she mumbled.

Leah's eyes widened as Ash stopped and went down on one knee in front of her. She no longer felt like vomiting but was suddenly dizzy. The room seemed to tilt. She gripped the chair arms with all her strength.

"Forgive me for interrupting your meeting, but I had to make sure you couldn't get away while I tell you a few things." He glanced around the table. "No one here is going to let Ms. Bellerose out of this room before I have my say, are they?"

Several heads shook firmly. No one was going to let her leave. Or miss a moment of whatever was happening.

Ash gazed at her, rich topaz eyes roving her face, her hair, her eyes, and at that moment they were the only ones in the room. In the universe. Her heart drummed so hard it hurt.

"Leah, from the second I laid eyes on you, I haven't been able to stay away. Whatever strange magic you possess cast its spell on me in that moment and I never had a chance." He reached up and briefly touched her cheek. His skin was electric on hers, a sizzle in her blood.

Ash continued. "My mistake was not realizing right away what was happening. I was so selfishly absorbed in trying to survive my father's gauntlet that I ignored the voice of my own heart. I tried to manipulate you so I could keep my job, prove myself to my father, and get the hell out of Charmant. But then…" He paused, a tiny smile at the corner of his mouth. "Then I fell in love with you."

Someone in the room sighed.

"I wanted to tell you the truth so badly but couldn't figure out how to do it. I knew it would ruin us. Every day that went by, it got harder and harder." His head shook ruefully. "I would do anything to go back and change things, to avoid hurting you. It would have cost me my job, but that would have been fine. As it turns out, I've left the company anyway."

Ms. Dennis made some kind of sound, but Leah ignored it. She could hardly breathe, in shock, feeling terrified, relieved, enraged, thrilled.

Ash reached for her hand, kissed it gently, then replaced it on the chair arm respectfully. "Leah, you and I are similar in more ways than we're different, and the ways that we're different are good for us. You changed me. You saved my life." He paused to look at her silently, trying to gauge her reaction. "My darling, I've come here today to explain. And to beg your forgiveness."

He withdrew a small box from the pocket of his tux and opened it. The twinkle of diamonds and emeralds dazzled as he plucked the ring from its velvet cushion and held it up. "Magnolia Evangeline Sebastian Bellerose, I love you with my whole heart. If you consent to be my wife, I promise to spend each and every day for the rest of my life loving you completely. Will you do me that honor?"

The room was deathly quiet. No one breathed. Leah's head and heart, her whole body, was a tumult of sunlight and thunder, flame and ice. As the seconds ticked by, she could see the hope in Ash's eyes fade into fear.

But the iron gates had shut and didn't open back up that easily.

At last, on a whisper, she shook her head. "I don't know."

Chapter 26

Economy was not a necessity but seemed a fitting penance. His motel room was small and designed for the budget-conscious traveler. Polyester bedspread. Cheap prints on the walls. The aroma of fried fish hung in the air, both inside and out.

He hated fried fish.

His phone chirped and he answered it with a sigh.

"Hey, Julius."

"Dear boy, I'm so sorry to hear."

Ash lay on the bed and stared at the ceiling of the musty little room. "I'm not giving up."

"I heard that, too." There was a sympathetic smile in the other man's voice. "Have you heard from her?"

"Nothing."

"How long are you staying?"

"As long as it takes. It's only been a few days. I'm prepared for the long haul." He glanced at the box of Cheerios on the night table. "She doesn't know I'm still here. I'm waiting to hear from her."

"William is taking it hard." Cranford sighed. "When he and Arthur arrived home, he was exhausted but insisted on coming in to talk to Karen. You know she's like a second mother to him."

Ash ran a hand over his eyes. "I shouldn't have involved him. My mistake."

Julius was reassuring. "He'll be all right. You take care of yourself."

Ash thanked him and rang off. He blew out a breath and hauled himself off the bed.

Walking by the marina bay, he drew in the fresh scent of ocean, of sunlight, and was reminded of something his mother had told him, not long before she died.

Life is short. Never waste a day.

He hadn't thought of that in years. Since then, he'd wasted far too many days—in carousing, anger, bitterness.

Losing his mother had felt like the end of the world. The sun had disappeared, leaving him in frigid darkness. The only person who had ever loved him was gone, and his rage at an uncaring universe had been turned inward on himself.

No more. Falling in love with Leah had brought life back to him, and he wasn't about to dishonor that by pouting or pitying himself. If Leah could care for him, that meant he was worth something. His mother's love was redeemed.

He stood at the water's edge, grateful for the wind on his face.

His phone chirped as a text came in. It was from her. Every cell in his body mobilized, his fingers shook as he punched in his passcode.

I'll be in the States next week. Can we get together briefly to talk, to get some questions answered?

He nearly dropped his phone into the bay scrambling to reply.

I'm still here on the island. Right around the corner from the hotel. Name the time and place and I'll be there.

He waited. No response. He paced the boardwalk, agitated, but still nothing. Sweat trickled down his back. It took every ounce of self-control not to text her again or try to call. At last, he went back to the motel, showered, and changed into fresh clothes. He stood outside his room, on the concrete walkway overlooking the parking lot, and ate a bowl of Cheerios.

It was early evening. It had been hours since he'd heard from her. His gut clenched with anxiety while a ray of hope persisted.

Never waste a day.

He ran down the street to an old-fashioned stationer and bought a set of letter-writing supplies. Breathing more easily having found a focus for the moment, he headed back to his motel, passing quaint shops and vendors.

Then, a chirp from his phone.

Bay Place Pavilion Apartments, number eighteen-eleven. Seven p.m.

Heart in his throat. It was six-thirty.

No tux this time. The velvet box was tucked into his jeans pocket. Dress-shirt sleeves were rolled up in the evening heat. He found the sleek apartment building next door to the hotel and stood in front of number eighteen-eleven, staring at his watch. The second hand ticked with agonizing slowness. At the stroke of seven, he knocked lightly.

The door opened slowly, cautiously, as if she were afraid of what might be on the other side. Leah was barefoot, wore cutoffs and a faded Indigo Girls T-shirt. Her hair was damp and loose, her face free of make-up. She had dark shadows under her eyes. His heart clenched.

"You're beautiful," Ash whispered.

She shook off the comment. "Doubtful. I left a ten-hour policy orientation and had to wash the bureaucracy off me." Her face was unreadable as she gestured for him to come in.

He scanned the enormous great room and open kitchen. "Nice place."

"It's awful." She sat on a broad gray sofa and gestured for him to sit across from her on a matching loveseat. "I hate it."

He hesitated, wanting to respect her wishes, but sat on the sofa next to her, giving her plenty of space. Her eyebrows rose but she said nothing.

"If we're going to talk, we can't act like strangers. Because we're not." He regarded her thoughtfully. "Why do you hate this place?"

She looked around but didn't seem to focus on the room. "It's cold. And loud." Her hands clasped in her lap and she stared at them, then back up at him. "Ash, how do you know my name?"

Oh boy, she was jumping right in. It took a moment for him to register what she was asking, then light dawned. He shifted to face her directly. "Okay, here it is. After I heard from my father where you'd gone, I headed back to Charmant to get my passport. I knew I had to come here, to explain." He paused, knowing he was moving into a minefield. "At the hotel, I ran into Dahlia, on her way to take Prune to your mother."

Leah's face went stony and she became eerily still.

He continued. "I went with her."

"You...?" Her face flushed. "You met my *mother*? You saw...the house?"

"I did." His chin tilted. "I had to know as much as I could about you—"

"Oh, Jesus." She dropped her face into her hands. "Shit."

"Listen," he hurried to say, "I get why you might not have wanted me to meet her right away, but honestly, it was fine."

Leah was shaking, hands still over her face. "No, no, no. It's not fine. You'll never understand."

"Leah. Honey." Without thinking, he closed the space between them and removed her hands from her face. "I get it. It was a violation of your privacy. But please give me some credit. I knew it was a risk to go there, but I took that chance because I need to...I *have to*...get you back. Knowing everything I could about you could only help my case." He held her stiff, trembling form close. "Sweetheart, I have my own demons, obviously, my own ugly origin story, and I'm far from proud of it. Listen, Cecelia's a character, but an interesting woman. And strong. I can see now where you get some of that steely backbone." He smiled even though her face was hard as she turned to him.

"You have no idea why I'm strong. And how much I've tried to leave her and that place behind." Leah's words were acid. "I don't hate her. But my past has to be that. My past. I've worked too hard not to get beyond it. It has to be separate. Totally and completely separate from my present life."

He shook his head. "Of course. I can see that, too, clearly." He chose his words judiciously. "That house is shadowy, Leah. There's no life there. Cecelia is a survivor of sorts, but she has none of your energy, none of your color. I don't know the full story and I don't have to. But I can see that growing up, you were a rainbow in the dark." He retook her hands and kissed the palms. "No one saw your magic, your brilliance. But you felt it and got yourself out."

She was watching him, listening, taking in his words.

"*I* feel your magic. *I* see your brilliance. Every day. That's why I'm here." He stopped, aware that the worst was yet to come.

She rubbed her hands on her thighs and stared down for a long moment, then back up. "Is that what you meant when you said that you and I are more alike than different? We both hid part of our identities?"

He nodded. "And I know that sounds like an excuse, but it's not. Our backgrounds are different, and our motives were different, but we each had strong reasons to keep our identities close to the vest." He blew out a breath. "Of course, you could say that my reasons were a lot less honorable."

Leah chewed her lip. "To keep your job?"

"At the time, yeah, I thought so. But in retrospect, I've realized I wanted...*needed* to separate from my history as well. Leaving behind my family name was a relief." He paused. "So did I keep my identity secret only to keep my job? No." He was on thin ice and he trod carefully. "It *was* part of the deal I willingly agreed to. My father, bastard though he is, had reason to require reparations from me. I wasn't exactly the model son, or employee, for several years."

She frowned. "You couldn't have been that bad."

He inclined his head. "Depends on who you ask. The thing is it was critical for me to break away from him. I know that now. We've always butted heads. My mother kept the peace." He paused. "After she was gone, the gloves came off." He realized as he said it how true it was. If Leah hadn't come along, he might still be scraping and bowing to a man he reviled. He'd be an angry man with a dead soul. He grimaced briefly.

"Strange as it may sound, I was committed to doing what he wanted me to do, mostly for financial reasons, and because I didn't have any other options at the time. It turned out to be harder than I'd thought when I met you."

Leah studied his face, considering. Finally she asked, "Why didn't you tell me? Why did it have to come to this?" Her voice trailed away on a whisper.

Ash's heart plunged, breaking for her. "I couldn't. My father had sworn me to keeping my identity secret to ensure my humility or assure his power over me or some such shit." He tutted in disgust. "But the real reason I was afraid was because I could lose you." His voice caught momentarily. "I knew it would hurt you, and not us and our relationship, but your career." He looked away, then back. "I knew how important your job was to you. If I'd said anything, it could have put your whole career in danger." He shook his head. "At least, that's what I told myself."

She watched him, tears filling her green eyes. "A message I'm sure Simon reinforced."

"Every chance he got."

For several minutes, they sat in silence. Ash's chest felt hollow, aware that this could be the last time he would see those green eyes, those freckles on her nose. But at least now everything was out.

At last Leah reached for him, touching his cheek. "Oh, Banks." Then, hearing herself, she smiled ruefully. "I guess that's not the right name to call you."

Ash took the hand that caressed his face and held it firmly between his own. "I like it," he said. "It was my mother's name, so I'll stick with it."

"Fair enough. As long as I'm still Leah, not Maggie." She leaned forward and placed her lips on his.

***

As she kissed him, Ash's taste, his smell, the warm touch of his lips was like a match thrown on gasoline. Every cell in Leah's body seemed to wake up at once.

Tears of relief rolled down her face as he lifted her and placed her back on the couch lengthwise. His weight on top of her was glorious. The strafe of whiskers on her face inflamed her more. She bit his lip, his neck, his shoulder.

He whispered to her over and over how beautiful she was, how he loved her more than life. She wanted him everywhere, all at once. Wanted to devour him, merge with him.

He threw his shirt onto the glass coffee table and lifted her T-shirt over her head, exposing her bare breasts. The hair on his chest rubbed and tickled her as the kiss went on, his breath moving into and through her.

She was living on his oxygen, he on hers.

This was the Ash she knew. The one who she'd always known.

The one she loved.

"It's you," she murmured, framing his face with her hands. "It's you." A tear ran down her cheek.

His eyes twinkled and he kissed her forehead, her cheeks, the tip of her nose. "It's me. The one who loves you. The real you. The real me."

They kissed softly, slowly. His lips moved over her tear-stained face. They lay, arms wound around each other, tightly bound, for what seemed like ages. The sun began to wane and orange light slanted through the windows. Purple streaks appeared in the sky.

It was forever before he reached down to unsnap her cutoffs. She thought she might combust as he pushed the shorts down her thighs and off. His fingers trailed the line of her panties as his mouth moved to worship her neck, her collarbone, her breasts. He bit a nipple gently as he pulled the panties aside and rubbed the apex between her thighs.

His breath hissed against her ear, feeling the wetness there. She palmed the hard evidence of his arousal through his jeans, causing him to groan again, more loudly.

It was fully dark now, the twinkling lights of the hotel next door lending sporadic color. Leah's heart sang as her fingers tangled in Ash's hair. He moved down her body, kissing and nipping, finally finding the lace of her panties and using his teeth to pull them down and off.

Then he stopped.

He rose over her, eyes glinting in the silver half-light. "I love you, Leah Bellerose."

Barely able to speak, she gripped his shoulders and drew his mouth to hers. "I love you, too, Asher Banks."

She gripped his derriere and pulled him to her.

"Come here," she gasped, and everything she wanted was right between her hands.

Epilogue

The bell over the door rang a happy chime as William Jones marched into the jewelry store.

"Hi, Mr. Jackson."

The jeweler looked up from his loupe and grinned. "William. What's happening today?"

William approached the glass counter and proudly held out a small blue velvet box. "This," he exclaimed. Chubby fingers opened the box to reveal a silver ring studded with pearls. He turned and pointed out the plate glass window.

Leah and Ash stood outside, looking in, waving, and laughing. Ash took Leah's left hand and raised it to the window, where the light bounced and twinkled from the brilliant emerald and diamond ring on her finger. Mr. Jackson beamed, gave them a thumbs-up, and high fived William.

ABOUT THE AUTHOR

Bronwyn Forest is a life-long lover of writing and all things romantic. She loves creating fun, dramatic, steamy fantasies that feature strong, interesting characters. When she's not writing, she can be found gardening, jogging, cuddling with her furry babies, and dreaming up new stories.

CONNECT WITH BRONWYN:

website: bronwynforest.com
blog: bronwynforest.com/blog/
instagram: @bronwynwritesromance
twitter: @BronwynForest
facebook: bronwyn.forest.9

www.BOROUGHSPUBLISHINGGROUP.com

If you enjoyed this book, please write a review. Our authors appreciate the feedback, and it helps future readers find books they love. We welcome your comments and invite you to send them to info@boroughspublishinggroup.com. Follow us on Facebook, Twitter and Instagram, and be sure to sign up for our newsletter for surprises and new releases from your favorite authors.

Are you an aspiring writer? Check out www.boroughspublishinggroup.com/submit and see if we can help you make your dreams come true.

www.ingramcontent.com/pod-product-compliance
Lightning Source LLC
Chambersburg PA
CBHW031326170626
46807CB00002B/590